The Devil On God's Doorstep

Daniel Lyddon

GWION PRESS

ISBN: 978-1-7396-6911-9

Typeset in Garamond
Cover design by: Daniel Lyddon

For Mam

Thank you for opening the door

Primo Edizione

When I decided to release *The Devil On God's Doorstep* through Amazon Kindle Direct Publishing, I chose to keep the novel as a Kindle Exclusive for the first six months of its publication. This initial First Edition print run of hardback and paperback copies will be available to purchase between June and December of 2022.

This copy comes with my heartfelt thanks: both for your interest in my story, and your investment in my creativity. I hope that you enjoy *The Devil On God's Doorstep* from cover to cover and that the words that follow give you cause to consider the themes of ambition and accountability that permeate the story.

Thank you for purchasing this copy, and joining me at the end of this path that I began to walk more than twenty-one years ago.

Haec est ara primo-geniti Dei

Here is the altar of God's firstborn

- Albunea, the Tiburtine Sybil

Author's Note

The following is a work of fiction - the result of an overactive imagination inspired by the combination of too many days spent admiring the artworks of Vatican City, and too many nights spent wandering the cobbled streets of Rome's Centro Storico.

Like any author worth their salt I have taken certain liberties with the urban topography of both cities: no matter how hard you look, you will not find the gated arch inscribed with the words Vicolo del Notte in the Eternal City, nor will you discover Il Capitano listening to Mussolini's speeches in a secret room atop the Tower of the Winds in the Vatican's Apostolic Palace.

That being said, every fictional work has some basis in truth. The talking statues are indeed real...

Prologo

R ome in the rain. Matteo was beginning to regret it already. He was having trouble keeping hold of both the umbrella and the package squeezed tightly beneath his arm. He regretted leaving on his driving shoes, which had turned out not to be waterproof, but after spending so much time driving around looking for a parking space he wanted to put as much distance between himself and the hire car as possible. He would've taken the Metro but it wouldn't have been the safest option – he didn't want to run into another angry mob.

He walked quickly, his wet map leading him away from the modern world and into side streets and alleyways that had remained unchanged for centuries. In some streets, the palazzi were so close on either side they almost held off the rain. The marble signs were barely visible here; everything was *via* something or *vicolo* other. A faceless statue pointed to the next street where an over-enthusiastic fountain made the floor more slippery than it already was. Matteo followed the muffled sound of a scooter and thankfully reappeared in the modern world.

This street was still narrow, the walls still old, but it was lined with potted trees and grubby glass-fronted shops. He was just two streets away on the map. It was a gamble, but he'd been told to come to this particular shop which, thankfully, was open. He would have left the job to someone else if the package under his arm hadn't been so personal.

And special, he thought as he opened the door with an elbow.

The word *Antiquaria* arched in peeling letters over the window. A ghastly clown marionette hung beneath it with a broken face that had transformed its laugh into a cackle. One of its arms was limp by its side; lifeless like the rest of the shop.

Matteo looked around at what was basically a front room cluttered with junk furniture. Dust-covered china-ware peppered the tables and cupboards. A lace cloth crumbled across the back of a chair. Old, yellowing tags labelled the goods in Lira, rather than Euros. The silent clocks confirmed the obvious – time stood still here; stagnant, rotting. The sounds of the street seemed kept just out of earshot – you could try and concentrate but the moment you heard them they were gone.

He shuddered. Whatever the reason, this was where he was supposed to be; and apparently, this was the man he was supposed to see.

The man sat in the doorway to the next room, absorbed in a newspaper of an unspecified date. He was so deep in concentration that he was practically eating the pencil in his mouth. Matteo's cough roused the man so violently that he almost choked on the pencil, jumping up and hitting a twisted birdcage that hung in the doorway.

'Mi scusi signore,' Matteo apologised, trying to steady the old man, 'Mi scusi!'

The man looked curiously at Matteo's mouth, squinted and asked 'American?'

'Sì. Well no, yes and no – sono Italiano...'

'It's okay,' the man said, reordering the newspaper, 'I speak good English.'

Matteo hadn't intended his sigh of relief to be so loud. He'd been dreading the thought of having a full conversation in Italian, yet this matter was so personal he hadn't wanted to risk bringing an interpreter. What little he remembered of Italian he had tried to forget as a teenager, rebelling against his parents' forcing him to embrace his heritage. They had taken him away from the country as a child and, until now, he'd had no desire to come back.

He regretted that now. The last few months would have been a lot easier if he'd had a full grasp of the language. For one thing, there would have been less misunderstanding, and less trouble. And maybe less danger.

'How can I help you signore? You want to buy something perhaps?'
'No actually – I was hoping you could take a look at something.'
'You want to sell?'

'Not really,' Matteo began, placing the package down on a table and unwrapping it. 'I want to find out more about this, and I'm told you're some kind of expert on this stuff.'

He had unwrapped a round object the size of a small melon and covered in carvings. The man picked it up and began rotating it in his hands. 'Roman...First Century...well-preserved...the markings beautiful...Proto-Christian.'

'Proto-?'

'...Christian. From the early Church. Do you see the markings? Roman gods, goddesses, but here - branches and vines.' He glanced towards the window and then beckoned Matteo into the next room. A stuffed parrot rolled its glass eye as the birdcage swayed in the doorway.

With a sweep of his hand, the man cleared a workbench for the object and began pulling books from a shelf above. He stopped on an old Italian Bible, threw it over his shoulder and pulled out a fresh, English version. He quickly flicked the book and began reading to Matteo.

'"I am the vine and you are the branches. If you remain in me, and I in you, you will bear much fruit." John, Chapter Fifteen.' He placed the book down slowly, thoughtfully, and picked up the object. 'Here, in between the vines – see in the light – these lines. They are a dove. Dove and vines, vines and fruit...early Christians disguised symbols to look Roman. The Roman Empire was no safe place for the Early Christians.'

The man ran his fingers around the carvings, twisting the object in the harsh light of a naked bulb. He looked at Matteo from the sides of his eyes.

'Have you opened it?'

'Opened it?' Matteo's eyes widened and he reached for the object. For the moment the man resisted, ever so slightly, to let go.

'It is a casket, Signore..?'

'Rossi. Matteo Rossi.'

If the old man recognised the name he hid it very well, flicking through a newspaper nonchalantly. 'Where did you find it, Signore Rossi?'

'My parents left it to me when they passed. I never did anything with it, but I moved here recently and I figured – what the hell? I'm finding out about them, why not find out about this? And you're the go-to guy they tell me.'

'They?' the man smiled, 'then as you say it - "I am your man". I can find out more but I will need money. And I will need to keep it.'

Matteo gripped the casket and looked alarmed. He was suddenly conscious of how precious it was to him and thought of the doorway behind him and the distance through the shop to the front door.

'For now, you understand. I have books, I have friends. You leave a number, I find out more, and I call you to come and open it. Not to worry – I am your "go-to guy."'

The man gave a reassuring smile, and Matteo relented. He remembered the rain, the cold, the car left under the pigeon-infested tree. All of it would have been pointless if he didn't get answers. It was a strange-shaped piece of his jig-sawed heritage – something that he had never been shown, and something that his parents had never mentioned. In ten minutes he had learned more about it than he had in the last ten years.

'How long?' he asked.

'Three days? Five.' The man said abruptly.

'You're sure?'

'I will have to make quiet phone calls, hushed conversations. Something like this doesn't come into the city without notice. I will call you, we will open it together, then you can pay me and never come back...Matteo Rossi.'

The man turned the newspaper around and Matteo saw his own face. He had to admit, it was one of the worst photos they had taken.

The man moved to the doorway and looked out through the shop. 'No one saw you come?' It was more like a statement than a question. 'You leave – you leave now! Don't come back until I call you.'

Matteo had closed the newspaper and weighed it down with the casket.

'Look, I'm not here for any trouble.'

'Get out! Get out of my shop!' The man pulled him back into the shop and pushed him through the mess to the door. 'And tell no-one you have been here. I don't want people coming here. No papers, no polizia!'

'Five days! You said five days.'

'Yes, five days, now leave. Please.'

The man seemed genuinely upset, looking out of the window in alarm.

'Look, here's my card: take it and call me.'

The man pocketed the card without looking at it and began swearing in Italian until Matteo was out in the street fumbling with his umbrella. He'd left his map inside the shop but there was no chance of returning and reclaiming it. The man waved him away, looked up and down the street, and slammed the door as much as its rusty hinges would allow. The clown trembled in the window, its head knocking against the glass. Matteo stared it out until the rain got the better of him and then stamped off, lost.

When he was sure that his visitor was gone the man bolted the door, retreated to the back room and did the same again. He shone a lamp over the box and, looking through a monocle, he scraped a scalpel around the carvings. With enough prodding and poking around the outside the casket clicked and a crack formed around the top. He found a knife and prised it open, the stiff metal fighting against him. The inside was black, defiled by the passage of time in the world outside. He bent down close, examining the contents then whistled to himself as he stood back. Without looking he reached under the workbench and retrieved a brand-new smartphone that looked out of place among the ailing, jaundiced contents of the shop.

He speed-dialled the only number programmed into the phone and trembled when the voice answered.

1

The press conference resembled a Renaissance fresco depicting lost souls writhing in agony within the gates of hell. Journalists elbowed photographers, who nudged the security guards; the security guards pushed back, and people stumbled and jostled to get out of the way. The moment a man vacated his space two more tried to fill it. The noise sounded like a swarm of insects – each person's voice individual yet contributing to a droning sound that invaded the head and made the teeth rattle.

Standing at the back of the room with one leg on a chair and the other higher up against the wall, Lorenzo L'Oscuro attempted to take pictures in between the flashes of the other photographers. He was twenty-two and fresh out of a journalism course and was determined to make more of himself than a junior correspondent at a local paper. The right story at the right time would see to that, and this could be both.

Less than two months ago the Italian government had made an abrupt about-turn in its policy on gene therapy and stem cell research. In what was said to be a scientific coup supported by American money, the controversial Law 40 that prohibited the testing of stem cells in human embryos in Italy was relaxed, and the outright ban on experimentation lifted. The backlash had been immediate, with public outrage fuelled by the Church and the far-Right. The use and destruction of human embryos in experiments was a hot potato in any country, but here at Catholic Central, it was a particular affront not only to a belief but to a way of life.

The Pope had condemned the move and the Vatican had criticised the experiments for violating the Sanctity of Life granted by God to each living thing – including the human embryo. The official line was that if it could grow, it was a living being; if it was a living human, it had a soul, and it was not mankind's lot to tamper with the soul. There were threats of ex-communication based on the grounds that, not only did the experiments violate the Sanctity of Life, they also violated God's law.

In the Italian Parliament's Camera Dei Deputati the opposition claimed that the move was governed by finance and not by ethics, pointing out the hefty sum that had been invested into the gene therapy trials by an American conglomerate. The policy change had opened the doors for investment into an otherwise fragile economy teetering on the edge of a collapsing Euro.

An American institution had installed itself in a suite of laboratories at the city's Ospedale Centrale which immediately became ground zero for every protester, preacher and fanatic within the city walls. The shouting could be heard throughout Rome's *Centro Storico*, with regular protests halting traffic in the narrow streets and students petitioning tourists in the many piazzas. On a good day, the sound could be heard from the Colosseum right up to St. Peter's on Vatican Hill. The rest of the time the autumn wind buffeted the placards and teased the banners. Rain-soaked pamphlets were pulped underfoot and became a carpet of mouldering slogans. From the clouds to the ground the city was in protest.

There had been an attempt to placate the people by installing an Italian-American, Professor Matteo Rossi, to oversee the experiments. It was hoped that the Professor's combined credentials and family history would give the Italian people a feeling of ownership, but all the move had achieved was to turn the respected scientist and Nobel Prize hopeful into a public hate figure. His life had been turned upside down by the combination of media frenzy and public hysteria, that at its worst had manifested itself in criminal damage and death threats.

So much for the Sanctity of Life, Lorenzo thought, as he adjusted himself to shift his leg cramp. Professor Rossi had just entered the room flanked by his colleagues. In front of him were the hounds of the press; behind him a projected diagram of something that could have been cells, molecules or anything that Lorenzo's mind filed under "science". As he looked through his lens the one thing he didn't have trouble working out was the expression etched on the Professor's face: fear.

The screen behind the Professor blurred momentarily and a title appeared: "Gene Therapy: the Future in our Past." Lorenzo swapped his camera for a notepad and watched as others did the same. Dictaphones whirred into life; pens clicked into action as Professor Rossi stood up and began to talk. The jostling and the arguing quickly died down.

'Good afternoon ladies and gentlemen, and thank you for attending this presentation. What I have to say will hopefully dispel some of the myths that have arisen about our work here in the past few weeks.

'"Gene Therapy" is a term that many of us have come into contact with in recent years, and along with cloning and genetic engineering represents the cutting edge of medical science and technology: the frontier where the present and the possible become blurred with science fiction and the future. Over the coming months, I plan to explore the ideas and grounding of these theories, as well as debunk some of the myths associated with them.'

He pointed a remote control over his shoulder and the screen displayed a rotating DNA helix that moved, zoomed and refocused as he spoke.

'Perhaps it is best to start with the genes themselves: the house of inheritance in the human body, our genes contain the information that determines who we are, how we live, and some would suggest, what we are capable of. Our genes control our physical characteristics, from shape and size to eye colour, and in recent years we have found that they can influence our disease resistance, and how illness affects us.

'Research is starting to confirm what we have suspected for a long time: that our genes could be harnessed to treat disease, could be altered to fight infection, and could be amended to ensure that we do not fall prey to certain viruses and bacteria. This, friends, is what is known as Gene Therapy: the manipulation of our genetic structure to treat, and to cure. It is both a dream and a nightmare: a double-edged sword that is open to abuse as much as it is to proper and efficient use. The questions about responsibility and regulation are well-founded: gene therapy could achieve both great good and great evil, but it is a possibility. It is a reality. It is here, it is now, and we have to deal with it as best we can, without sticking our heads in the sand.'

Professor Rossi clicked the remote control again, and a reproduction of a woodcut engraving appeared behind him.

'The story of genes and gene therapy begins, somewhat ironically, with an Augustinian monk, Gregor Mendel, who conducted early genetic experiments in the nineteenth century. Working with pea plants from his home in Bohemia, Mendel discovered the dominant-recessive gene influence on inheritance and discredited the contemporary thought that genetics was based on similarities rather than differences.

'In reality, our inheritance is governed by the variations in the genetic information passed down from mother and father: stronger dominant genes result in a particular trait manifesting itself, whereas weaker recessive genes often result in certain traits remaining dormant until subsequent generations are made free of the influence of dominant genes.

'It is therefore ironic,' the Professor said, raising his voice on the last word, 'that a science which traces its origins to the work of the Church should, through the passage of the centuries, find its progress impeded by the superstition, dogma and outdated views of several world religions.'

This was what the journalists had been waiting for, and Lorenzo's handwriting automatically switched to capital letters. The primary effect of the Professor's words was a further deepening of the silence in the room, and he seemed momentarily taken aback that he had not provoked some form of outrage, but quickly resumed his speech without losing his fervour for the material.

'Despite persecution, victimisation, bad press and general suspicion, science has managed to flourish, and we stand here today in the sight of a new world: as we defeat one illness, another, worse one rises to cripple and claim the lives of our loved ones. Pain and suffering can be eased by manipulating the rules of evolution: dwarf species of grain, manufactured by scientists, have proved successful in averting the starvation of malnourished peoples in desertified regions. In recent years there has even been talk of using gene therapy to re-introduce extinct species, thus reversing some of mankind's less desirable effects on the planet. The possibilities, friends, are endless.'

An image, appearing on the screen behind him, of Da Vinci's *Vitruvian Man* with arms outstretched, morphed into a picture of a modern-day man before zooming through the skin and past organs, deep into his being, to settle upon an individual cell.

'A typical human cell.' The Professor announced. 'Identifiable by most schoolchildren, with its membrane, cytoplasm, and most important of all: the nucleus. Those of you familiar with the science behind gene therapy will know that its operation entails the replacement of a cell nucleus, or specific genes inside it, with a modified, more healthy version.'

The image on the screen zoomed into the nucleus and picked out a particular chromosome, zooming in again to reveal the genes that constructed it. A short animation followed, depicting the process of gene extraction and replacement, with the entire cell emitting a healthy glow when the new gene was fitted into place.

'Here we see the proposed replacement of the faulty gene,' Professor Rossi continued, 'and its effect on the rest of the cell. Damaged cells can be rejuvenated and go about their duties with a lengthened lifespan, making proteins, and fighting infections, rather than being rendered redundant by age. The operation seems simple in itself, but that simplicity comes from the fact that it exists, only at present, in theory. There is much work to be done before we see this miracle replicated across the face of the earth.

'If trials prove successful, this technology could be used to correct defective genes in the womb, thus eradicating certain hereditary illnesses from entire bloodlines. Subsequent generations may be freed from some of the most debilitating conditions known to man. Genetic abnormalities that we know to cause problems in later life can be rejuvenated, lifespans could be increased, and diseases treated quickly, and with minimum pain. The future of medicine is at hand: it is in our hands. It is up to us to grasp it, to make that future possible.'

Matteo knew that no matter how simple the diagram behind, or how easy the words in front, he had already lost. They weren't here to listen: they were hoping to see him sweat; to hear him stammer. To watch him lose it.

'Before we continue,' he said leaning over his microphone, 'I would like to repeat what has already been said to the press: the experiments that we will be conducting here will not involve cloning or the destruction of human embryos. This has to be understood or nothing will come of the wonders of science that we can achieve here. The constant portrayal, this demonisation of us as 'mad scientists' gets in the way of what we're working towards: a giant leap forward in medical treatment, cures for some of the most horrendous afflictions to the human body.

'How many people do we know who are living, or have lived with a loved one suffering from a debilitating condition? Motor Neurone Disease. Multiple Sclerosis. Alzheimer's Disease. They occur all too frequently in the world today. What if they just became names? If they just became words in a history book? Imagine a world where these conditions – and more – could be prevented as well as treated. Imagine that. That is what we are here to work for – it's work that we have to do. We can't do that with these misunderstandings getting in the way. My colleague, Doctor Karin Leibowitz will now make the presentation to explain – again – exactly what our work entails.'

He leaned back as Karin took over. There was the briefest of silences between them that usually allowed for applause. Not this time. A shutter clicked and that was it. Matteo was used to being lauded for his work, not lynched. All that he saw now were narrowed eyes and pinched faces as Karin told them that the experiments would harvest cells from the same patient being treated. There would be no need for human embryos to be tested upon.

The presentation continued behind him – an infographic explaining how the cells were scraped down to their genes, with 'bad' genes being replaced with 'good' genes. Matteo saw a few faces soften and hoped that meant there would be marginally less furious column inches in the morning.

Lorenzo was bored. He had quickly lost interest in the science and had put the notebook down. A man was looking at him from outside the room without any attempt to hide it. He was dressed in a dark trench coat and what looked to be an oversized fedora. Lorenzo looked away wondering whether he had somehow drawn the attention of the Mafia. He was already tuning out as the first question, from one of the national newspapers, was picked above all the others,

'Professor, what do you consider to be the effects of your treatment on Eugenics technology and the genetic makeup of people as a whole?'

'A good question' Matteo answered, 'the treatment, if successful, could revolutionise the possibilities for eugenic science: it may open up the door for greater improvements of mankind's genetic makeup on a global scale. Future generations may well have different DNA to our own: enabling them to work harder, achieve more, live longer, and stay healthier. The possibilities are endless, with as many negative outcomes as there would be positive, but all these dreams are a long way off because the technology simply doesn't exist yet.

'We have the power to change that, by supporting projects such as this and by continuing research in the field of gene therapy we can bring the future closer to the present. We can make a difference to the future of mankind by beginning that work; by taking on the responsibility to improve our lot, and to safeguard our descendants from suffering and disease.'

When the questions with the scientists came to an end Lorenzo hadn't recorded anything. In his pocket, his lonely notebook was waiting to ask its questions for his article. It was too late now and Lorenzo's attention was already elsewhere. He looked back to the door: the man was gone.

The frenzy kicked in again when the scientists got up to leave. Lorenzo pulled himself down using a pole at his side and stretched across the floor to release the cramp in his groin. Other journalists were bumping past him now at varying speeds: for some, the story was over; for others, there might be a potential exclusive waiting for whoever could chase after the scientists leaving the building. Lorenzo fell in with the latter – perhaps there was a way of making up for his lack of questioning.

He walked swiftly to the doors with his head down only to be brought to an abrupt stop as someone stepped on his foot. The profanity that rose inside him stopped at his throat as he looked up into the face of the man in the hat.

The man was as ugly as his battered attire. It was hard to judge his age from his face – a deep frown and disgruntled grimace, stubble flecked with grey and what looked look like rust where his forehead met the hat. Lorenzo studied him quickly – square shoulders, square jaw, thick neck. He wouldn't have been surprised if there was a gun beneath the coat.

'Be careful where you tread.' The man said accusingly.

'Careful? Me careful? You're the one-'

'I am Serafino.'

'What?'

'Serafino. That is my name.'

'Lorenzo.' He replied, offering his hand.

Serafino reluctantly shook it, his grimace deepening as he did so. He was wearing fingerless gloves and what skin was showing was coarse and cold. He tilted his head to check out Lorenzo's press pass.

'L'Osservatore Calabria?'

'We're a local paper.'

'You're at the wrong end of the country for a local paper.'

'It's a national story.'

'Ah yes,' Serafino mused, looking over Lorenzo's shoulder to two women clearing the room. 'Professor Rossi and his sinful experiments. Wretched, isn't it?'

'That's one way of putting it,' Lorenzo retorted, noting his assailant's apparent joy at the word *sinful*.

Serafino stepped forward and raised his head to look at Lorenzo with round, staring eyes that caught the light. He spoke with urgency as if he was afraid of losing his audience's interest.

'A storm is about to break over the Eternal City that will have consequences reaching far beyond its ancient walls. The Professor has unknowingly waded into a battleground, and knows nothing of the effect his work will have over the coming months. War will be declared.'

'War?' Lorenzo laughed, 'In Italy? Where did you get that from?'

'Do not think to mock what you do not understand, Signore L'Oscuro: the fight will break out before your eyes and you will have to choose a side.'

Lorenzo took a step backwards. 'You...you know my name?'

'Your press pass.' Serafino pointed reassuringly at his chest; Lorenzo couldn't even remember whether it was facing the right way.

'Who are you?'

'I am here to tell you about the war of good versus evil,' said the stranger, 'and the fight for the Seat of Peter.'

'Sounds more like a Church matter to me: I'll be staying on the fence on this one. I'll make my own up about the arguments between the Professor and the Church.'

'You cannot see what is laid before you. Open your eyes, or your blindness may become your undoing.' He pressed something into Lorenzo's hand. 'When you see that the battle lines are being drawn, call me on this number.'

Lorenzo looked down at the card in his hand and rubbed it with his fingers. It was a thick, textured card, plain but for the word *Serafino* calligraphed in the centre. He turned it over and scowled.

'There's no number on it.'

The stranger shook his head, and taking Lorenzo's hand, led him to the door where he raised the card.

'When in doubt, look to the light.' The sun shone through the card, revealing a telephone number watermarked in the paper.

'It's original, that's for sure,' Lorenzo started, but Serafino had disappeared and the gloomy hall was empty.

2

Rain lashed the cobbles of St. Peter's Square, cleansing it of tourist trash and sweeping the sou'westered crowds under the huge colonnades. Rolling clouds rumbled overhead, obscuring the sun and draping the buildings of Vatican City in a pall of darkness. Minute camera flashes sparked from the lantern crowning the cupola of St. Peter's Basilica as pictures were taken of a sodden, soaking, Eternal City.

The crowds kept one eye on the clock, and the other on the small window second in from the end of the Apostolic Palace. The curtains were closed, but outside a maroon banner hung from the balcony, dripping wet, dishevelled and tossed by the wind. Children strained their hooded heads to get a slightly better view of the balcony; tourists uttered rain-soaked monologues into their camcorders. Policemen, priests, tour guides and their flocks - the faithful and the unfaithful alike – congregated beneath the colonnades, the wind whipping the rain into their faces.

Tired children cried as their parents set them down on the floor and attempted to mop away the cold water with whatever tissues or handkerchiefs were to hand. The more entrepreneurial street tradesmen wove through the crowd selling umbrellas at extortionate prices, avoiding the eyes of the watchful policemen. The air was scented with the stench of sweat, clouds of expensive, overpowering perfume, the smell of damp hair, and worst of all: that of wet pigeon. Above their heads, the rain, wind and thunder conspired to dampen people's spirits and douse their faith.

Further along the street, beyond the stone walls of the Passetto that stretched from the Vatican to the Castel de Sant' Angelo on the banks of the river, a black umbrella emerged from the guarded Porta Sant'Anna, one of the few thresholds in the Vatican walls. The crowds flocking to St. Peter's, either in faith or need of shelter, parted before the umbrella and rejoined as it passed.

'It is uplifting to see people still making the journey to see His Holiness, despite the conditions of the day.' Cardinal Luis Sanchez remarked to Rodrigo, his umbrella-toting companion, who simply nodded in silence and put an arm forward to part the sea of cagoule-clad Catholics in front of them. The umbrella bobbed up and down as they waded their way against the wet and miserable pedestrian current, charting a course along the Vatican wall.

The two men walked to where the crowd whirled around a small space empty of bobbing heads and umbrellas. People eddied about the space, careful not to step inside of it and to keep their eyes away from street level. The clouds cracked loudly overhead, releasing a heavy downpour of stinging rain. The pace of the crowd quickened; people headed for the colonnades, the nearest newspaper stand or phone booth. In a matter of minutes, the umbrella salesmen doubled their profits.

The large black umbrella came to a stop in the space beside the wall. There, in smelling distance of a restaurant now feeding a throng of wet and hungry people, with her clothes and hair plastered to her cold, sodden skin and a small boy curled up in her lap, a woman sat with her back to the wall rattling a cup at the passers-by. The Cardinal stepped forward, the umbrella moving with him to give the woman a little shelter. A thunderclap tore the heavens apart, startling her child and making him cry.

The woman looked up into the venerable face of Cardinal Sanchez and gasped at what she saw: his crooked nose, the dark shadows under his staring eyes where the skin folded in great wrinkled swags, the eyebrows arching over his eyes like bristling white hoods. It wasn't the most pleasant of faces to behold, but at that moment, he was trying to warp his mouth and brow into an expression of sympathy for the destitute woman's plight.

Cardinal Sanchez motioned to Rodrigo who produced a small bag and handed it to him. He reached into it, selected a handful of coins, and kneeling beside the woman, dropped them into her cup. He attempted a smile and patted her child on the head.

She burst into life all of a sudden, taking him by surprise, and started kissing the hem of his robe, all the time wailing 'Multo grazie! Multo grazie signore!'

Cardinal Sanchez turned to look at Rodrigo and gave a slightly embarrassed jerk of the head in the woman's direction. Rodrigo stepped forward, his face expressionless as the stone of the high wall, and pushed the woman away with his foot, all the time waving a finger at her and shaking his head. Tears mixed with the rain that dripped from her chin onto her son's head. Shivering with cold and fear in equal measures, she reached inside her shawl and pulled out a scrap of paper, holding it up to the Cardinal in her cold, trembling hand.

The Cardinal duly accepted it, nodded and turned on his heel. The umbrella moved with him, exposing the mother and child to the elements once again. Cardinal Sanchez looked around him: people rushed in all directions, covered by umbrellas, coats, and newspapers opened above their heads. The trams arriving and departing at the station in the centre of Piazza del Risorgimento were crammed full of people determined to stay dry. Birds huddled together in the surrounding trees, preening their damp feathers. The two men turned around and retraced their steps to the gate in the wall. The crowds making their way to the colonnade were thinning now.

They walked back in through the gate; the guard saluting as they passed. None of the people they had passed in the street had recognised Cardinal Sanchez, or known anything of the considerable amount of power that he wielded at the Holy See. Such ignorance would have annoyed some of his fellow Cardinals, but Cardinal Sanchez enjoyed secrecy and appreciated its benefits.

The two men made a hastened journey past the Apostolic Palace into the Belvedere courtyard, and into a corridor beneath the Vatican Museums. One floor above them tourist groups were perusing the Gallery of Maps on their way to gawp at the ceiling of the Sistine Chapel. Had they waited in the quiet they may even have been able to hear the shuffle of the hundreds of feet above their heads.

They exited via a nondescript side door that opened out onto the road leading to the heart of the Vatican administration: the Palazzo del Governatorato. Rodrigo opened the umbrella again and they walked along the road through the gardens, smelling the scents of wet pine and damp foliage. Ahead of them, the many windows of the huge building reflected the washed-out grey of the clouds. As they approached the entrance, Cardinal Sanchez stopped and pointed to a window on the third floor of the building.

A small, grim face: grey and heavily lined, looked down on them. Through the rain, Cardinal Sanchez was sure he could discern a scowl. Recognising that it had been discovered, the ashen face withdrew from the window into the shadow beyond, leaving the glass to reflect the miserable sky. Cardinal Sanchez quickly scanned the other windows, certain that they were still being watched.

'Our friend Cardinal Romano seems pleased to see us.' Rodrigo remarked. 'No doubt he wishes we had taken him with us to give alms to the poor.'

'Do you think he would have come with us if the sun had been shining?' Cardinal Sanchez asked with a chuckle. 'No Rodrigo, I fear his compassion doesn't stretch that far. Cardinal Romano is suspicious enough of the people he knows: he avoids strangers as if they harbour the Plague.'

Cardinal Sanchez dismissed Rodrigo once they had entered the building and walked along a corridor, listening to the rain tapping at the windows begging to be let in to wet the halls. He climbed a staircase to the second floor, his knees creaking quietly as he ascended each step. In annoyance, he noticed that the chandelier hadn't been switched on, leaving the stairwell in darkness, save for the gloomy light that permeated through the clouds.

He placed his hand on the bannister of the staircase and began to climb to the third floor, where the windows were smaller, and there was less natural light. Halfway up the stair, that light was suddenly cut off. Cardinal Sanchez looked up to see a dark figure standing in front of the window, haloed by the pale grey light.

'Did you enjoy your walk?' Cardinal Romano asked, in a low, grave voice devoid of pleasantry.

'Indeed I did. It was quite refreshing; the air is much clearer when the rain cleanses it of the dirt and dust of the city. The streets are surprisingly full, given the weather. I was glad to see so many people making their way to San Pietro: I could almost feel the faith coursing through them. Tell me, how does the world look from your side of the windowpane?'

'The same as it did before you went out: grey, wet, cold, dangerous.'

'Dangerous?'

'I have received most distressing news this morning: the professor, this...' he looked at a letter in his hand, '...Matteo Rossi held a press conference this morning in which he dared to say that his experiments at the Ospedale Centrale are continuing work begun by the church.'

Cardinal Romano hissed the word *experiments* as if it were an insult.

Cardinal Sanchez climbed to the step above his peer and looked down at the piece of paper in his hand.

'Rossi? I am not familiar with him.'

'You will be – I have convened a meeting to discuss the matter further. We have to take the necessary action to remove him from our city.'

'When is the meeting? I have matters to attend to this afternoon.'

'Tomorrow morning.'

From the corridor beside them, a clock chimed midday. The Cardinals looked at one another, then looked out of the window.

'He'll be coming out now.' Cardinal Sanchez said. There was no more conversation: they stared silently out of the window. The world seemed silent save for the thunder rumbling overhead.

In Piazza San Pietro, the bells marked the hour, and the crowds stepped out of the sanctuary of the colonnades to see a small figure dressed in white shuffle out onto the balcony. A ripple of quiet applause passed among them. Umbrellas quaked and hats bobbed. Children were lifted onto shoulders for a better view. The sounds of the outside world fell away, the rain softened, and even time itself seemed to slow down as the Pope addressed his audience.

3

Cardinal Luis Sanchez closed his eyes and remembered. He remembered his life before the call of the Church. He remembered his younger self: a guerilla fighting the Franco regime and dreaming of a free Spain. Spain before the War came. With a shiver he remembered the atrocities, the things that had been done by his own hands in the name of freedom; and shivering now, those hands unrolled the piece of paper given to him by the wretch outside the Vatican wall. The plain, bold letters made him feel sick:

NON INNOCENTE

NON INNOCENTE

NON INNOCENTE

His hand rose to his mouth to stifle the scream he was half-afraid would come out. Those words, or rather the meaning behind them, had plagued him his whole life long. The guilt almost brought tears to his eyes. *Not Innocent.*

He thought back to the woman in the street. She had given the paper to him as arranged, which meant that someone else had copied it, as arranged, from the original text, wherever that might be. And in their own way, the words confirmed two things: that the casket existed, and that the man who held it was still alive.

He opened a drawer and pulled out a well-worn address book. There, among the entries under 'A', written in someone else's hand, was the word *Antiquaria*. He tapped it with a finger and reached for the phone on his desk.

The phone rang before his hand reached it.

'Your guest is here, Your Eminence.' His secretary said from the antechamber outside of his office.

'He is? He's early. Bring him in.'

He stood up, brushed the creases out of his robe and smiled in the direction of the doorway. The boy was ushered in and Sanchez was struck by how much like the father the son had become.

'Take a seat, Lorenzo.'

'I'm sorry if I'm a little early.'

'No, no, you're right on time.' He dismissed his secretary with a hand gesture signalling that should the meeting run over a phone call would be put through that needed urgent attention.

'The weather's so bad I needed to be indoors and it was easier to get here than I thought, so I guess I'm here before time.' Lorenzo looked around the room for a clock and found none.

'It's not a problem – any time I have with my Godson is a blessing How are you finding the city?'

'I'm seeing it with adult eyes for the first time. It's a lot smaller than I remember – especially with the scooter. And everything's pretty much within walking distance anyway.'

'What do you think of the hotel? I'd have you stay with me but I didn't want to obstruct your independence.'

'You've done more than enough to help me, Your Eminence. I wouldn't have got the press pass without your intervention. Your kindness has certainly made things easier. And I appreciate your offer to pay for the hotel but I really should be paying my way. I owe you enough as it is.'

'I only help where I can, Lorenzo, and who I can. Other people might not have accepted my help so freely. The press pass was the least that I could do. I hope that it was of some use.'

'It was perfect, thank you. I've got some great photos to accompany the article...not as much as I'd like for the article itself, but I can flesh it out and the paper's not looking for much anyway.'

'Indulge an old man's curiosity: tell me what it's about again?'

'It's a lot to go into – I can forward you the article before it goes to press – but essentially it involves cutting damaged genes out of our cells and replacing them with healthy ones. The scientists say the treatment could be effective in the womb...or in embryos.'

Cardinal Sanchez sucked the air in through his teeth. 'Those building blocks of life again. Why science can't leave these things to God I have no idea. Always the same tests, the same arguments, the same threats. When will people learn to just leave things be? I have a meeting about this tomorrow and part of me would like to be informed, whereas the rest of me wishes that the question hadn't arisen in the first place.'

'It's fascinating really, it's just that it goes against Church doctrine.'

'We do have other views on it besides outright condemnation you know. Our Pontifical Academy for Life deals with the promotion and defence of Life, and our Academy for the Sciences keeps us, or rather the Church, up to date on scientific development. I myself have little understanding of it – my duties fall elsewhere.'

'I had no idea.'

'Very few people do. People are all too eager to draw a line between religion and science and claim that the two are polar opposites. Today's Church takes a much more tolerant approach to scientific advancement. Come to think of it, I may be able to make an appointment for you with one of the Academy delegates. Perhaps it would bring balance to your article?

Lorenzo blinked vacantly and shook himself out of a brief stupor.

'Seriously? You could do that? Would you do that for me?'

'Of course, let me see if I have someone...'

The Cardinal picked up the address book knowing full well that all it would take was a call to his secretary and then he wouldn't have to bother any further. He made a deliberate search of the book before opening to A once more and running his finger once more over the name of the antique shop.

'Now that I think of it perhaps there is something else that I could do for you too – pointing you in the direction of another story for your newspaper perhaps.'

'Really? What is it?'

'There is a certain antique shop in the Centro Storico that has recently suffered a burglary of sorts. There were no signs of forced entry and nothing has been reported to the police but I have been assured that there has indeed been a burglary. The proprietor, however, seems reluctant to talk about it.'

'Why would somebody not inform the police?'

'Why indeed. The logical answer is that someone doesn't want the police to know. '

'But if there isn't a record of the crime and the owner won't talk about it, how do you know that anything has happened?'

'Because two days ago an item was delivered to this particular antique shop. Two days later, the item is still there, but now it is empty.'

'I don't understand.'

Cardinal Sanchez leaned forward over steepled fingers as if he was about to impart some serious and confidential information.

'Lorenzo, I am the Prefect of the Vatican's Congregation of Divine Worship and the Discipline of the Sacraments. As part of our mandate, we verify and venerate relics attributed to our saints and the events described in the Gospels. We have at our disposal some of the world's best archivists, archaeologists and historians in this field. Whenever a purported relic surfaces we are notified of it, and it becomes our job to support or debunk the claims made about the object.

'Two days ago we received a phone call from a certain antique shop; the proprietor has worked for us on occasion.'

'Freelance?'

'If you like. He is a good man, and trustworthy. When he worked for us he specialised in First Century Roman items, with an interest in Christian artwork.'

'Obviously.'

'Obviously. Like I say, he is trustworthy, to others as well as to ourselves. From time to time he is approached to value pieces that he feels could be important to us and we receive a phone call to alert us to the item's existence. We usually have a meeting with the owner, and more often than not begin a dialogue which results in us purchasing whatever it is. The Vatican Museums hold many artefacts that have been acquired in this way.

'The call we received two days ago concerned a casket, believed to be First Century, made of silver, carved with both Roman and Christian symbols. It's an interesting find that we're keen to look at, but it may also be useful to you and your story, in that the owner of the casket is Matteo Rossi.'

'The Professor?'

'The very same. It was a legacy left to him by his parents.'

'And the casket has been stolen?'

'No, no; the casket is still at the antique shop. Its contents, however, are missing. I fear that in his excitement our friend also called people other than ourselves and that someone broke into his shop, opened the casket and emptied it.'

'Why didn't he contact the police?'

'It's a delicate matter. If the police become involved, the story becomes public. We have to keep a lid on it until the contents have at least been recovered, ideally until we have secured it and are working on verifying whatever it is.'

'And yet you think this could be a story for me?'

'Yes: an exclusive. Your article about the scientists is just that: an article. One take on an existing story. This could be *your* story. You, and your paper, would be the ones to break the story; the first to make it public.'

Lorenzo noticed that the Cardinal's steepled fingers were now gripped together as if in prayer, the knuckles' white skin stretched over bone. A sheen of sweat illuminated the old man's forehead.

'Investigate the story: find out who stole the item and where it has gone, and find a way for us to recover it before it falls into other hands. All I ask is that you keep this secret until the item is safely within our walls. Please understand, if it were public knowledge every detective and treasure seeker in the city would be looking for it. Mobsters, politicians; everyone. We might never have a chance of recovering it.

'Keep this to yourself, however, and you will have our full cooperation, our support, and access to the resources necessary. And of course, I will set up your meeting with one of our delegates from the Academy for the Sciences.'

'Of course I'll help,' Lorenzo said with a nod, 'although I don't know what use I will be. Do you even know what I should be looking for?'

'To be honest, no. To begin with, you won't be looking for the item itself; only the mention of it. Concentrate on finding where it is.'

'But do you even know what it is?'

'We have some ideas, and I myself have my own opinion.'

'Which is..?'

Cardinal Sanchez leaned back and let his head rest against the back of his chair. He closed his eyes momentarily and when he opened them his pupils seemed dilated beyond their natural size.

4

This time the rain was just what Matteo wanted: rain kept people inside, kept prying eyes away from the Ospedale. The more people there were inside, the less chance there was of anybody paying too much attention to the refrigerated lorry reversing toward the Ospedale's rear entrance. Two bedraggled security guards closed the gates behind it and waded off through the drenched courtyard. Water rushed through the gutters and surged down the drainpipes, flooding the drains and drowning the plants in the landscaped garden.

He watched the lorry reverse under the porch area where the building's upper storeys overhung the rear entrance. Through the rain he saw it shudder to a halt: two beams of light lancing across the courtyard in the direction of the gates were extinguished as the headlights were switched off. For a moment, nothing moved in the rain-darkened world outside. The passenger door opened and the blurred shape of a man jumped down from the cabin into the downpour, his uniform turning a more saturated shade of blue.

Matteo pushed off from the windowsill and turned to look for Karin: she was already standing by the door waiting for him, holding a tablet computer in her hands. They took the lift down to the rear lobby, where Karin took a wet clipboard from the deliveryman. She signed the form, the ink running instantly down the page, and nodded to two technicians who accompanied the deliveryman out to open the back doors of the lorry, sending clouds of frozen air curling out to meet the rain. An electric-blue glow pulsated from within the glacial gloom of the vehicle.

'Could they have parked any closer?' Matteo observed, noting the ramp now extending of its own accord from the back of the lorry and down through the doors of the lobby. Cold clouds rolled down the ramp and across the carpet to his feet. The temperature dropped quickly.

'At least this way prying eyes don't get to see what we're unloading.' Karin said, turning to face him. 'The big day's here at last, Matt. How do you feel?'

'I feel like it's all coming together now: all the years of theory and planning, the months of creeping around setting up the operation. It's like I've planted a tree, and it's just starting to bear fruit. We're going to make history Karin; we're going to change the world!'

'There'll be a lot of trials to get through before we do any world-changing. You know that. And there's no guarantee of success. Not all theories can jump off the page and survive in the real world. History is a little out of our grasp; we have a lot of hard work ahead of us if we're going to try and reach for it.'

'I know, but I can't help feeling excited. Don't you feel it? These experiments could be a major turning point for all of us. If everything goes to plan, there won't be a person on the planet who doesn't know who we are.'

His eyes were fixed on the huge silver chest labelled "FRAGILE" being unloaded from the lorry. Matteo reached out and touched the cold steel as the container passed him, feeling his fingers sticking to the frozen surface. Karin thought he looked content.

Another two technicians walked up the ramp, silhouetted in a halo of blue light as they crossed the threshold before being enveloped by the mist. There was a bright, stellar quality to the light: it flashed across the back of the eyeballs and up to the brain like a tiny power surge.

'Here they come.' Karin whispered, her breath rising in a plume of vapour.

The shapes of the two men loomed up out of the fog, pulling two large freezer units down the ramp, dragging white clouds in their wake. On the front of the first was a huge padlock and the words "MANEGGIARE CON CURA." Matteo and Karin looked at each other, their eyes sparkling in the crisp cold. *Handle with care* indeed: the contents were priceless.

As the first unit rolled past Matteo took it from the technician and began to push it up the corridor. The glass top was etched with a layer of complex frost patterns that obscured the precious contents from view. Karin took the second unit and followed a few paces behind. Matteo held the lift door open for her to catch up; the doors closed and they stood side by side in silent awe of what was inside the containers.

The freezer units lowered the temperature of the lift, and Karin shivered, unsure of whether it was the cold creeping over her skin or the excitement that was creeping under it. It seemed like an ice age before the lift started to rise: they were encapsulated in the cold, glared at by the red digits that counted the passing floors, and blinded by the fluorescent light above. Matteo stroked the glass lid of his container with paternal love. The feathers of ice fluttered in the light as his shadow passed over them.

Maria, their receptionist, held the door for them as they pushed the containers into the reception of the Gene Therapy Unit, leaving cold wisps of air behind them. Security cameras followed their journey to the glass door and through the restricted area behind it. The corridor came to a claustrophobic end, with three doors close to one another on the three walls, each sporting a swipe card mechanism.

'I still wonder if all this is really necessary.' Matteo whined.

'Only until they install the retinal scanners.'

'What?'

'I'm kidding! Look: they don't even work yet.' She pushed open the door and pulling her freezer unit behind her entered a small, glass-walled vestibule that opened out into a laboratory. Pristine white coats hung on one wall, gleaming in the clinical bright light that bathed the room. Every corner and every handle of the work surfaces, refrigerated cupboards and computer equipment in the lab reflected the bright, opalescent glow from above. It was sanitised, sterile, and almost pure in its cleanliness.

Two spaces on either side of the room had been left empty: the freezers rolled under the worktops to fill them snugly. With the freezers in place the laboratory become whole; looking around, Matteo thought of the experiments that would take place in the room over the following months; he could almost see the project coming to life. With the arrival of the freezers, something had begun ticking inside of him. Something began counting time until the success of the experiments and the world-renown that would come with it. He couldn't wait.

'It feels right, Karin; as if the final pieces of a puzzle are coming together, and the picture looks better than I ever thought it could be.'

'Which picture is that?' She asked, reaching inside a fridge and retrieving a test-tube rack.

'The one of our future. We'll be treading in places no one else has been. History will be ours for the making. What we do over the next few months could change the world. We could be heralding in a new era; not only in medicine and science but also in the way that we live and die.'

'Not to mention the way we're born.' Karin said from within the fridge.

'We'll change the rules, and the rest of the world will change with us.'

'And what if the rest of the world disagrees with the changes we're making?'

'What choice will they have? If we perfect the treatments, the world won't be able to ignore them. It won't want to.'

'And when we tell them what we've really been doing? What then?'

Matteo leaned against one of the worktops with folded arms. 'You're losing faith aren't you?'

'Not at all,' she said, concentrating on the test tubes and not meeting his eye, 'it's just that this is all very real now. It's not on a page or a presentation.'

'Which is what we want: an end to the theory, and the beginning of practicality.'

'But the opposition is real too. I've had to be moved to two different hotels since we got here, and how you've managed to drive that hire car without suffering some an accident I don't know.'

'You're not afraid are you?'

'Yes. What we're doing is amazing, and life-changing. But a lot of people don't want their lives changed. We need to tread with caution, and hide what we're doing as much as possible.'

'But at some point, they'll need to know. The reality of Synthetic Embryology will be so shocking the world will have no choice but to sit up and pay attention. It will be a watershed in medical science, and once we've reached it, there'll be no going back.'

'If we're the ones to reach it.'

'What do you mean?'

'You've seen that memo from the Board, haven't you? We have to provide results on a tight schedule to stop funding going to other teams. To secure the funding for years we have to produce something within months. We can't risk the chance that some other facility gets allocated our money.'

Matteo took the test-tube rack from her hand and held her by the elbows. There was an uncomfortable moment between them before he let go.

'No one else is trying to do what we're doing. Everyone else is planning to use existing embryos. No one else is planning to build them from the bottom up, create them out of nothing. People will be interested in the experiments in a more positive way: they'll log onto the website to watch our video diaries and read our news feed. They'll become familiar with our terms and processes from our regular updates. We won't just educate the opposition – we'll let them do it themselves until they see the benefits of the experiments and come to appreciate our point of view. We will become household names; public interest will ensure our continued success.'

'Sounds like you've got it all planned out, although there's no guarantee the experiments will be a success. Have I mentioned that?'

Matteo slapped his hand against the side of the freezer unit.

'We *will* be successful, Karin.' He spoke through clenched teeth, 'You must have faith in the project: faith in us. We will be known the world over as pioneers of genetic medicine.'

She gave him a sideways glance. 'Seeing as you're in such a good mood and all, what do you say to going out and celebrating tonight? I know a great place for Italian food.'

'Very funny.'

'I'm serious! There's this great-looking place two blocks from the hotel: it's got a balcony with little tables looking out onto a cobbled piazza. Come on; it's not every day you start work on something that you've planned and dreamed about for as long as you can remember. We've talked about this project for years: now it's finally got off the ground, we should celebrate. It'll be perfect: good food, a few bottles of wine, a balmy Italian evening.'

'It's raining.'

'So we'll eat inside. What do you say?'

5

Il Capitano slept. He dreamed of younger years when the City was more complicated, and his life was easier. The years after the War had seen him at his most free: unencumbered by his past life, and all of his trespasses forgiven. He had been at his strongest, his most influential, and people had feared him. He had been powerful and in control, but now?

Now he dreamed of the future, what little of it might be left. He was almost in power now – a better place than his younger self could have ever imagined him being. Millions of people were at his command. Billions in riches to surround himself with. Il Capitano dreamed of the future and dreamed of Glory.

He was awoken by a knock at his door. His housekeeper apologised and told him that he had a visitor, even at this most ungodly of hours. The dream sunk beneath his pillow awaiting his return. He donned his usual robe, rubbed the sleep from his eyes and found his glasses by the door. Hovering on the landing was a Deacon.

'Deacon Fuentes. Have the clocks stopped working at the Vatican?'

'I am so sorry to be waking you at this hour-'

'Apology accepted; get on with it.' He was still too tired to snap but impatience was beginning to yawn inside him.

The housekeeper opened a door from within another room: she had already lit a fire and there was a carafe of water on a table. Il Capitano thanked her and she disappeared. His senses heightened as Deacon Fuentes closed the door behind them.

'Take a seat, friend, and tell me why I am blessed with your visit at this time of night.'

'The Congregation for Divine Worship is to meet in the morning.'

'All of them? Why?'

'No; just a small, select group. I heard of it just an hour ago. Something important has happened: something has been *found*.'

'Tell me more.' Il Capitano said, pushing a glass of water into the other man's hands, all the while never looking away from his face.

'One of the sisters at the switchboard listened in on a call two days ago from an antiques dealer in the Centro Storico. He has been asked by a foreign client to identify an artefact.'

Deacon Fuentes pulled out a note and looked at his hastily-scribbled handwriting.

'A box made of silver. Solid. Engraved with details of the Crucifixion. Roman in origin. The client had been unable to open it but the dealer has since succeeded and called the Congregation to say that he had found...fragments.'

'Fragments of what?'

'I've no idea. I don't think that he did either. The Musei Vaticani will have someone at the meeting to discuss potential verification of a relic.'

Il Capitano finally woke up.

'A relic? What else can you tell me?'

'There's nothing else – it's all being kept quiet until the meeting tomorrow.'

'Good. There's no sense in exciting people if it turns out to be nothing. Do you have the antique dealer's phone number?'

'I can get it.'

'The address too?'

'Yes. First thing in the morning.'

'I need them before then.'

'I don't know if I can-'

'I'm not asking.'

Deacon Fuentes tried to stare him out but somehow found himself looking at the floor, ashamed at even trying.

'I should go now – I should be able to find something.'

'Find everything that you can,' Il Capitano interrupted, then added gently' and thank you for coming, Deacon Fuentes. Your help is always appreciated and I look forward to the day that you formally enter the Priesthood.'

Deacon Fuentes bowed with unashamed ambition, excused himself and left. Il Capitano waited for his housekeeper to come back and close up the room before returning to bed, where he knew he would not sleep. There were too many things to think about now, both exciting and alarming.

A relic had been found. He was sure of that because someone in the Congregation of Divine Worship and the Discipline of the Sacraments was also sure. Sure enough to call a meeting of the most senior Cardinals first thing in the morning. There was obviously some kind of time limit. The Vatican would have to own the relic in order to look at it, identify it, test it, verify and possibly venerate the...fragments.

Fragments of what? Carvings of the Crucifixion didn't narrow it down: there were too many items purporting to be relics from Christ's Passion as it was. So many sections of the True Cross existed that it would have had to have been gargantuan. Enough holy thorns to make multiple crowns. Enough of everything. Except that this must be different, and the section of the Church's administration with the responsibility for relics seemed eager to find out what it was.

Il Capitano thought about ownership and began to dream again. The Vatican would need permission from the owner, currently the antique dealer's client. If he could find the dealer, he could find the client and things could change all over again.

Il Capitano dreamed of his days of influence at the Vatican when men had other names, and the gold was ill-gotten. He remembered when honesty and information could be bartered like currency. In post-war Europe, when a man's life rested on who said what to whom, Il Capitano had shepherded men to God and back, making many friends and few enemies in the process. Without meaning to, he fell into an uncomfortable sleep as birds began to sing outside his window.

6

Cardinal Giancarlo Romano rubbed the sleep from his eyes, poured himself a glass of wine, and yawning, turned his blinking eyes to the dim glow in the East that heralded the new dawn. The air was cool, the streets almost silent as the world made the transition from night into day. He shifted in his chair slightly to ease the pain stabbing at his lower back: years of slouching were beginning to take their toll on his aged body. His back hurt on most days, and a small hump had formed at the top of his spine where his shoulders had gathered into his neck. His joints ached in the cold and clicked at even the slightest movement.

An early breeze rustled through his robes and stirred the leafy vines entwined around the balcony. In the darkness above him, a bunch of wrinkled grapes eagerly awaited the ripening sun. Romano had always liked to grow things: fruit, vegetables, flowers. Anything that he could fit onto his small balcony. He had once derived much pleasure from watching the plants grow and bloom, but he rarely had time to tend to them anymore: they were left to grow wild, their roots bursting through frost-shattered pots, their flowers dead and drying on the floor. Consequently, he took little pleasure from sitting among them now, a testament as they were to a life that had gone to seed.

He rarely had time to do anything but work, although there were plenty of hours in his day: he got up in time to see the sun rise every morning and usually retired a little shy of midnight. Nevertheless, the time seemed to fly by uncontrollably. Romano felt that time was passing him by; that his own time was running out, that he never seemed to make the most of it. Then again, he mused, perhaps it had always been like this, and only now was he beginning to take notice. The hours and minutes ran perpetually like water through his fingers, the pain of the years building up in his body like debris in a stream. He couldn't help thinking that sooner or later time would come flooding towards him, and he would be washed clean away.

Pale light spread across the horizon, dimming the stars and diluting the darkness. A speckled moth fluttered gracefully about the shrivelled grapes before flying away to chase the moon into the West. Slowly and steadily, night receded and the cityscape appeared before him, released from the grip of the dark. Churches stood tall and proud, their cupolas and spires reaching to heaven from among the rooftops of the city.

For the moment the streets were quiet, populated only by the last of the night's revellers and the earliest of the morning workers. The rest of the city slept under the tawny haze that floated above it like a blanket of low clouds. A lone bat snapped its jaws over the distant speck that was the moth. The light, now golden, began to intensify behind the hills to the East.

Dawn broke like an egg cracked over the city; its new light oozing slowly between every tower and obelisk, church and house. With a flap of its leathery wings, the bat changed course for home, and sanctuary from the sun. The golden orb rose in the sky, momentarily catching the bat in its brilliant light, making the skin of its wings glow rose pink before it dived into the trees of the Vatican Gardens. The sun climbed over the rooftops, promising a fine autumnal day; the leaves falling along the banks of the Tiber flamed russet and gold. The river itself was a flowing artery of verdant green glistening in the fresh light: it was morning in the Eternal City.

As the sunlight reached his balcony, Cardinal Romano offered a quiet prayer. He prayed to God, giving thanks for being allowed to see another beautiful morning; he prayed for the souls of friends and family who had passed from the world, and for those who had not; he prayed for his soul, begged forgiveness for his mistakes, and asked that his prayers be answered, his ambitions fulfilled.

A small part of him also prayed to the other gods, for Cardinal Romano recognised the existence of other powerful forces that held sway over the world. There were spirits, he knew, that haunted places old and crumbling; entities that had power over the inhabitants of the mortal world; and Rome was a city built on a foundation of ancient faiths. One only had to dig below street level to find the remnants of previous pagan civilisations, and there were many temples, both public and private, dedicated to heathen gods. Having spent a great part of his life in Rome, he knew that in the older and more sacred of these sites, something lingered still.

Cardinal Romano eased himself up from his chair, his joints creaking in protest, and raised his glass to the reborn sun. As he finished his prayer, he drank the wine and cast a glance over the city. It was this private ritual that he performed every morning that reaffirmed his commitment to the people of the city; that he would look after them, and defend their souls from sin. With a contented sigh, he brushed a smudge of dust from his robes, tucked a few stray hairs under his *zucchetto*, and returned to his room to begin another day's work.

He was soon passing behind the Holy See's Ethiopian College on a pleasant route through the Vatican Gardens that he wished he could walk more often. Romano muttered a curse against his aged body: he was out of breath despite having only walked half the distance to his destination. He stepped off the path and crossed the leaf-strewn grass to lean against the trunk of a tree. As he stood catching his breath, he noticed the patches of sunshine that permeated through the otherwise dark shade of the tree. Autumn was taking its toll on the world, he noted as he watched the spots of light swirl around him with the swaying of the branches and falling of the leaves.

The Cardinal became engrossed in the patterns of light as they formed, joined and separated again on the ground under the tree. Light and shadow chased each other around the trunk, spinning and dancing outwards across the grass: his eyes followed them until his vision spun and danced with them. He suddenly became cold, and the back pain he had woken up to seemed to have burst through to his chest. Shocked by this intense combination of cold and pain, and paralysed by some unknown fear, he coughed in short, spluttering breaths. Dark spots appeared before his eyes: negative images of those on the floor. Looking downwards, he saw a sickening riot of light and shade; the world tilted slightly and his stomach heaved. Pain knifed through his chest as it expanded, and his body bucked; backwards then forwards. Floor became sky, and sky became floor;

he fell to the ground and looked up to see the leaves falling to join him as he slipped out of consciousness.

He awoke confused, alarmed, and unsure of where he was. His limbs felt stiff and his left side seemed subject to the points of a thousand cruel needles when he tried to move. After a few minutes of agony, he managed to sit up and brush himself down. Crawling to the tree, he managed to pull himself up using the trunk; his pale, translucent hands grasping at the dark and twisted bark. An intense pressure on his chest made it hard to breathe, his head swayed drunkenly as he took his first tentative steps away from the tree. He felt an urge to claw at his skin, to scratch some unseen, inner wound. He felt bruised and weakened, his left arm felt heavy, and swung limp at his side.

Panting, with a cold sweat spreading across his skin, he decided to make for the Palazzo del Governatorato in whatever stumbling, shuffling fashion the pain allowed. As he came within sight of the building, he was approached by a Deacon; a man in his thirties, a young boy by his own account.

'Cardinal Romano, I have been looking for you everywhere!' he exclaimed with what Romano was sure was exaggerated exasperation. 'The senior Cardinals are waiting to start the meeting. Where have you been?'

'Taking a stroll through the grounds, Deacon Fuentes. Today is a good day to appreciate the gardens in their autumnal fashions, don't you think? The way the leaves move around one another as they fall, the way that the light flickers through-'

'Cardinal Sanchez requests you come immediately, Your Eminence.' Deacon Fuentes interrupted.

'Does he? I fear that my colleague is premature in making his demands: the meeting doesn't take place for another half an hour.'

'It's gone half-past seven: the others are tired of waiting.'

'Is it? Already?' Cardinal Romano asked, his voice confused and distant. He looked back along the road, wondering how long he had lain on the floor. 'If that is the truth then we must hurry. Please, take my arm; help an old man whose legs are weak.'

'Are you feeling alright, Your Eminence?' Deacon Fuentes enquired, looking the Cardinal in the eye, 'you seem a little out of sorts; and you look rather pale. Would you like me to bring help?'

'No, no: just you will be fine. I'm not as young as I used to be, that's all, and my mind sometimes forgets how large the gardens are.'

The two men walked slowly, the younger supporting the older, towards the Palazzo. Cardinal Romano hobbled and stumbled continuously; in Deacon Fuentes' eyes, purposefully. Their pace was lethargic: Cardinal Romano paused quite often to admire the plants, or to complain of the tightness of his chest. A full fifteen minutes had passed before they reached the main entrance

'Is the meeting in the usual place?' Cardinal Romano asked in a quiet voice. 'Could you please go upstairs and inform Cardinal Sanchez that I will be along shortly?'

Deacon Fuentes gave a curt nod and did as he was asked, leaving Cardinal Romano to make his way to the meeting room at his own slow, painful pace. By the time he reached the fourth floor, he was out of breath, and rested for a while, leaning against a marble bust of Saint Peter. The pain in his chest increased with every breath: jabbing at his left lung and pricking his skin from the underside. Having slowed his breathing to small, shallow breaths, the pain subsided enough for the seventy-year-old Cardinal to walk the short distance to the meeting room, where Deacon Fuentes was waiting, holding the door open.

As he neared the doorway, Cardinal Romano straightened his back and stood tall despite the pain. He abandoned his shambling gait, forcing his legs to move smoothly. Thrusting his shaking hands into his robe, and altering the position of his head to relieve it of a painful twitch, he entered.

Deacon Fuentes closed the door and with a look down the empty corridor made his way to an alcove between two pillars. A large statue filled the alcove but left enough room for a slight man to squeeze in sideways and stand in the recess behind it. Deacon Fuentes took up position behind the statue and carefully pulled at a section of the wall decoration which came away in his hands, revealing two eye-holes. He leaned in and watched Cardinal Romano take a seat.

A stained-glass light fixture illuminated a table in the centre of the room, bathing the Cardinals seated there in various hues from crimson to indigo. At the far end of the room, three orange bulbs cast a soft citrus glow over a marble sculpture of a young woman cradling a severed head in her lap. With the closing of the door, the spotlights shuddered, and shadows quivered across the effigy's expression of sublime pleasure.

This was the seldom-used Salome Room at the Palazzo del Governatorato. It adjoined no office, it had no natural light. It sat at the end of a corridor on the top floor forgotten by most and ignored by the rest. It was here, out of sight and out of mind, that on occasion the senior cardinals would meet to discuss the things that were not ready to be discussed elsewhere.

The assembled cardinals looked up from the table as Cardinal Romano entered the room. There were six of them in all, none under the age of sixty, with the eldest being Cardinal Pierre Beauclerc who at eighty-two still retained the role of Prefect Emeritus of the Congregation for the Causes of Saints. His was the responsibility of presenting potential saints to the Pope, and he held an influence that many of his peers envied.

Each man was highly skilled in the principle of *romanità*; the time-educated waiting game of ruthless patience, veiled threats and whispered instruction implemented to gain success. However, for all their years of practising it, they had all been affected by the long wait: their various expressions ranged from boredom to anger, via impatience and fatigue. Cardinal Sanchez, dark-eyed in the dim light, was the most impatient and alert.

'Where have you been?' He demanded.

'You don't look so well Giancarlo; is everything alright?' One of the others asked with compassion, shooting a look of censure in Sanchez's direction.

Cardinal Romano took his seat, avoiding the eyes of his colleagues, and only answering them once he was comfortable. 'I was walking in the gardens and lost track of time. I am fine, Michel.'

'We were going to start without you,' Sanchez said icily.

Romano waved by way of apology and sat down in a creaking chair.

'Summoning old men to an early meeting is bound to be met with some difficulty Luis,' one of the others joked.

'Still, the subject is something that cannot wait. Time is against us.'

'What is it?' Cardinal Beauclerc asked as he shifted uncomfortably in his seat, 'and why here of all places?'

'As per usual, what we discuss here has to stay among ourselves until further discussion and decisions have been made. Something has happened that affects each of our departments within the Curia – a relic has been found in the city.'

'Then shouldn't this be a meeting for -?' Cardinal Romano began.

'No – this is different. A relic unlike any other has been delivered almost to our door, only to be snatched away before we could even grasp it.'

Cardinal Beauclerc leaned forward on his elbows and looked imploringly at Sanchez. 'Another relic Luis? How many times have we had this very same meeting? Have the item verified before you bring it to our attention.'

'I can't – the item in question has been stolen. And even if it were in my possession I couldn't release it for assessment without consulting everyone here. This is no ordinary relic – no scrap of material or shard of bone. This is a collection of fragments arranged to form a dish or at least part of a dish. From my own research, I believe the relic to be the remains of the wash-bowl of the Roman Governor Pontius Pilate. The bowl in which he absolved himself of the responsibility for Christ's death and suffering.'

The spotlights quivered in the silence. Cardinal Sato, the only member of the group born beyond the borders of Europe, stared intently at Sanchez, trying to detect any sign of doubt or deception.

'Could such a thing exist?' He asked.

'Apparently so.'

'How?'

'The fragments are, or rather were, stored in a silver casket before they were stolen. The silver casket hadn't been opened in a hundred years or more. It was a family heirloom, a seemingly well-looked after one. How long it had been with the family is unsure. What we do know is that it exists, and has to be found before it falls into some kind of private collection.'

Cardinal Beauclerc looked down the polished table at Cardinal Sanchez. 'What is the name of the family. Are they collectors?'

'Rossi. They were originally from Rome but moved to America. They are not known to us as collectors. There is only one son – Matteo Rossi, the scientist who has been in the newspapers of late.'

'The man gets everywhere.' Cardinal Romano said, with spittle flying through the air. 'What does he say about it?'

'He doesn't know. Or doesn't yet. He knows nothing of the casket or its history. He took it to an antique shop in the Centro Storico – the owner has served us well in the past. I assume that he wants it valued, most likely to sell it. I'm sure you'll all agree with me when I say that this should not be allowed to happen.'

'Tell us about the casket Luis,' Cardinal Beauclerc asked, his words sounding more like an order.

Cardinal Sanchez opened the portfolio on the table before him. He smoothed the already-flat piece of paper as if fearing that reading it might make it fly away.

'The antique dealer believes it to be a first-century work, an early-Christian reliquary, most likely Roman in origin. Its carvings are simple yet crude and tell nothing of the contents, yet an inscription on the inside of the lid identifies the relic that, until recently, was held inside.'

'Have you seen the casket for yourself?' Cardinal Romano asked.

'No. Not yet. But I will be there when it is returned to the owner – I will ask that he relinquish it to us for further investigation. I will say nothing of the relic.'

'And you haven't seen the relic either. How do you know it even exists?'

'I trust the antique dealer. He has worked well for us in the past and serves to gain nothing through dishonesty. I believe that this is something that must be pursued. The sheer magnitude of this relic – it's almost too much.

'Too much to believe.' Cardinal Romano snorted.

Cardinal Beauclerc silenced him with a wave of the hand. 'If you proceed with your inquiry it must be done so quietly and carefully.'

'I have someone who I trust to do this discretely,' Sanchez assured him, ' and I will personally speak with the owner and convince him that the best thing would be to allow us to verify the casket.'

'Other than that no word of this casket or its supposed contents must leave this room.' Cardinal Beauclerc ordered. 'A relic such as this is a reminder of the great evil that took place during our Lord's Passion. It must not fall into the wrong hands.

Deacon Fuentes had heard all that he needed to. He re-covered the hole in the wall and stepped out of the recess. He wavered for a minute at the door, wondering whether to interrupt the meeting, but couldn't think of an excuse. Instead, he walked briskly down the corridor and onto the marble staircase that descended throughout the whole building. A Cardinal and a Priest nodded at him as they passed by but he paid them no attention. It was only once he was outside, his breath panting and his palms sweating, that he pulled the phone out of his pocket and dialled the number.

7

Cardinals Romano and Sanchez were late for the second meeting. The two men disliked each other, and both men hated the fact that they had to walk together with not a word spoken between them. At one point they had both been considered for the position of Pope yet neither man had won enough votes during the conclave, and knowing this soured an already strained relationship between the two.

Cardinal Sanchez hid his portfolio in his robe as they entered the room and Cardinal Romano welcomed everyone to the meeting.

'We waited for you Giancarlo,' one of the other Cardinals said, with calculated enthusiasm intended to disperse tension in the room, 'after all, it is your meeting.'

On this cue the others around the table opened their own copies; sparks flew the length of the table as the portfolio covers, embossed in gold with the tiara and crossed keys of Saint Peter, caught the light.

'Understand this is a preliminary meeting to inform you all of the considerable threat that has arisen in the city, and to canvas opinion on how best to act against it.' Cardinal Romano began. 'I would like this meeting to be kept secret until a course of action has been decided upon and approved. For now, this information should be kept to our own, select group.'

'Not that it matters,' interrupted the Cardinal seated directly opposite him, 'in an administration such as ours, where information is the most valuable currency, rumours accrue a great amount of interest.'

Cardinal Romano looked into the eyes of Cardinal Benedetto San Marco, Prefect of the Congregation for the Doctrine of the Faith, wondering what purpose that comment had served, and whose side the Cardinal would take during the debate.

'As I was saying,' he continued, 'I would like this to be kept to ourselves for the time being. I trust you have all had time to read the dossier I distributed?'

'We are all of us busy men, Giancarlo,' came the reply, 'none of us has that much time left to us, but we all managed to read over the information.'

'If you have read it, then you must all appreciate the serious implications of the threat, and the situation that is soon to develop in the city.

'This is my research to date on the man heading the gene therapy experiments that have begun in the city. His name is Matteo Rossi: he was born here in Rome and grew up in America. He is an Ivy League graduate: an all-American Professor known in his own country for his devotion to the cause for genetic engineering.'

Eyebrows were raised, and he heard a gasp to his right: he had won over his audience. He looked around the table at the enraptured faces and continued.

'Among his published works, I discovered the papers "Gene Therapy: the changes that lie within." and "Synthetic Embryology: a revolution in human reproduction." Both tractates discuss and applaud the use of genetic engineering in the medical field; the latter even outlining the possible uses of manipulating the way that embryos are formed. In another thesis, Professor Rossi advocates the use of human embryos in experimentation, even going to the extent of describing it as a necessary practice in medical science. The man is an abomination: everything he stands for conflicts with our faith, and our respect for life.'

Romano sat back, content, and folded his arms. His colleagues absorbed the vitriol of his words; the shock quickly became apparent on their faces, many of which contorted into expressions of disgust.

'Abominable indeed!' spluttered Cardinal Arroyo, a passionate Latin American who Romano knew could be counted upon to quickly rise to the defence of all that the Church held sacred. 'Clearly, this man has no qualms with violating the Sanctity of Life that we fight so hard to respect and preserve. These new experiments of his: do you know whether they will involve the abuse of human embryos?'

'Towards the back of the portfolio, you will find a copy of the Professor's mission statement for the experiments.' The other Cardinals followed him to the relevant page in a rustling of thick, hand-crafted paper. 'The Professor and his team plan to "Implement a four-step programme of experimentation to research the methods, practice and possible benefits of a new form of gene therapy: Genetic Manipulation and Substitution."

'In short, this new technology, he refers to it as "GMS", includes the manipulation of the way genes are formed, isolating defective genes or gene components and replacing them with synthetically created versions. Human embryos must undoubtedly play some role in the experiments, most likely as the testing ground for Professor Rossi's theories.'

'It all sounds very involved,' Cardinal Sanchez grumbled, 'I think we would be working a little out of our depth if we were to attempt to combat this ourselves. Are we absolutely sure that the Professor intends to use embryos here?'

'Perhaps it would be best to involve the Pontifical Academy of Sciences: let our scientists debate and investigate Giancarlo's "threat"?' Suggested Cardinal San Marco.

'And for every hour that they spent debating the subject, Professor Rossi's team would have free reign to carry out their experiments.' Romano countered. 'No, Benedetto: that is not acceptable. The experiments cannot be allowed to continue. We must voice our concerns now: act swiftly and we show the world how seriously the Holy See regards this matter. These modern times bring with them many troubles that infringe upon our beliefs: we must make an example of Professor Rossi to show the world that such insults will not be tolerated.'

'An insult as well as a threat?' Cardinal San Marco questioned from beneath raised eyebrows.

'Yes! An insult! A threat! A violation, a disrespect, a problem! One that we have to act against now, or else others all over the world see us as weak, and the faith will be compromised!'

'This shouldn't have been allowed to happen!' Cardinal Arroyo added to Romano's outburst. 'The government must have known the full ugliness of these unholy experiments: why was the Professor not prevented from setting up in Rome? Not only are the experiments an affront to our religion but they also show a clear disrespect for life in its simplest form. We should demand that these experiments cease, and also ask questions as to why the Italian government gave the experiments the go-ahead in the first place!'

A few gentle nods moved through the silence following the accusation. Cardinal Sanchez lifted the tumbler from the top of the crystal carafe that sat by his elbow, and upturning it, filled it with water. Heads turned, and attention focused on the water as it filled the silence as well as the glass.

'I think we may be letting our fears run away with us, my friends,' he said once he felt he commanded their attention, and with no attempt to drink from his glass. 'We don't want to be seen to be throwing accusations at random politicians and scientists; we can't let people think we are afraid of these experiments. By all means approach them cautiously, and logically, but don't take action until we have the full facts.

'Cardinal Romano has done an exemplary job of researching this Professor Rossi and his experiments, but I have seen nothing here that proves his accusations. What evidence is there that these experiments will involve the use of embryos? Although we can say without a doubt that they *probably* will, the information here neither confirms nor denies it. We need concrete proof before the Holy Father is involved, and before we make a statement or take any other action.'

'Isn't it obvious to you that this Professor is looking to offend the Church? Why else would he come to Rome?' Cardinal Romano's exasperation simmered at the surface of his usual composure.

'Please let's not get into an argument,' Cardinal San Marco pleaded, 'it's too early in the day. Both of you make good points: I think it may be more than just a coincidence that Professor Rossi chose to come to Rome, yet I think we need to keep level heads regardless of what action we may take: if we can't agree amongst ourselves, how can we stand together against the experiments? What do you say, Giancarlo?'

'I – I think it would be wise to investigate the experiments further before we consider taking action against the scientists. There seems to be something clandestine about them, but I couldn't find anything to prove my suspicions.'

'Who should take up the task?' Cardinal Arroyo asked.

'Ordinarily, it should fall under my jurisdiction.' Cardinal San Marco answered.

'But I have the necessary contacts, Benedetto, and have already begun making further enquiries. It also falls under my remit as Prefect of the Pontifical Council for the Family: I will be able to liaise better with the Academy for Life and Social Sciences. I have started my investigation, and would like to be the one to finish it.'

The varied opinions were evidenced by a mix of nodding heads, shrugging shoulders, and slick sneaked looks from one Cardinal to another.

'Very well,' Cardinal San Marco said, 'I think we're in some kind of agreement. Pursue this matter to your heart's content, Giancarlo: we'll meet within a month to discuss your findings and draft some kind of statement.'

There was a distinct finality in his tone that somehow declared that the meeting, although not started by him, had most certainly been finished by him. Cardinal Romano glared at Cardinal Sanchez as he closed the portfolio in front of him. Both men now had their own investigations to conduct, their own secrets to keep. Once again they found themselves at odds with one another: their respective investigations gave them the chance to either impress the Pope or else ruin their reputations among their colleagues and the wider Church.

8

Rodrigo stood guard at the doorway into the room behind the shop looking out towards the main door. He had taken an instant dislike to the shop when they had arrived: everything from the malignant clown in the window to the yellowed fingernails of its owner spoke of stagnation. Nothing moved in the Antiquaria, nothing changed. Who knew what hid in the dark and dusty corners of the shop?

He shivered and turned his attention to the back room, where Cardinal Sanchez sat with the shopkeeper, looking at the casket through an eyeglass.

'Primitive, yet exquisite,' the Cardinal declared, 'I'll be honest: it would prefer it in my personal collection rather than the Musei Vaticani.'

'You can see the marks where the fragments were eased out of the dirt,' the other man pointed out.

'A heinous crime. The relic has been defiled in its removal from the casket. I only hope it has not been destroyed as well.' He paused. 'You can guarantee that it was there?'

'I saw it with my own eyes, Your Eminence, although I didn't dare touch it.'

'Curiosity didn't get the better of you?'

'No. This is one relic I would not like to handle: the bowl that condemned Christ. By using this relic, the blame for Christ's death was passed on to the Jews.'

'Yes, I am more than familiar with the Gospel.'

'This cup is, or was, the source of the enmity between Christians and Jews throughout the centuries. Imagine the power that it has.'

The Cardinal's eyes flashed to Rodrigo in the doorway and then back to the shopkeeper.

'Or had, Signore. We have no idea whether the relic still exists.'

'My instincts tell me that it does – why else would someone go to the trouble of taking the relic but leaving the casket, if not to keep it somewhere else? Whoever stole it knew what they were looking at.'

'Who else did you tell?'

'One or two other traders. But I only talked about the casket. I said nothing about its contents. None of this makes sense, Your Eminence.'

'And nothing else was stolen?'

The shopkeeper looked over his shoulder at Rodrigo and moved his chair closer to the Cardinal. He leaned toward him, and Cardinal Sanchez did the same.

'There was a small bust, a copy of Madama Lucrezia.'

'The talking statue? Why would you have such a thing?'

'It was sold to me by a struggling artist a long time ago. I kept it for good luck.'

'Luck?'

'You know what they say...'

'Indulge me.'

'They say she still lives.'

'Who?'

'Madama Lucrezia.'

Both men jumped to see Rodrigo standing beside them. The shopkeeper coughed nervously and looked at the Cardinal with pleading eyes.

'What is it, Rodrigo?'

'He is here.'

The rusted bell stopped mid-ring as it stuck in place. Matteo did his best to ignore the clown in the window as he stepped into the shop. His feet kicked up small clouds of dust as he walked towards the doorway of yellowing light at the back.

'Hello?'

The shopkeeper appeared at the door, looking back into the room and then out into the shop again. Even through the thick gloom, Matteo could see that the man was nervous.

'Matteo Rossi. *Benvenuto*. Come and take a seat.'

Matteo quickly crossed the shop floor, taking care not to knock against any of the items placed precariously on the furniture. The dead bird in the cage stared blankly at him from its place in the doorway. The shopkeeper welcomed him into the back room and it was then that he saw the two other men; a Cardinal and a Deacon.

'Professor Rossi,' the Cardinal, the older of the two, said, 'welcome. I hope you don't mind us attending this meeting. My name is Cardinal Luis Sanchez, head of the Vatican's Congregation of Divine Worship and the Discipline of the Sacraments. This is my assistant, Deacon Rodrigo Fuentes. We are very interested in your casket.'

'You are?' Rossi did little to hide the suspicion in his voice.

'Indeed. The Vatican takes a special interest in historical artefacts that relate to the early Christian eras. There are so few items remaining that each one, if found to be genuine, is priceless. Although we do our best to compensate the owners.'

'Compensate?'

The Cardinal sat down and gestured to the casket. That part of the conversation was over for now.

'Are you ready to see inside, Signore?' The shopkeeper asked.

'Have you opened it already?'

'No. I thought it best to wait for you. But I have found out a great many things about the casket since you first brought it to me. We believe that it is of Byzantine origin, possibly from Dalmatia or Roman Macedonia, both of which form today's Albania. It most likely moved between churches or monasteries although how it came to belong to a single family, I cannot guess.'

'The point is,' the Cardinal interrupted, 'that it is a Christian item, that it has always belonged with the Church.'

'It's a family heirloom,' Matteo corrected him.

'Of course.'

The shopkeeper coughed again and picked up a small palette knife. It was probably made of silver but the patina had tarnished it so much that it looked more like lead.

'I have tried to open it already and it is a little stiff, but I think that I can manage it now.' He shot a look at Cardinal Sanchez and then returned his attention to the casket.

'May I?' Matteo asked, reaching forward for the knife.

'Of course.'

Matteo picked up the casket, weighed it in his hand, turned it around to examine the carvings on the surface, and slipped the knife into the thin gap beneath the lid. The casket groaned as he prised it open, his face filled with boyish anticipation. Slowly, carefully, the casket revealed its insides.

'It's...it's empty.'

'What?' The shopkeeper said with what sounded like genuine surprise.

'Nothing in it at all?' The Cardinal asked.

Rodrigo turned to face the doorway just in time to hide his smirk.

'Wait...there's something on the inside of the lid...an inscription I think.' Matteo opened the lid fully and pointed it towards the naked light bulb in the ceiling. Crude markings were indeed visible, scratched into the metal, but blackened by time.

'What does it say?' He mused to himself, and then remembered the others in the room. He handed it carefully to the shopkeeper, who in turn inspected it theatrically.

'I'm not sure. It doesn't look like Latin. Coptic maybe? Or perhaps some kind of early Christian glyphs? I'd have to look into it.'

'And how long would that take?' Matteo wondered aloud.

Rodrigo turned around in the silence and cast a look in Cardinal Sanchez's direction. The old man made a deliberate show of considering the professor's question.

'We have scholars at the Vatican who may be able to solve this riddle. Yes, I'm sure there would be someone at the museums who could help us. I could get an answer in days. That is if you were willing to relinquish the casket for a little while longer.'

Curiosity got the better of Matteo and he agreed to leave the casket with Cardinal Sanchez, exactly as the old man had hoped. The shopkeeper remained silent as the deal was struck between the two men: besides his finder's fee, his part in the affair was now over. The Cardinal thanked Matteo and Rodrigo escorted him from the room.

Everything had gone according to plan and now the casket would reside in the Vatican where it belonged.

The relic, meanwhile, had yet to be found.

9

'Take a seat, Lorenzo.' Cardinal Sanchez said, carefully trying to make it sound like more of a request than an order.

Lorenzo did as he was told, and sat in one of the Cardinal's plush red chairs. The soft fabric in the back cushioned his spine.

'Have you had any luck researching the missing casket?' He asked.

'As you said, Your Eminence, there was no report of the break-in. I spoke to a few private detectives and none of them has been engaged to find the relic.'

'Did you tell them about the relic?'

'No, but one of them hinted that he knew what I was talking about. He said that there were rumours of a shop burglary where nothing had been taken.'

'Ah. It's possible that he was thinking about something else. It seems that something was stolen from the antique shop.'

'Besides the relic?'

'A small marble bust, a replica of the statue of Madama Lucrezia.'

'Is it significant in any way?'

The Cardinal paused, wondering once again how wise it was to continue. How far would he allow the boy to go in the search for the casket? If he continued, he set Lorenzo on a path through the Roman underworld. If he held his tongue he might lose the relic and by extension, his salvation. His immortal soul got the better of him.

'Lorenzo, do you know anything about the talking statues of Rome?'

'The what?'

'I'll take that as a no. The talking statues of Rome: you'll read about them in most guidebooks, and find them scattered across the Centro

Storico. The most renowned are Pasquino, Il Babuino, Marforio...and Madama Lucrezia. Since the Renaissance, they have "spoken" in the form of verses and slogans drawn or pasted onto them. From satires to outspoken rebellion the statues have spoken the mind of the people in matters that would otherwise have landed the speakers in hot water. They remain a bastion of rebellion against authority; agents of chaos carved from stone.

'Madama Lucrezia is a large Roman bust, possibly of the goddess Venus, but she has come to represent something more: she is the voice of the underworld.'

'The underworld?'

'The gypsies, the undesirables, the criminals, and yes, the thieves.'

'And you think that the theft of this small bust is connected to the original statue somehow?'

'I do indeed, and therefore the theft of the relic is linked to Madama Lucrezia. It goes deeper still.' Here, the Cardinal turned over his notes, and ran a finger down the page, coming to rest against a name and a question mark, 'There is a rumour I have heard, that Madama Lucrezia is in fact, a person; an idea made flesh. Someone has taken on the persona of the talking statue, some figurehead in the underworld. Find that person, and you may indeed find the relic.'

'And how do I find this person?'

'If I were you, I would start with her statue. You will find it in the corner of Piazza di San Marco, near the Vittoriano monument.'

'I will not let you down, Your Eminence.'

'Nor would I expect you to, my boy.'

The Cardinal dismissed him, and Lorenzo found his way to the statue of Madama Lucrezia as directed and had staked out the piazza for most of the day. Late afternoon, bold as brass, a dirty-faced young boy had marched up to the statue and pasted something on the wall behind it. It was a poster that decried the treatment of the Roma population by the authorities. Lorenzo was vaguely aware that the government had recently intensified its attempts to rid the streets of Rome of the gypsies, in an attempt to appease the tourists with their fat wallets and foreign currencies.

As the day crawled to its inevitable end, Lorenzo found himself following the course of the Tiber, not high on the street-level embankment, but along the weed-strewn towpath far below. The sun threw a feeble attempt at light across trees and buildings, casting long cold shadows that grew by the minute as Lorenzo walked upstream. Ahead of him, the elaborate Ponte Vittorio Emanuele II spanned the river, carrying the roaring traffic, and beyond it, a few birds watched the sun set, upon a rock that rose defiantly out of the water.

His task had been simple so far: follow the boy. The urchin had not seen Lorenzo as he tailed him through the streets to the river, passing under bridge after bridge as the waters of the Tiber hissed against the stone embankments that encased it. Eventually, in sight of the angels that graced the Ponte Sant'Angelo, the boy stopped before a small collection of tents and tarpaulins, where a family of Roma had taken up residence between the walls and the water.

Plain for all to see yet ignored by the tourists, pilgrims and pavement artisans who congregated daily on the levels above, a small band of people lived among the pillars supporting the bridge. Groundsheets and lines of washing marked out individual homes in this shanty street no bigger than the average bus shelter. A small fire burned at the water's edge with a misshapen pot boiling above it. Two children in ragged clothes played with a dirty, unkempt puppy; they waved to the boy, and then got up and ran away when they saw Lorenzo following behind. The boy seemed not to care as the puppy ran past him and on to Lorenzo, its tail wagging and tongue hanging out in welcome. Lorenzo recoiled at the dog's frothing mouth, then saw the animal was blind in one eye and stopped to stroke it pitifully.

When he looked up again, he saw the young boy pointing him out to a burly man with skin the dark colour of the streets. Something about the man's stance commanded that he stay rooted to the spot, and as he approached, Lorenzo saw the man had a face so wrinkled it seemed as if the pattern of the city streets had somehow been carved into his skin. Behind the man, Lorenzo could just make out the two children peeking from the slats of their packing-crate home.

'Come posso aiutare?' The man asked, in a strong deep voice befitting his build.

How can I help you? For a moment Lorenzo considered the irony of a man, clearly in need of some form of aid, offering to help someone like him, who in comparison had everything he might want.

Lorenzo mustered the courage to speak, all the time fighting the urge to run and climb the nearby steps back up to the world of streetlights and pizzerias. The traffic roared menacingly overhead, the birds cackled at him from their rock amid the churning waters.

'I'm looking for Madama Lucrezia. She is supposed to be in the city.'

'I have never heard of this Madama Lucrezia. I know of no such person. Go from here and never come down to the river again.'

'Look, if it helps, I can pay you for any information you have.' Lorenzo pulled a wallet from his jeans and began to count out some crisp bank notes.

The man looked Lorenzo up and down, taking in the clean clothes and the warm-looking jacket.

'There are many layers to this city, boy. Below the surface of tourism and politics, the world of everyday living, there is a whole world of the unwanted, the unloved. In the underworld, power is the currency, not money.'

The man stepped forward and batted the wallet out of Lorenzo's hand, sending it to the ground in a flurry of Euros. As Lorenzo stooped down to save the money from the hungry puppy, the man reached for the small white business card that had fallen out with it. He picked it up, and turning it over, saw Serafino's name written on it. Lorenzo looked up and saw the recognition on his face.

'Perhaps I may be able to help, after all. This underworld too has its layers; the gypsies, the thieves, the drug lords, the assassins; and these layers are ruled by two regimes: one of kindness and one of fear. The man who gave you this card: crosses the chasm between both.

'On the one side, Madama Lucrezia rules with her heart and cares for those who are unfortunate enough to enter her realm. She helps the homeless, she looks after the sick. But she is in constant struggle with the criminal elements of this underworld: the world of fear, ruled by the cruelty of Il Capitano.'

'Il Capitano? Who is he?'

'This man, Serafino, will tell you, but you would do better by not asking questions about him. Madama Lucrezia has great influence here: no decent person would see harm come to you whilst you seek her, but the same cannot be said of Il Capitano. Know this: you will not find her unless she wants you to. It is more likely that *she* will find *you* in time..'

'I don't understand.'

'Her ways are not for the likes of you to understand. What would you know of our suffering? Our sorrows? If you are worthy, Madama Lucrezia will seek you out.'

'What do I do until then?'

The man handed Serafino's card back to Lorenzo.

'If I were you, I would follow what few leads you to have. ' He looked up at the sun setting beyond the high walls of the embankment, 'And I would do it when there is still light left in the world.'

Lorenzo thrust the wallet back into his pocket and turned away as the man dismissed him. He felt foolish; he felt like he had failed the Cardinal. The puppy gambolled about a few steps ahead of him, begging for him to stop and play, but a shrill whistle from beneath the bridge sent the animal running back among the tarpaulins. Lorenzo ignored the dog, his eyes drawn up to the Ponte Sant'Angelo as he climbed the steps in front of him. Stone angels raised the icons of Christ's Passion high above the tradesmen selling counterfeit goods.

As he crossed over the bridge, the colossal Castel de Sant'Angelo rose out of the ground ahead of him. Crowning the castle was a verdigris statue of the Archangel Michael brandishing a sword above his head; looking at it, the man's words echoed in his head.

What would you know of our suffering? Our sorrows?

He wondered how many of them were left: the unwanted, and the unloved, hiding in the crevices among the city's ancient stonework. The thought made him shiver as he walked through the avenue of trees that encircled the castle. Dried dung from the birds in the branches above him crunched underfoot, filling his nostrils with the duel aromas of feathers and excrement. Dodging a late horse-and-cart transporting tourists along the embankment, he threaded his way through the lingering groups of people bartering for fake designer handbags and leapt over the white chains at the entrance to the park surrounding the castle, where he found peace and solitude.

Sitting himself down on a bench, he pulled out Serafino's card and held it up to the last rays of the sun to see the watermarked phone number.

'When in doubt, always look to the light,' he mused.

'I'd save that call for another time,' a voice answered, and Lorenzo looked to his right to see Serafino replacing the receiver on a nearby payphone.

'Have you been watching me?' He asked.

'No,' Serafino said, and then shrugged in supplication, 'and yes. A man like you, with his couture outfit and coiffed hair, stands out among the unwashed folk of the riverbank.'

'How long have you been following me?'

'How long have you been searching for Madama Lucrezia?'

Serafino sat down on the bench and produced a cigarette case, offering Lorenzo the first cigarette.

'Do you always speak in riddles?' He asked, dismissing the cigarette with a wave.

'Do you always ask the obvious questions?' Serafino lit the cigarette and inhaled deeply, 'It seems to me that a man in your profession would do better to seek less obvious answers. To look beneath the surface, and find out what moves in the depths.'

'And how do I do that?'

'You can start by answering my question: how long have you been searching for Madama Lucrezia?'

'Since the...since a friend told me about her.'

'What sort of friend?'

'A family friend.'

Serafino took another drag on the cigarette, 'I see. And what might this "friend" want of Madama Lucrezia, do you think?'

Lorenzo thought silently for a while. A middle-aged couple in evening dress passed by, the soft fur of the woman's mink stole teased by the evening breeze.

'It's about appearances, isn't it?'

'What is?'

'The Car-' Lorenzo stopped himself, but Serafino seemed not to have noticed, 'my friend, he wants me to look into Madama Lucrezia. A bust of the talking statue was stolen from a shop across the river.'

Serafino looked down at him from the side of his eye, 'Go on.'

'Apparently, the bust wasn't worth anything, but it might have been stolen along with something of more value.'

'Why steal a statue of no value? Especially if you have already stolen something of great worth?'

'Because perhaps the statue is worth something after all?'

'To whom is a worthless statue worth something?'

'I don't know.'

'Let me put it another way, Lorenzo: those people you saw down at the river. Do you think they have worth?'

Lorenzo looked at Serafino's weathered face, crowned by the battered fedora, and shrugged.

'Do you think they contribute to society? Did they look as if they had any value at all?'

'Not really.'

'Then who are they worth anything to?'

'Who?'

'Their Creator. He who creates something: be it a life, or a work of art, with always ascribe value to his creation.'

'So...'

'Find the creator of your missing statue, and you might just identify the thief.'

'Is it really that simple?'

'Does it need to be any more complicated?'

'What about Madama Lucrezia?'

'You know that is the name of the statue.'

'And I know there is someone in the city who uses her identity. Someone who helps people.'

'Then if you find the artist who carved the statue, he may be able to shed some light on the situation. He may even point the way to Madama Lucrezia.'

'How will I find out who the artist is?'

'You are investigating a crime, Lorenzo: do as a policeman would, and begin at the crime scene. In the aftermath of a robbery, there is always confusion. Mistakes are made, and facts are jumbled. Sometimes to get a better picture of what happened, you have to wait until the dust has settled. Until the smoke has cleared. '

Serafino breathed a deliberate cloud of cigarette smoke into Lorenzo's face. Lorenzo closed his eyes and waved it away, trying not to splutter.

'How long should I wait?'

But when he opened his eyes, Serafino was gone.

Lorenzo looked left and right, and finding no evidence of his companion, even looked upward. The dark clouds above were stained amber by the city lights. Looking down, he saw two small dark circles, droplets, on the bench where Serafino had sat. The liquid appeared to have a red tinge in the electric light, and with a shiver, Lorenzo wondered whether it might be blood.

10

'So you have a new lead?' Cardinal Sanchez asked, scratching his chin with the blunt brass *gladius* that he kept on his desk as a letter-opener. The sunlight bounced off the miniature gladiatorial sword as he placed it down on the green leather inlay of the mahogany desk.

'Yes, Your Eminence,' Lorenzo beamed, flipping open his notepad 'I visited the Antiquaria and the shopkeeper, Signore D'Eustachio, showed me the listing for the statue that was stolen, which as it happens included the name of the original artist.'

'How very enterprising of you, Lorenzo, however did you come by it?'

Lorenzo looked guilty, 'I may have mentioned your name in connection with the story.'

'I see. No, my boy, I was asking how you came by the idea of visiting the antique shop?'

'I...' Lorenzo paused, and Cardinal Sanchez could tell that he was considering his words carefully, 'I just thought about going back to the beginning. You know, like a policeman would do. Start at the scene of the crime, and work from there.'

'I wonder whether your investigative instincts would have been put to better use in law enforcement than in journalism? The *carabiniere*'s loss is L'Osservatore Calabria's gain, it seems.'

'Thank you, Your Eminence.'

'Of course, if anyone else were to help you along with your investigation, you would tell me, wouldn't you? So that they can be included in the letter of thanks.'

'Of course.'

The Cardinal watched him carefully, waiting for some twitch, some tick or sign of a lie, but none was forthcoming.

'What did you say the original artist's name was?'

Lorenzo looked down at his notepad, 'Amadeo Bertoli. I've asked around and apparently he still runs a workshop somewhere in the city, so I shall be visiting him this afternoon to see if he can tell me more about Madama Lucrezia.'

'Well done, Lorenzo, although that visit may have to wait, a I have a little news of my own. I remember you said that you might need more content for your article on those gene therapy trials.'

'Ideally, Your Eminence, but I was grateful enough that you managed to get me access to the press conference. You don't need to do anything more.'

'Nonsense,' the Cardinal said in mock protest, 'I was happy to pull some strings for my Godson, and so I have pulled a few more. I have managed to secure you an interview with Professor Rossi this very afternoon!'

'Thank you so much, Your Eminence! How did you manage it?'

'I followed up with the Professor about the casket that we are investigating, and thought it would be the opportune moment to ask that he meet with you.'

'Your Eminence, this is too much!'

'Look at it this way, in agreeing to an interview, Professor Rossi is doing me a favour. And in speaking with him about the casket, you are also doing me a favour. Find out whether he knows anything about how it came into his family's possession.'

'Of course, Your Eminence.'

'He has agreed to give an interview at four o'clock at the Ospedale Centrale. I look forward to your findings.'

'Thank you so much-'

The desk phone rang, and the Cardinal raised a hand to silence Lorenzo. 'Do let me know how you get on,' he said as he picked up the receiver.

Lorenzo nodded and left the room silently, almost walking into Deacon Fuentes in the doorway. He excused himself and hurried by as the Deacon narrowed his eyes.

Cardinal Sanchez beckoned the Deacon in with a wave as he spoke to his secretary on the other end of the phone.

'Yes, he's just left. He'll be attending the meeting at four, as arranged. One more thing: can you arrange a car for half-past three? There's a workshop in the Ghetto that I wish to see. Studio Bertoli. Thank you.'

He replaced the receiver and smiled at his new guest. 'Rodrigo.'

'Bertoli? Wasn't he the artist who sold you that *Aracoeli* painting?'

'Yes, he was.'

'Are you in the market for more artwork?'

'Of a sort. I am in the market for *information*.'

'Perhaps I can be of service?'

'How so?'

Deacon Fuentes handed the Cardinal a gilt-edged folder with a sheaf of yellowing papers. Cardinal Sanchez thumbed through it and raised his eyebrows as he recognised the words.

'This is Spanish.'

'From the Secret Archives. It seems that, in Nineteen Thirty-Six, Benito Mussolini sent a large contingent of Blackshirt soldiers to Spain to assist in General Franco's war.'

'This I know, yes,' Cardinal Sanchez said dreamily as he flicked through the pages, his mind drifting back through the decades.

'It seems that one of them brought something back.'

'Indeed.'

'A certain casket, matching the one that you are assessing for Professor Rossi, allegedly held the remains of an ancient clay bowl. The fragments were allegedly all that now exists of the Washbowl of Pontius Pilate, Roman Governor of Judea at the time of Christ: the very bowl that condemned Christ to death. Mussolini thought of it as a link between the Roman Empire of old, and the New Empire he desired to carve with the Fascist sword.'

Cardinal Sanchez mouthed silent Spanish words as he traced his fingers over the fragile paper. Rodrigo continued to recite his memorised summary.

'After the fall of the Fascist Party and Mussolini's death, the relic was taken by one of his guards, who brought it to the Vatican hoping he could bribe the Church into helping him flee the country. A deal was brokered but collapsed when the full extent of the man's brutal past was discovered. Later on, it was understood that the relic had ended up in a gambling house, where it was given as a prize in a game of cards to a young doctor, who later emigrated to America, taking it with him.'

'America?'

'That doctor, Alberto Rossi, was the Professor's father.'

'Ah. So that is how he came to inherit it. Thank you for this, Rodrigo. Although I have never seen it for myself, I have heard many of the stories of the relic's purported existence. I have spent countless years searching for it, and yet it has always eluded me. Even to this day, I have the casket in my possession, but its precious contents are missing. Such a thing should be in the hands of the Church.'

'Agreed.'

'Tell me, does anyone else know of this?'

'I haven't told anyone.'

'Good, let us keep it that way. At least until we have the relic safe within the walls of the Holy See.'

11

Lorenzo tapped the top of his pen repeatedly with his thumb, pushing the ballpoint at the other end in and out with a rhythmic clicking sound that echoed around the antechamber. The receptionist was bristling at the repeated sound but was doing her utmost to ignore him. He told himself that he was supposed to be there, was *meant* to be there, but at that time he would rather be anywhere than in the gene therapy lab at the Ospedale Centrale, waiting on the scientists to meet with him as agreed. He would have preferred to have been investigating the theft of the relic or else seeking Madama Lucrezia out on the streets, but the Cardinal had been good enough to arrange the interview, and the gene therapy trials were the reason he was in the city in the first place, so here he was, stuck inside, waiting.

After what seemed like an age, and many glances at the steel clock on the wall, Lorenzo finally looked up at the automatic doors as they swung open to admit Professor Rossi and his second-in-command, Doctor Leibowitz. They stood there, arms folded in the doorway, a scientific Don and his *sottocapo*, Lorenzo mused. He was about to enter another world, yet another layer below the surface of his understanding, and these two were his guides.

'Signore L'Oscuro?' The Professor asked.

Lorenzo stood up, smoothed his chinos down, and stepped forward to shake both their hands. 'Buongiorno.'

'You have friends in high places, it seems,' Doctor Leibowitz said, fixing him with a stern glare as she shook his hand mechanically.

'And some in low ones,' Lorenzo countered.

'Welcome to our facility,' Professor Rossi waved him in through the door, 'Cardinal Sanchez told me that you were in Rome to write a newspaper article about our work?'

'That is true.'

'We've made a point of being open and honest with the press, and I hope that the Cardinal's phone call signifies a cooling of the hostilities that we've felt from the Vatican. Perhaps your article might go some way towards bridging the divide?'

'Perhaps. The Church is very steadfast in its stance against the kind of experiments that you are proposing.'

'They're more than a mere proposal now,' the Professor said with a smirk, 'you have just crossed the threshold into the future, Signore L'Oscuro.'

'Lorenzo, please.'

'Lorenzo. The future is here, and now. We are here, at the vanguard of the fight against disease and death itself. We are experimenting with new methods of gene therapy that will alter how our bodies respond to sickness, improving our quality of life, and ultimately our longevity.'

'I've read a little of your work, and I was at the press conference the other day. What you're basically saying is that you'll be able to change the genes in people's bodies to cure them of disease?'

'Eventually, yes.'

'Providing they're genetic diseases,' Doctor Leibowitz added, 'we won't be able to combat viral and bacterial diseases yet: they have to be treated by building up the immune system, training it to defend the body against a particular disease. In time, gene therapy may be used to protect against existing infections, providing that we know enough about them. But there will always be others.'

'So you're saying that as we treat and eradicate other diseases, we might become susceptible to far worse conditions?'

'There will always be new diseases, Lorenzo,' Professor Rossi said somewhat patronisingly, 'everyone has to die of something. As we eradicate the diseases we know about, we will inevitably discover ones that we're unfamiliar with. And in time, we will treat those, too.'

'My understanding is that you advocate altering our genetic code to combat these illnesses.'

'We do, yes. Gene therapy involves making changes to the human genome to improve our quality of life.'

'But if you change our DNA to make it resistant to an illness, and then another illness comes along, and you make more changes, and then you say there will be worse conditions to come...when do you stop making changes?'

Professor Rossi stopped in his tracks, and Lorenzo could almost see the resistance rising in him, 'We don't stop. We never stop the fight against illness. There will always be new diseases, new ailments, new infections; so we must never, ever stop our work.'

'Then that means you'll never stop changing our genetic code, right? So with that in mind, I'd like to ask: at what point, when you're making all these changes, do we stop being human?'

'We will always be human, Lorenzo.'

'Can you guarantee that? How do you know that making changes to our genetic code won't change who and what we are as a species? And what if the very tampering that you do is what makes us vulnerable to these new diseases in the first place?'

'I'd counter that with a question of my own: what if it makes us *more* than what we are as a species?'

'More than God intended us to be?'

'Religion has been wrong about so many things, Lorenzo.'

'So has Science.'

Doctor Leibowitz cut through with a loud cough, 'Our work here is for the betterment of all people, regardless of what their beliefs are.'

'And if people believe that what you're doing is against God?'

'You sound like the Cardinal who came here this morning.' The Professor grumbled.

'Cardinal Sanchez was here?'

'No, one of his colleagues: Cardinal Romano.'

'Interesting. And what did he think of your facility?'

'I think that Cardinal Romano had made up his mind about us before his visit. He came with certain preconceptions about our work.'

'Misconceptions,' Doctor Leibowitz added.

'And he left with them, too. He didn't take on board any of our comments and listened to no explanations. In all honesty, I think he just came to deliver a sermon about how we were messing with

God's work; how we were sinners; how the Church would fight us at every step.'

'He just came to let off some liturgical steam,' Doctor Leibowitz said, with a roll of her eyes and a shake of her head.

'He demanded to see our laboratories,' the Professor continued, 'and when we told him we couldn't let him inside them because of our decontamination procedures, he went lost it. He threatened to get some kind of search warrant: said he would get the police to launch an official investigation to uncover whatever we were hiding.'

'And what are you hiding?'

'Nothing! You can read our reports on our website as we publish them. We engage with the public via social media. We want to involve people, and share our results, as and when we can finalise them.'

'And when will that be?'

'When the Church leaves us alone to do our work in peace, Lorenzo.'

'If that's what you want, why set up in Rome? Why not go somewhere far from the Catholic crosshairs?'

'Rome has a particular resonance for me: it is the city of my birth. It is *caput mundi* for many, and the Italian government's new stance on the subject of genetic testing is encouraging. I believe it will be healthy for the country in the long run, and lucrative, too.'

'So nothing to do with the publicity that you generated by setting up this facility in the shadow of St Peter's Basilica?'

'Nothing whatsoever.'

Lorenzo scoffed, and his eyes settled on a door at the end of the corridor, marked with chevrons, and the words *Accesso Limitato*.

'If you're so open to sharing with the public, what's behind that door? Why the "Restricted Access" signs?'

'Like I said,' came the Professor's answer, 'we will share the results of our work as and when we can finalise them.'

'So we won't be going in there today?'

'Lorenzo, you may have friends in high places, but trust me when I say this: God himself couldn't get you through that door.'

Lorenzo made a show of writing the Professor's words down, but he had already committed them to memory and would recite them to himself over and over in the coming weeks until his article was finished.

God himself couldn't get you through that door.

That was it; that was all he needed. That last quote would tell his readers everything that he wanted them to know about Professor Rossi and the gene therapy experiments. Cardinal Sanchez would be pleased, and so would his editor at L'Osservatore Calabria. Lorenzo promised himself that the Professor would come to regret those words, and his blatant ego.

12

Cardinal Sanchez rapped his bony knuckle against the glass screen in front of him and the car slowed to a stop opposite a small alley across the street so deep in shadow that it seemed to drain the light from the streetlights, darkening the whole area. The chauffeur got out and held the door open for him, reaching a hand in to help him out of the vehicle. He bade the driver wait in the car, and then crossed the road, disappearing into the alley and leaving the world of light, traffic and friendly faces behind, to enter a world of darkness, whispers and muffled sound. His footsteps echoed along the narrow alley as he walked through the ink-black darkness, looking for a doorway that he only half-remembered. From a window high above, he heard a steady whimpering; a sound that almost struck pity in his heart, before it became a scream that was silenced both suddenly and suspiciously.

A small trickle of water fell down the side of the building to his left and followed a well-worn path through the cobbled floor. The Cardinal could just about make out a streetlight winking at the far end of the alley, casting nervous rays of light into the darkness. He dragged his hand along the wall, counting the door frames, coming to a halt before a doorway in the centre of the alley, the darkness stretching out either side of him. Cardinal Sanchez raised his fist to knock against the door, but thought better of it, and instead flattened his hand, and pushed against the brittle wood. The door gave way with an oaken groan that barked loud in both directions along the alley; shapes moved in the darkness, suddenly alerted to the Cardinal's presence. He crossed himself and entered the building.

The hallway directly inside led to a courtyard decked with dried creepers and dead vines that draped themselves over the balconies above and tumbled to the ground floor. Recalling long-forgotten memories, Cardinal Sanchez found his way to a stone staircase and climbed three floors. Trampling the desiccated leaves of past winters underfoot, he followed the cloistered gallery along the top floor of the building to a door that hung open on its hinges, barely clinging on to its purpose. To the right, a metal plaque pocked with rust bore the words:

STUDIO BERTOLI

Cardinal Sanchez pressed on, stepping into a suite of small, sparsely decorated rooms that was in complete disarray. He flicked the light switch in each room, engaging naked light bulbs that illuminated broken sculptures, smashed vessels, and canvas paintings slashed to such a degree that it was impossible to tell what their subjects might once have been. In the furthest room, a set of curtains that had been rendered almost lace-like by the mouths of hungry moths hung limply from a curtain rail, framing a set of warped shutters that the Cardinal pulled back to reveal a brittle wooden balcony perched above the street below.

The Cardinal looked out of the shutters, admiring the view over the next street and the Tiber beyond. To his left, in the middle of the river was the boat-shaped mass of L'Isola Tiberina, the sole island that disrupted the river's path through the city. The cluster of buildings on the island; the hospital and the church especially; enjoyed the effect of subtle yellow lighting on their ancient stonework. It was a picture-postcard view, a golden reward glimpsed beyond the decrepit artist's workshop. When he finally dragged himself away from the cityscape and turned to face the room, his eyes were met with two words, repeated over and over, in wretched capital letters across the wall opposite:

NON INNOCENTE

Cardinal Sanchez retched, and fought back the urge to vomit. He had seen enough and hurried from the rooms as soon as his old bones would allow. Without so much as a glance over his shoulder, he returned along the alley, to the safety of his waiting car, and instructed the chauffeur to forgo the congested embankment route in favour of the relatively empty Via Giulia. The driver negotiated the narrow, cobbled street slowly and carefully, for fear of scraping the car against one of the vehicles parked along the road.

The Cardinal stared blankly out of the window. Ahead of the car, there was a movement in the space between two buildings: a flash of red. Cardinal Sanchez ordered the chauffeur to stop, and pulled his face away from the window, but remained close enough to see a face emerging into the field of vision granted by the nearest streetlight.

It was a face he recognised immediately: another Cardinal stepped out of the shadow, cloaked in black, yet with the red trim of his cassock still visible beneath. A black hood covered his head, keeping half of his face in shadow; but half a face was all that Cardinal Sanchez needed to identify the man. Here was Cardinal Romano, another man of considerable power. Here was his rival.

'You look as if you've seen a ghost.' The chauffeur commented, observing him in the rear-view mirror.

'No, not a ghost,' Cardinal Sanchez mused, 'a man of flesh: living and breathing. But not where he should be at this hour. Please, drive on: there is much for me to do.'

13

Reeling from the rejection of the scientists, and with Professor Rossi's flippant comment rebounding around his head, Lorenzo had left the Ospedale Centrale and set himself in the direction of the convivial ambience of the cafe-clad Piazza Navona. The rush hour traffic along the Tiber was thick with mopeds swarming around irate taxi drivers, mounting pavements, and running red lights. Emergency sirens screamed along the length of the river, causing havoc with the traffic lights that displayed maddening sequences of light, giving rise to a soundtrack of blaring horns, angry yells and revving engines. Ghostly parking tickets waved from the windscreens of cars lying dormant at the roadside under the darkening canopy of trees.

Bank-breaking price tags drew Lorenzo's eye to the glowing window displays of the fashionable boutiques opening up for the evening punters. Nuns jostled with students to ogle the latest lines being unveiled, all imagining themselves in designer threads they had no means of purchasing. Crossing the road, he passed a toy shop prematurely setting out a range of Christmas stock, and entered the aromatic, colourful Piazza: a wide space among the warren of ancient streets and alleys where he could breathe easily.

Nestled among the grand palazzi, Piazza Navona provided a refuge from the overwhelming traffic, whilst still preserving the hectic buzz of the city's tourist trade. Three fountains graced the square, providing the endless, calming sound of water to soothe the distraught minds of the tourists battling with language barriers and exchange rates. The subtly-illuminated fountain waters, combined with the rich restaurant aromas, created the feeling of a tranquil oasis among the smog-choked city streets.

Lorenzo stalked the fringes of the Piazza, seeking a bar with enough noise to drown out all thought of his experience at the gene therapy lab, yet quiet enough to let him gather his thoughts of the relic. Legions of people, congregated under huge umbrellas, talking in innumerable languages. Busy waiters, every one of them smiling, hopped from table to table, taking orders, bringing sizzling meals, and carrying trays overloaded with drinks. A juggler entertained the patrons of one restaurant, singers stood outside another, and a man in harlequin costume stood in the bowl of the smallest fountain breathing plumes of fire into the evening air.

He stood for a while watching a girl sitting for a caricaturist, who Lorenzo felt had captured her likeness well: her high cheekbones, dancing eyes, the gently flushed skin. The picture almost breathed life, and as interest grew in the artist, he melted into the thickening crowd. A man opened his coat to reveal six lines of glimmering watches, but Lorenzo waved him away and walked on. Laughter and clapping filled the air as the artist signed the bottom of the completed portrait. He could hear the girl squealing from somewhere behind him.

Eventually, Lorenzo settled on one of the smaller perimeter restaurants and he sat down to watch people photographing the nearest fountain. A waiter approached with a menu and a beaming smile; he hadn't intended to eat but ordered bruschetta and beef straccetti with a bottle of red wine. He had picked a good spot, under the warmth of an incandescent patio heater, yet not so far under it that he couldn't feel the breeze against his bare arms.

As Lorenzo drained the first glass of wine, a drab band of entertainers entered the square and began to walk among the tables, singing to the seated tourists, before they were chased away by irate waiters. Two had guitars, one played a mouth organ, while another rattled a bucket for small change. Their dark clothes enabled them to retreat swiftly into the shadows and reappear in other parts of the square to try their luck, unlike the other brightly clothed street entertainers who stuck out like a sore thumb. Dirty-faced children that reminded him of those he had seen at the river threaded their way through the tables selling roses to overly-romantic couples.

The troupe launched into a murderous rendition of something that may, or may not have been by Puccini, as they approached the restaurant that Lorenzo had chosen. Although it sounded familiar, he didn't move in the right circles to know one opera from another. The men wove around the crowds, their faces contorted in song, arms waving, eyes closed in strained effort to reach the high notes. They finished in a devastating crescendo that sounded more like caterwauling than anything else. Lorenzo applauded with the rest of the restaurant's patrons, glad it was over, more than anything else.

He rolled his eyes as the man with the mouth organ produced a tambourine and began shaking it. One of the guitar players began beating rhythmically against his instrument, while the other stood beside him strumming a few chords. Behind them, as a splash of bright red danced through the air, he heard the sound of castanets. The men began to sing, in tune this time, oblivious to the movement behind them. Lorenzo craned his neck to try and see: there was another flash of red. A scarf perhaps, or else one of the children throwing a rose.

Some of the patrons began to tap in time to the music; others cuddled up to one another over the candles illuminating their tables. The rhythm of the song got inside their heads: hands and feet tapped, and one or two drunken notes were hummed. The singers gathered together, crooning louder, playing faster, and then stopping abruptly, leaving only the tambourine, the castanets, and the rattling money bucket playing a slow drum roll. The drum roll picked up quickly, and with a chorus of shouts, the men parted to reveal their best money-spinning weapon.

Clothed in a revealing crimson dress so tight it seemed like a second skin, yet covering enough to be considered tasteful, a young woman danced provocatively for her audience. The sound of castanets came from her stilettos, which she stamped against the cobbles to the staccato beat. It was as if Carmen or Esmeralda had been made real by the songs and music of her people, although she lacked the tanned skin more commonly associated with the gypsy stereotype. Her skin was pale as the moon above and looked almost translucent compared to her scarlet dress.

Desire flamed in Lorenzo; from the first glimpse, he wanted her, had to have her. There was no denying it: from her dark silken hair, and her perfect curves somehow defying the laws of physics to stay in the dress, right down to her dainty feet in the bejewelled shoes that she struck against the floor, Lorenzo wanted every last inch of her. His mouth gaped open as she rotated her hips rhythmically, moving in wider circles in time with the music. The whole world seemed to stop and look as she moved through the crowds and the tables of the restaurant. The waiters ignored the rose-selling urchins; husbands ignored their wives, and a few wives even ignored their husbands.

Watched by everyone around her, she danced, twirled, pouted and winked, bewitching them, drawing them into her world of movement and rhythm. She picked up glasses of wine and drained them, she teased the awestruck waiters, and danced, all the time accompanied by the singing of the men at the edge of the crowd. Lorenzo was so stunned that she was almost on top of him before his brain had even registered her approach. He had forgotten about the relic, he had forgotten about the scientists: in his mind, there was only the dancing woman, aflame in her dress.

Somehow, he had come to purchase a rose, although he couldn't recall ever taking money from his wallet. Speechless and shy, he gave it to her, and to his complete astonishment, the siren; this woman that every part of his body ached for; sat down at his table. The people around him clapped as the music stopped, and the children ran among the tables grinning, rattling small buckets. She reached a slender hand forward and closed Lorenzo's mouth for him with an enticing laugh that drew him further into her thrall until there wasn't a clean thought left in his head.

'Mi scusi signore, are you being bothered?' A waiter asked, gulping as he looked the woman up and down. She looked up with a look of belligerence that made him take a step back, then looked back pleadingly at Lorenzo.

'Not at all,' he said dreamily as he stared at her breasts moving beneath her dress, 'we were just going to have dinner.'

'Dinner?' The waiter scoffed.

'Yes! Dinner! Would you like dinner?'

'I'd love dinner.' She said, sliding one of her smooth legs in between his.

'And what will the lady be having?' The waiter said, bemused, handing her a menu and setting down a fresh wine glass. Lorenzo picked up his glass and drank, as calmly and nonchalantly as possible.

'Manzo con salsa verde,' she said, with a sultry accent that Lorenzo felt belonged somewhere on the Italian border, 'I like to have meat on a first date.'

Lorenzo nearly choked on his wine.

'Grazie, signora; enjoy your meal.'

She waved the waiter away and gave a little smirk. Lorenzo filled her glass with wine whilst trying to think of something witty to say. In the event, she was the one to fill the silence.

'My name is Maddalena.'

She held out her hand for him to shake, but he raised it to his lips and kissed it. He'd seen it happen in the movies, but it didn't work so well in real life, yet here he was doing it and making a fool of himself in the process. Her perfume was intoxicating: he breathed it in, letting it work its way into his head, soothing him, disarming him. From that moment on, he was hers: completely, and probably forever.

'And you are?' She asked.

'I am?'

'Your name?'

'Oh, Lorenzo. Lorenzo L'Oscuro.'

'That's an interesting name you have, Lorenzo L'Oscuro.'

'Is it?'

'Some would say it means "Laurelled by the Dark One".'

'Really?'

She nodded, as she drank from her glass.

'And what does Maddalena mean?'

'Some would say it means "From the Tower".'

'What do you say it means?'

'What would you like it to mean?'

Lorenzo saw the waiters gathering in the doorway over her shoulder, watching with suspicion. Maddalena's musical companions had moved on to the next restaurant, yet she remained.

'Do you make a habit of sitting at the tables of men you don't know?' He asked.

'Only the ones sitting alone.'

'What brings you to Rome?'

He arched an eyebrow as he drank from his wine glass, and returned it to the table. 'What makes you think I don't live here?'

She smiled, 'If you lived here you wouldn't choose to eat at a tourist trap from a menu created for foreigners.'

He nodded, 'I'm a journalist. With L'Osservatore Calabria.'

'And how do you like Rome, Lorenzo?'

'Oh it's...beautiful.' He tried to recover himself, thinking of some quick comebacks.

'Really? How much have you seen?'

'Not much. I'd like to see more.'

'Would you like a tour guide?'

'You're a local? I thought from your accent you were from further North.'

'We're all *from* somewhere. It's where we *are* that is more important.'

She smiled, and he felt her leg brush against his. Her touch was electrifying: it made every nerve in his body jump and made his hair stand up on end.

'And where are we, exactly?' He asked.

'The edge of a public open space that has been used to entertain crowds for thousands of
years. Before the restaurants, there were markets. There were also times when the Piazza was flooded and naval battles were recreated for the masses. Going further back, there were gladiatorial contests: this was the site of the Stadium of Domitian, dating back to the First Century, used mainly for athletic contests, but also recorded as the site of the martyrdom of Saint Agnes. The church dedicated to her is right there.'

Maddalena indicated a Baroque building with a dome flanked by two towers. Lorenzo found himself wondering how many similar places he had walked past without knowing what they were. To take the city at face value was a mistake: there was so much to be missed.

'Are you a professional tour guide?'

'No, I'm a fortune-teller.'

'A real gypsy?'

'We prefer Romani.' She said with a hint of severity. 'My people are originally from Romania, but we've done a lot of travelling. I've been everywhere.'

'I'd never have guessed.'

'Have you been to many places?'

Lorenzo tried to stop himself from blushing; pushed all thoughts of his cloistered small-town upbringing aside, 'I'd like to see more than I have so far.'

'I can show you everything.'

It seemed like they talked for hours: Maddalena lead the conversation, first giving details of her background, then asking Lorenzo about his. They talked about their jobs; he told her about the interview with Matteo Rossi, and how powerless it has made him feel. The crowds came and went until they were alone, looking at each other across the stump of a candle whilst the waiters cleaned the other tables.

The more they drank, the more Lorenzo lost track of time. He'd bought her food, flowers, drink, and dessert. When the time came to leave, he found that he didn't want to get up, and not just because his legs weren't working properly: he wanted to preserve the moment for as long as possible. He gave his credit card to the waiter and felt her bare foot moving up his leg, intent on distracting him. She was smiling again. He wanted to see more of that smile.

He wanted to see more of her.

He mumbled something about walking her back to her home. She laughed, and leaning over the table so that their cheeks brushed together, whispered in his ear the words he'd been wanting to hear all night.

'How about your hotel?'

That made his night, although he didn't realise then how important the night would be. He had no way of knowing that the events of the night would dramatically change his stay in Rome; change the way he worked, and even change the story he was working on. Leaning on one another, they staggered away from the restaurant. Lorenzo was amused to find himself humming along to the music that had earlier ensnared him.

The street traders had long ago packed away their wares, the shops had closed, and the only sound echoing around the square was the soft splashing of the fountains. The smells of garlic, olive oil and roast chestnuts were fading now; the patio heaters were being switched off, and the lights extinguished.

14

Lorenzo woke up naked with a breeze blowing across his body. The top sheet was gone and the cold made every hair stand to attention. It had been so hot last night he'd forgotten it was autumn. He came to life as if synchronised with the heartbeat of the city waking around him. Lorenzo had always been a city boy at heart: he loved congested streets and bright lights, the fast pace of life; and although the oily stench of traffic left a lot to be desired, he preferred it to the manure-and-dried-grass aroma of the countryside.

He propped himself up on his elbows. The room was a mess. The chair on its side, papers all over the desk; clothes everywhere.; the lamp on the floor and the clock yanked out of its socket. No wonder he'd slept through – the night must have been wilder than he remembered, although he quite wasn't sure what he remembered. Or if it had even happened at all.

Her clothes were still on the floor. She was still here, somewhere. The breeze blew through open doors, which had been closed last night, and he saw her foot on the balcony on the other side. He pulled on a pair of jeans, stumbled through the mess and joined her.

She was sat against the railings wrapped up in the sheet. The sun was in her face as she looked up, wrinkling her nose.

'Buongiorno.'

'Morning,' he whispered, scratching the back of his head and yawning. He sat beside her, manoeuvred himself beside her into the corner of the balcony and pulled her towards him, unwrapping and wrapping the sheet so that they were together, warm bodies pressed against one another. He buried his face in her shoulder to hide from the sun, managing to steal a kiss from her skin at the same time.

'I didn't want to wake you.'

'I could've done with waking.'

'How's your head?'

'Hurts like hell. I must have drunk more than I meant to.'

'You hit your head.'

'How?'

'If you don't remember, perhaps it should stay that way,' Maddalena said with a smirk.

'What time is it?'

No idea. Does it matter?'

The question disappeared as they sat there warming in the sun. A tram rolled beneath them, passing a group of nuns; one of whom looked up, scowled and crossed herself. The newspapers in the small *edicole* on the corner of the block had already forgotten about the gene therapy trials. Most of the headlines belonged to the footballers and the juicy, sinning celebrities; others screamed about a rising crime wave in the city and the fact that the streets were no longer safe.

They both jumped as the room phone started ringing inside the room. He jumped up leaving Maddalena with seconds to cover her modesty. She leaned into the door to listen to the conversation when he finally managed to find the phone.

'Pronto. Buongiorno, Your Eminence. No, I haven't had a chance to investigate the Bertoli lead yet. Yesterday's interview with Professor Rossi didn't go as well as I'd hoped, unfortunately,' he turned to see Maddalena drifting in through the curtains with the morning breeze, 'I found other ways of making up for it.'

He winked at her and she smiled. He barely registered the Cardinal's words coming out of his phone, so they took a few seconds to sink in.

'You found Bertoli's studio? Does he know anything about Madama Lucrezia?'

Maddalena froze, momentarily statuesque in the early light, and then began gathering her clothes and getting dressed with increasing urgency.

'So where do we go from here?' Lorenzo continued his call, confused by her sudden urgency. 'How do we find Madama Lucrezia without finding Bertoli? Yes, yes of course I'll come in. This afternoon? Of course, I'll see you then. Grazie.'

Lorenzo put the phone down and crossed the room to join Maddalena, kissing her neck.

'I have to go.'

'What's wrong?'

'Nothing. I just didn't realise how late it was.'

'It's early, not late. Do you have to go right away?'

'I have to go now,' she was forcing her swollen feet into her shoes, 'my Nonna. I have to see her. I sort of look after her; she's kind of dependent. She'll-'

She stopped abruptly and straightened her back. She shook her head and looked at him. 'She's waiting for me.'

Before Lorenzo had a chance to open his mouth she had snatched up her shoes and was out of the door, the beads at the hem of her dress clicking a morse distress code as she hurried. He ran after her and caught her elbow before she opened the elevator cage.

'At least let me call you a cab.'

'I don't want your money!' she shouted, and then looked hurt at what her own words had just implied. She went to kiss him, checked herself and placed a finger on his lips.

'I'm sorry.'

She left Lorenzo at the elevator and used the stairs instead; the steps didn't sink fast enough for her and by the time she had reached the ground floor, she was running. Out of the hotel, out into the street, out into the morning chaos, away from the boy she had met the night before, and the phone call that he had just received.

Cars growled endlessly past in both directions on a street flanked by a growing throng of pedestrians. Glamorous women in designer threads trilled into their cell phones; shopkeepers rolled up security shutters to reveal enticing window displays; two builders carried a plank through the crowd, jostling for space among nuns, children, and the early-morning businessmen beginning to sweat in their tailored suits.

Mopeds carried leather-clad, slick-haired adolescents in and around the lanes of traffic, leaving chaos in their wake. Pedestrians and motorists alike seemed colour blind to the lights at the crossings, choosing to use the road as and when they liked. It was a hectic morning, bursting with life; closing her eyes, she absorbed it all, and let her mind be guided along by the shouts of stallholders and the clinking of loose change. She felt safe among the crowd, anonymous, tapping into its energy, letting it revive her, awaken her.

Maddalena allowed herself to be buffeted along by the people around her, flowing with them towards their destinations, adrift in a tide of other people's lives. As she brought her breathing under control she felt herself reaching out, beyond the confines of her body, the limits of her consciousness. As she walked, she felt not only the cobbles beneath her feet, but the layers of history beneath them: the cellars, the subterranean tunnels, the streets that had not known daylight for a thousand years, and beneath that still, she felt something else. Something had shifted. Something had moved. The world felt different; changed somehow.

She let her feet carry her home, to safety. To her grandmother, sleeping in her chair in the ground floor room beside the window. Maddalena could see the old woman's shape through the window in the dim light filtering down to the courtyard of the palazzo that they had taken residence in all those years ago. It wasn't their property, and they had no legal right to be there, but for as long as she could remember, Maddalena had called it home.

She closed the door as lightly as she could, and yet still managed to wake her grandmother, who looked up from her seat at the table.

'Where have you been? It's morning.'

'Didn't your cards tell you?' Maddalena teased playfully.

Her grandmother looked down at the tarot cards spread before her, 'I was worried about you. You know I can't see clearly when I worry.'

Maddalena sighed, and took up position in the chair opposite her grandmother, 'I was out enjoying myself, having fun. What is there to worry about?'

'I fear he has returned?'

'Who?'

'Il Capitano.'

Fear flickered over Maddalena's face, but she blinked it away, and reached for her grandmother's hand, patting it tenderly, 'Are you sure? As you say, you can't see clearly when you worry.'

'The world feels different this morning,' her grandmother said, 'something has changed.'

Maddalena let go of the old woman's hand and moved her chair closer to the fire. She leaned forwards, rubbing her hands together over the last of the night's embers.

'It's getting cold, isn't it?' She said, 'I think we're going to have a harsh winter this year.'

'You've felt it, too.'

'I can feel the change in the seasons.'

'Maddalena.'

'Fine!' Maddalena threw her arms up in supplication, and moved the chair back to the table, 'I thought it was just me; for once, just me. I met a guy last night, and I had a good time. That's all; no meaning to it. And then...'

'And then?' Her grandmother fixed her with a cold stare, telling her with a look that it was pointless to keep anything from her.

'And then this morning, he took a phone call...from a Cardinal, I think. He called him "Your Eminence". He's looking for you, you and someone called Bertoli.'

Her grandmother began to gather the cards between them on the table., dealing herself a card, turning it over, wincing, and then placing it back into the deck before Maddalena could make out which card it was.

'*Nonna*...who is this Bertoli? And why is Lorenzo L'Oscuro looking for you?'

'I know not this Lorenzo L'Oscuro, but Amadeo Bertoli? His is a tragic story which would take too long in the telling. Let's call him a suffering artist: a man with dreams so big that he could never fully grasp them. Creative intent, and an artistic temperament; but he was never grounded enough to make his dreams a reality. I haven't heard his name for many a year, and I thought he'd stopped working altogether.'

'Lorenzo seems to think that Bertoli will lead him to you. Why?'

'If he has linked Amadeo Bertoli to me, it is because of the statue. As you know, I have spent a great many years hiding behind the assumed identity of Madama Lucrezia. Hers was the first statue that spoke to me when I arrived in the city when I was carrying your mother. Amadeo once showed his devotion to me by carving a copy of the statue, with my face in place of hers, you understand. Whoever holds that statue holds my identity in their hands. If your young man is looking for Amadeo Bertoli, he obviously thinks that Amadeo has the statue once more.'

'I didn't tell you Lorenzo was young.'

'You didn't have to.'

Maddalena looked at the small carriage clock on the mantelpiece; its face was empty of hands as it marked a time beyond the conventions of hours, minutes, and seconds.

'You said that Il Capitano has returned.'

'I believe so, yes. I can feel him, I think. Something is happening at the Vatican: a shift in the balance of power. Il Capitano is waking again, after decades of slumber, and like the bear who spends too long in his cave over winter, he is hungry.'

Maddalena shivered, 'What do you think will happen?'

Her grandmother stood up and shuffled to the window to look out at the dim world beyond the cold glass panes. A statue reared up through the gloom from the middle of the courtyard, guarding the entrance to her haven.

'When Il Capitano last ruled the streets of Rome, he cost your mother her life. If he returns to power, I cannot guarantee your safety any more than I could guarantee hers.'

'Who is he?'

'I do not know. He is so shrouded in legend that his identity is as concealed as mine. I believe that your mother came to learn his name, and that is why he came to her, in this very room.'

Maddalena stared at the space before the hearth, fighting the pricking sensation of fresh tears welling up for an old pain, 'If he has returned...'

'If he has returned,' her grandmother said, 'we should leave.'

'We should fight! Now might be our chance. For-'

'For what? Revenge?'

'For justice. For Mama.'

Her grandmother wrapped the tarot cards up in a well-worn cloth and deposited that in a velvet drawstring bag.

'It is not worth the risk. It wasn't then; it isn't now.'

'What are you so afraid of?' Maddalena threw her arms up again, this time in frustration. The answer; so small, so simple yet so profound, shocked her.

'*Him.*'

15

Cardinal Sanchez stood over the table snuffing out votive candles. They lost their heat one by one as the brass snuffer captured their warmth, their light submitting to darkness as he passed over each flame. Had there been a mirror in front of him he would have seen the shadows under his eyes darken. Instead, he watched the pale alabaster icon of the Holy Virgin above the table grow darker as he extinguished each flame.

Little lights that go out.

The soft footsteps that approached from behind suggested a man deliberately walking without the intention to disturb. A man used to creeping and following.

Lorenzo stopped at the Cardinal's left elbow and looked straight ahead to the icon on the wall.

'We couldn't have done this over the phone?'

'Phone lines can be tapped, Lorenzo. Calls can be traced. You should know this, especially in your line of work.'

'I've never stooped so low myself, but others don't have the same principles I have.'

'But you have no qualms in doing it in person. Following a person; asking questions about him. Lines can be tapped.'

Lorenzo picked up a thin taper and lit it from one of the few remaining flames. Cardinal Sanchez hovered over the candles as Lorenzo lit one, and then another, undoing all of his hard work. He calmly put the snuffer down and reached into a pocket for a photograph, which he handed to Lorenzo.

'There's no easy way to say this,' he said with a quiet sigh, 'but one of my brethren; a fellow Cardinal, and a senior one at that; has been seen leaving the Vatican late at night and wandering the city streets. He takes these walks every two or three weeks, and won't tell anyone where he is going. He walks down to the end of Borgo Pio and gets into a car, without aid or protection, and we in the Administration fear for his safety.'

'You want me to follow this man?'

'Yes. Tonight.'

'It's a bit last minute.'

'Consider it a personal favour, as my Godson, for the help I have given you in researching your story.'

'Where will he lead me?'

'I'm not entirely sure. You must keep your distance from him so that he remains unaware of you. Proceed with caution and without disturbance.'

Lorenzo crossed himself and placed the taper in the pool of wax. 'Anything else?'

'That will be all, Lorenzo. God bless you.'

The Cardinal bowed his head slightly and watched Lorenzo leave. Almost instinctively the snuffer was in his hand and before he realised it, he had blackened all of the candles.

16

Cardinal Romano pulled the hood over his head and, nodding to the sentry, walked through the gateway. Via di Porta Angelica was quiet now, the tourists and policemen having retired to more pleasant parts of the city, leaving the beggars to look through their rubbish. Sounds of laughter and clinking glasses bounced off the buildings as he crossed into Rione Borgo, the cluster of streets that, in years past, had provided the Vatican with all the servants it could need. Now, however, the streets were home to restaurants, hotels and souvenir shops.

On either side of the street, the buildings rose six storeys; enveloping the Cardinal in oppressive darkness. Windows blinked into luminescence, only to darken and die just as quickly. The Cardinal stopped to look in the window of a shop selling religious apparel; although the lights had been switched off, and a lattice of steel had been pulled down in front of the glass, he could still make out the shape of a replica Papal Mitre, and under it a ghostly white robe. He stooped in front of the window so that the hat sat on top of his reflection, looming out of the darkness like some pale spectre of temptation that inflamed the ambition smouldering inside of him.

He had wanted for so long to wear that raiment, and accept the responsibility that accompanied it, that he could no longer remember ever wanting anything else. After a few minutes of cruel introspection, he pulled himself away from the vision in the window and continued walking down the street. He waited on the edge of the road until a set of headlights flashed in a dark street to his left. A black unmarked car rolled towards him, and he got inside.

Behind it, a light shone in the darkness as Lorenzo turned the key in his moped. Pulling his coat up around his neck, he followed the car, always staying two or three vehicles behind.

The car crossed the river just as Cardinal Sanchez had predicted, then turned onto a narrow street that ran parallel to the river. Small flags waved in the breeze, proclaiming the name of the street to be Via Giulia, and the road suddenly narrowed as a line of potted citrus trees materialised on either side. Realising that he was the only vehicle in the street other than the car, Lorenzo slowed down and fell back to what he thought was a safer distance. In front of him, the car slowed to a halt, and the door opened. His quarry stepped out into the glare of a streetlight and disappeared down an alley that opened up on the right. The driver of the car killed the lights and drove off, concealed in darkness.

Lorenzo dismounted and followed on foot. Reaching the corner of the alley he peered cautiously around the corner: he could just make out the shape of a man reaching the other end and turning to the right, doubling back on his journey. Paying careful attention to where he was putting his feet, Lorenzo continued his silent pursuit.

The Cardinal reached a small piazza from which the road split into two even narrower lanes; bare skeletons of defunct market stalls occupied the otherwise empty space. Away to his right, behind the dark buildings, he could hear the muffled sounds of the late-night traffic. Somewhere back up the street behind him, he heard the unmistakable sound of a footstep splashing into a puddle as Lorenzo lost his footing.

'Is anyone there?' He called out, gazing intently back down the street. The city answered back with the hushed sound of mopeds and the smashing of a plate in the next street.

A light came on in a window above his head, illuminating him with golden stripes streaming out through the wooden shutters. He turned around, and brushing away a cloud of midges that hovered lazily at head height, picked the left fork in the road and walked on, keeping as close to the wall as possible.

Lorenzo exhaled quietly and crept out from behind a rubbish bin. The surface of the puddle was still again, laying in wait in the middle of the street for the next person to step in it. Creeping slowly through the darkness, he followed the Cardinal along the street until it branched in two again. The Cardinal paused momentarily, apparently deliberating which road to take, when a hotel door vomited a drunken man onto the cobbles at Lorenzo's feet.

Hearing the man's inebriated moans, the Cardinal turned around and for a fleeting moment saw Lorenzo caught in the light from the doorway, bending over the drunk. Their eyes met in the instant before the hotel closed the door and darkness took the street. Panicked by the realisation that he was under surveillance, the Cardinal darted up the street on the left. Lorenzo stepped over the man sprawled at his feet and stumbled on in pursuit, still blinded by the darkness. He had lost his prey, and couldn't help thinking that the mission had been a waste of time. The Cardinal, whatever his purpose, was surprisingly agile for his age, and cunning enough to evade his pursuer.

Lorenzo's eyes scanned the darkness for signs of life. He had no idea of where he was, or how he would find his way out of the darkness, let alone follow the Cardinal. The scream of hinges up ahead gave him some hope: a gateway was being opened towards the end of the street. Footsteps disappeared into the right-hand wall beneath a carved sign with the words *Vicolo della Notte*, and then the gate sang as it was shut. One foot in front of the other, he approached the gate, feeling around for a latch or handle, gasping as a cold hand took hold of him.

'Why are you following me?' The Cardinal demanded from behind a veil of darkness. All Lorenzo could see was a pale thin hand, grasping his with surprising strength.

'I-I'm looking for someone.'

'Who?'

'Amadeo Bertoli.'

'I know no such man.' The Cardinal spat derisively. He released his grip and disappeared into the darkness, his footsteps echoing into the shadows.

Fighting against some primal fear that had taken hold of him at the touch of the Cardinal's hand, Lorenzo felt around the gate for the latch and opened it. With every step, he was rewarded with a growing vision of his surroundings. He found himself in a low, arched passage that ran under the side of a building; a narrow space rendered claustrophobic by a litter of crates, bags and other rubbish.

Hiding among the waste, Lorenzo was horrified to discover thin, haggard forms that barely registered as human. On a boarded-up doorstep, two of the wretches held up dim torches that illuminated children playing cards for cigarettes among the filth. Their eyes were wild and threatening in the weak light, despite seeming less than half his age. He straightened his back and tried to walk with an assertive, self-confident air; but it was hard not to feel afraid in such a cruel, unforgiving place.

At the end of the passage, he saw the Cardinal silhouetted against a faint red light. Lorenzo followed to the end of the passage, where it opened out onto a small courtyard formed by the rear walls of Renaissance palazzi. There were three old doorways, now boarded up and cloaked with cobwebs, and another free of obstruction; Lorenzo thought they were most likely the service entrances to the grand buildings in centuries past. A tall statue groped by vines stood in the centre of the courtyard, serving as an anchor for the web of washing lines radiating out to the windows on the first and second floors.

Dimly lit by the electric light that filtered through grime-encrusted windows, grey washing hung limp and dripping in the cold night air.

'Go home, boy.' The Cardinal ordered.

Looking across the square, through a line of dripping tablecloths, he saw the Cardinal framed in a rose pink light that glowed from a window behind him.

'You cannot come any further.' He waited for a moment, and then, in the absence of any reply, turned on his heel and opening a door in the wall behind him, disappeared from view.

Lorenzo stayed where he was, confused and dejected, looking at the strange place he found himself in. Between him and the door in the opposite wall fell a steady rain of grey water from the lines of shawls and towels, rugs and clothes hanging above. The courtyard was a veritable pond of dirty water in which every cobble was a tiny island. Shutters barred the windows on the lower levels; blinds restricted the light from the upper ones. The only thing of beauty amid the grime was a glass lamp that shone in the window next to the door.

It was made from clear glass and seemed to have some design painted on it in red. He could make out the swirls and shapes of a pattern, but nothing more. The effect created was that of a mottled light of red, orange and yellow hue, that gave the courtyard a warming, almost pleasant feel. The more he looked at it, the more comfortable he felt. He found himself drawn to the light; as if all the happiness and love he needed could be found within its glass. It shone in front of thick red curtains that caught the colours of the glass so that the whole window seemed to be aflame with the warmth and love offered by the light.

He stepped towards it, and felt a drip of cold water strike the back of his neck and slither down underneath his shirt. Instantly the illusion of warmth melted, and he found himself back in the dark and dirty courtyard. The candle now seemed to be nothing but a weak flame that offered little light. Despair seemed to creep out from the dank corners of the square to mock him for ever thinking that anything good, anything wholesome, could be found in such a place.

Nevertheless, Lorenzo had come this far. Cardinal Sanchez had told him not to make his presence known, and he had failed at that; he may as well press on. He rallied his courage and was about to step into the courtyard when he was stopped by a voice he knew.

'I wouldn't venture any further if I were you.'

Lorenzo turned to look up into the grim face of Serafino, darker than usual beneath the brim of his battered hat.

17

Piazza della Rotonda had settled down to sleep after a busy day spent amazing the wide-eyed and the open-mouthed. The camera-wielding tourists had marched back to their plush hotels, the local drunks had stumbled off to the nearest bordello, the cafes had folded their umbrellas and closed, and the bronze doors of the Pantheon had been shut for hours. Now, with the fountain's song filling the air, only the roosting pigeons were around to hear the sound of an engine dying.

A black, unmarked car parked in the short street running directly behind the brick bulk of the Pantheon, and switched off its lights. The driver, wearing a plain uniform devoid of any identifying badge or crest, stepped out and opened the door for his passenger: a tall, formidable figure; who gave him a nod of thanks.

'Wait here for me: if all goes well, I won't be long.' The passenger commanded and walked off. The driver watched the statesman-like figure descend a flight of steps at the rear of the Pantheon, and then got back into the car. He rubbed his gloved hands together, and ignored the temptation to turn on the heating: he was not allowed to power up the car until his passenger returned.

High above street level, clinging to the roof of the Pantheon, Amadeo Bertoli watched the driver get back into the car. He waited a while longer, hoping to see signs of another passenger in the car, then slowly turned himself around and crawled back from the edge. Fumbling in the darkness, he clasped at the line that had been earlier secured to the roof and pulled himself up. The roof of the Pantheon was the largest dome in the city: even the cupola of St. Peter's had been made smaller in deference to the feat of engineering that had created it. A temple to all the Roman gods, the Pantheon had survived the ravages of time largely intact, due to its conversion into a church.

When he judged himself far away enough from the edge, he stood up gingerly, and slowly ascended to the top of the dome. He looked down through the Oculus: the eye in the centre of the roof that exposed the interior of the church to the elements. He could hear footsteps rapping sharply against stone: the sound bounced around the Pantheon's interior, growing louder with every echo so that by the time it reached Amadeo, stood at the edge of the Oculus, it sounded as if a host of men marched across the marble floor.

An electric torch shot a beam of light across the floor, swaying as the man who held it entered the Pantheon's circular main chamber. Amadeo watched as an old man came into view; a man he hadn't seen in years and had hoped to never see again.

'Amadeo?' The man called, with concern in his voice, 'I know you're here, friend. Show yourself.'

Amadeo peered over the edge of the Oculus to look down upon the man below. He had seen him many times before; there was once a time when he had even looked upon him in friendship, perhaps even admiration. Now, however, the only thing he felt was a rising tide of anger towards the old man standing in the middle of the chamber. Try as he might to contain it, the anger overpowered him.

'Friend?' He shouted, 'When was the last time you and I were friends, Your Eminence?'

Cardinal Sanchez looked up at him, the light of his torch spearing up at the night sky through the circular hole in the roof.

'We have known each other a long time, you and I: we know each other's dreams and nightmares; we know what it is that the other wants. Why hide from me now? Come down here, sit in the light with me, and we'll discuss what it is we want.'

'I know exactly what it is you want,' Amadeo growled, 'but I will not give it to you: it is not yours to have.'

'Amadeo!' The Cardinal called with feigned sympathy, stretching his arms up to the ceiling. 'Come down to me, and let us talk face to face. We can reach an agreement, you and I, in which we shall both find some contentment.'

'I will not bargain with you anymore, old man: our days of allegiance are long over. I will not give you what you want.'

At the words "old man", the Cardinal dropped all pretence of caring. 'Thief!' He spat the last word out, and marched to the scaffolding, rubbing the candles up against the dry wood.

'You dare use that word to describe me?' Amadeo shouted down, 'You who stole my artworks, who took them for your private collection?'

'I took them for the Church!'

'You took them for yourself! Your promises mean nothing to me: there is no honour in your word!'

'Amadeo, come down. Tell me what it is you want, and I will deliver!' There was a desperation in the Cardinals' voice that had displaced the threat. A brooding silence enveloped the interior of the Pantheon once more, underscored by Amadeo's sharp, swift breaths.

'I trusted you! ' He shouted down to the floor below, 'And you took my work. You ruined me. So when I heard that the Relic had finally returned to Rome, and was within your reach, I took it from you.'

'Amadeo, please...'

'All your life you have sought it. For years you have wanted to cleanse yourself of sin.'

'The Bowl of Pontius Pilate is not some simple piece of crockery you can carry around with you,' Cardinal Sanchez pleaded, 'It carries a great weight with it: the weight of responsibility. The responsibility that Pilate washed from his hands still lies on it, and the one who carries it. You know this: even now you feel the burden. Give it to me, let me carry it, and you will be free from the pain. Free from the madness.'

The last word drifted up through the cold night air to reach Amadeo's ears. He snorted with laughter. 'You waste your words, Cardinal Sanchez. You are the last person I would consider giving it to. I won't be the one to give you the relic so that you can use it to further your schemes.'

'Amadeo, Amadeo,' the Cardinal muttered, 'did I wrong you so badly that you would hate me so much?'

'So much, that I would hide the very thing you seek, ' came Amadeo's answer, 'hide it from you at all cost.'

The thief looked down at the Cardinal through the hole in the roof from which the old gods looked down on those worshipping the new.

'I do not have it, and you will never find it,' Amadeo muttered. It seemed to him, at that moment, that Autumn became Winter. A cold breeze, natural and untainted by the warmth of the city, wafted around him now, bringing clarity and hardening his resolve. In his mind's eye, Amadeo Bertoli saw the brushstrokes of his favourite painting, and he remembered the work of which he was most proud.

He looked up to the sky. By some fortuitous movement of air, the clouds parted, and he could see stars winking in the dark sky above. A word came to him on the wind, and he smiled.

Aracoeli.

'Amadeo, no!' The Cardinal shouted as he watched the artist lean forward into the abyss of the Oculus, and fall forward, turning over once, before smacking into the floor below with the harsh crack of bone, and the soft escape of his last breath.

Cardinal Sanchez remained frozen for a moment; as if staying still would freeze the passage of time, and movement in any direction would condemn him to live in a world where he must acknowledge what he had just witnessed. Amadeo Bertoli was dead, having confessed to stealing the relic and hidden it somewhere. All hope of finding it was now gone, and in its place lay a jumble of bone and skin, broken, ruptured and bleeding over the polished marble. The very lifeblood of the artist now drained away through the holes in the floor that were designed to channel away the rain and snow that fell through the Oculus.

The Cardinal switched off his torch, enabling the darkness to gain a greater hold within the Pantheon. He backed out of the chamber without turning away from the grotesque scene before him until he had retreated far enough into the shadow that Amadeo's body was obscured from his old eyes. He made his way back to the car, stumbling and groping through the darkness, before heaving the door open and collapsing into the back seat. The driver turned to look at him through the glass divider.

'Are you alright, Your Eminence?'

Cardinal Sanchez shook his head as he caught his breath, 'Something terrible has happened, Rodrigo.'

Deacon Fuentes drew back the glass panel and leaned in to address his trembling passenger, 'Whatever it is, you can tell me, Your Eminence. I will not tell another soul.'

Gradually, through recovering breaths, Cardinal Sanchez told Deacon Fuentes about the man who had just fallen to his death inside the Pantheon. Rodrigo appeared not to believe him, and coaxed the Cardinal into taking him back inside, where they inspected the broken body of Amadeo Bertoli.

'Who was he?' Rodrigo asked.

'A troubled soul,' was the only answer the Cardinal offered.

'We need to dispose of him.'

'How?'

Rodrigo looked about the chamber, his eyes alighting on the scaffolding that had been erected for the restoration of some of the frescoes. The oil paints and canvas for protecting the work, along with the scaffolding itself, were all flammable.

'I'll take care of it,' Rodrigo reassured the Cardinal, and the old man watched as the Deacon gathered together the materials to construct a pyre large enough to cover Amadeo's remains, doused them in a slick of oil paint, and then set them alight with a match. They stood at the fireside and paid their respects momentarily before the smoke began to curl up through the Oculus and into the night sky.

'We should get you back to the Vatican,' Rodrigo said, and Cardinal Sanchez nodded in compliance, and allowed himself to be led out of the church.

18

Cardinal Romano stepped over the threshold and closed the door behind him; he was confident that his stalker would not attempt to follow him. On his left was another door, beyond which he could hear a fire crackling. Composing himself, he turned the knob and opened the door.

The small room within was warmed by a glowing fire that cast shadows towards the window, where Madama Lucrezia sat, shuffling a deck of cards.

'Buonasera, Carlo,' she said with a smile.

The Cardinal took off his coat and hung it on a hook behind the door. He joined her in the opposite armchair, the firelight highlighting the years on his face. He was old and tired; a new darkness seemed to have fallen behind his eyes.

'It is good to see you again Lucrezia,' he said, 'I should have liked to have come sooner, but Cardinal Sanchez has been watching me in the days since I announced my plans to oppose the gene therapy experiments. I think he fears that my work will place me in a favourable position for the next Conclave. Your warnings were right: he seems intent to find some fault in me, and thus secure the Papacy for himself.'

'Dark indeed is the man who wishes to occupy the Holy See to satisfy his greed and lust for power. Continue to heed my warnings Carlo: Cardinal Sanchez has a thirst for success that is matched only by his taste for seeing suffering in others. He is more than a rival: he is an enemy.'

'It is true that his ambition knows no bounds. He would occupy the seat of God Himself if he thought it achievable, but I cannot see that he would breed injustice to further his own ends, though I do not dare underestimate him. You are right to call him greedy: he looks only to consolidate his power base.'

'I worry about you, Carlo. I worry about the both of us: we are reaching the end of our days, and I fear that we cannot survive the battle that lies ahead. In my dreams, a darkness lies between us that I cannot see through. The ambition of Cardinal Sanchez may prove to be the one force strong enough to sunder our paths.'

'Worry not, Lucrezia,' he said with what he hoped was an encouraging smile, 'he is as old and infirm as I am. His ambition is not so strong that it cannot be contained by the College of Cardinals.'

'How can you be so certain? The news that you have brought to me in recent years leads me to believe that he has a firm following in the Vatican; that his will prevails over that of the other Cardinals. He has power: a dominion over his peers that can only be dangerous in a man as ambitious as he is. My instincts tell me that his grasp reaches further out into the city than we know.'

'Your instincts can advise you depending on how you interpret them: I see little need to worry over Cardinal Sanchez. I have been his match all these years, and will be for many yet to come.'

The look she gave him caused him to doubt his own words for a moment. Her lips trembled, and her eyes watered with a grief that comes from one who has witnessed a horror that they were powerless to prevent. No sooner had the Cardinal noticed her expression, she changed it to a mask of grave seriousness.

'My mind tells me otherwise, Carlo. That and my heart.' She turned to stare into the flames, and he saw a tear glisten as it formed in her eye.

He reached out and turned her face back to his; holding it there, he looked into her frightened eyes. 'Sometimes it is best not to believe what our hearts tell us. They can be fickle and deceptive at times. Better to trust logic and common sense. I can handle Cardinal Sanchez, and my plans may yet come to thwart his own. Aid me in evicting this scientist from the city, and the glory I gain may allow me to overcome my opposition. I need you with me Lucrezia; I need your help to find a way to get rid of Professor Rossi and his experiments.'

Lucrezia sighed and shook her head. 'How long did it take for the young priest with a view to changing the world to become a wrathful Cardinal intent on trampling over others to realise his ambitions?'

'The same amount of time it took the sweet and gentle woman I knew to close her doors to the world and turn away from the simple acts of living.' He spoke softly, without anger, although his grim words brought sorrow to her face.

'I will help you, Carlo, for I still believe that you mean to do well, but you must know that my abilities are not what they once were.'

Cardinal Romano noted the tremble in her voice, and for the first time saw a weakness in her that, having been finally revealed, now frightened him. As Lucrezia got up from her chair and shuffled to the sideboard on stiff legs, he realised how old she had become; how fragile and insecure on her feet. Her spirit was still strong, but her body had become a frail, decaying prison.

Lucrezia picked up a shallow bowl and a pitcher of water and set them on the table. Motioning for Romano to bring the chairs to the table, she filled the bowl to the brim. She took the pitcher back to the sideboard and returned with a small glass phial and a plastic bag full of leaves.

'As always, I cannot guarantee that you will hear anything of use.' She said whilst emptying the phial into the bowl. Blood-coloured oil spread across the surface of the water in a swirling, churning film. She took a pinch of the dried leaves from the bag and crumbled them over the water in her fingers.

Romano took out a pen and paper and nodded expectantly. Lucrezia gave a weak smile and closed her eyes, breathing deeply. As the depth of each breath increased, she pulled the bowl toward her until it sat in between her elbows, and then hung her head over it.

The oil formed swirling patterns that swamped and drowned the leaves like waves sinking an armada. The leaves, caught up in the tempestuous oil, began a frenzied dance around the bowl. Lucrezia opened her eyes as the hallucinogenic scent of the oil and leaves began to take hold. The surface of the bowl writhed in the firelight, sending snatches of reflection up into her face. A haze developed in front of her eyes as they opened and closed dreamily. She felt parts of her brain shutting down as she relaxed and slowly withdrew from the world around her; deep inside, to a place where there was no sound, no light, no feeling. The last thing she felt before her mind and body fell asleep, was the rush of elation as something else took over.

The room became still save for the crackling of the fire, and the faint ticking of the clock above it. Leaning over the table, Romano saw that the water in the bowl was now rippling, causing the oil patterns to spin rapidly.

'What do you see?' He asked gently.

'I see a man.' Lucrezia answered sullenly after some time. 'The one who brings the end. He is known to you. He is strong now: stronger than you know. He sits in darkness, coveting the prize that is not yet in his keeping. He plans to seize control, to take power. He will use his prize and be victorious. None will withstand him.'

Lucrezia's face became contorted in sorrow. Three mournful tears fell, like droplets of glass aflame in the firelight, and disrupted the oil patterns in the bowl.

'Is it Matteo Rossi? Is he the man you speak of? What is his prize?'

'Matteo Rossi?' She considered the name and laughed.

'How can I get rid of Professor Rossi?' Romano pressed.

'That question is not yours to ask; the words are not for you to hear.'

He stabbed his pen clean through the page and bit into his lip. Lucrezia began shaking, and dry coughs rattled her lungs. She strained to get up from her seat as if to escape the convulsions. Romano felt a pang of concern but reminded himself that all would be well. He had seen this happen before. The convulsions subsided, and Lucrezia's eyes burst open, roving across the surface of the water wildly.

The old woman's head lifted from the bowl and stared at him, now freed from their enclosure. With horror, he saw two dark recesses where her eyes should have been; two vast pits into nothingness. He felt drawn in by them as if a powerful vacuum existed within her, and only he could fill it. As he recoiled in horror, her voice moaned four final words.

'My heart is broken.'

Lucrezia's head dropped down and once again her body was wracked with convulsions. Romano got out of his chair and moved the bowl out of harm's reach as the convulsions began to take control. Her arms thrashed wildly, her eyes rolled up into her head, and she cried hysterically. He bent down beside the chair and held her, firm but gently, and whispered into her ear.

'It's alright Lucrezia: Carlo's here. I am here; like I have been these past fifty years. I am beside you always. I won't leave. You are not alone.'

She pushed her head into his shoulder like a dog nuzzling its master, and wept. She gripped his robe and twisted it between her fingers as the pain intensified.

He closed his eyes and recalled the first time that he had held her like this. Both of them had been a lot younger, a lot stronger. He had helped deliver her child, and looked after her, nursing her back to strength. It had barely been months since she had walked into his life; she said she felt so comfortable with him that she wanted to share her gift.

Amazing though the spectacle had been, he had been horrified by the toll it had taken on her, almost repulsed by the fits that followed the use of her supposed "gift". He couldn't believe, and still failed to, that God would inflict so much pain and brutality on one so clearly in communion with divine beings. Over the years that he had known her, he had cradled her like this many times, slowly becoming used to the spasms that shook her. Tonight, however, the horror of that first sight was rekindled: this was the worst fit he had seen her endure in years.

Cardinal Romano couldn't help but think about the end that had been prophesied, and sitting half in darkness, half in light, he felt a sense of impending doom press down upon his shoulders. One side of him was warm and glowing, the other cold and uncomfortable. Instinctively he reached for his rosary and began thumbing through the beads, reciting the prayer aloud.

Lucrezia recovered slowly, her head nodding with the rhythm of his words as he brought her back to herself. Eventually, she spoke; her voice more present than during her trance.

'Neither of us is getting any younger Carlo, or stronger. We cannot fight these battles much longer. You cannot compete forever with

Cardinal Sanchez; and, I fear that I will not be able to control my gifts for much longer. After a lifetime of dreaming, and planning our tomorrows, I think it is time that we called time on our work in the city.'

The faceless clock on the mantelpiece marked off the silent seconds between them.

'I won't give up my ambition Lucrezia; I have come too far. We've come too far to let the opportunity slip away. I am already favoured as a successor to the Holy Father; by continuing my crusade against the gene therapy experiments, I am seen to be upholding the ways of the Church. I will be the saviour and custodian of the things we hold sacred. If you help me to work against Cardinal Sanchez, I can consolidate my position, and achieve my ambition.

'Think of the good I could do as Pope; the things I could do to help the people of this city. The impoverished need no longer be poor, the damned can be saved. The Church could reach out to help heal the wounds of the world, and no longer turn people away. Long ago, we both talked of bringing about a better world: we have come too far, to give up on that dream now.'

'Carlo, the time for us to change the world has passed. The world now belongs to those of advanced technology; those looking forward, not back. Yes, we had dreams once, but they belong in the past. We are old, and the number of people who would listen to, or care for what we have to say is dwindling. You talk of events that neither of us has much power over. Your proposed deeds will put you at great personal risk: I see that much.'

'It is worth the risk, any risk, if I can both depose Cardinal Sanchez, and rid the city of these experiments. I would sail through any storm to accomplish the goals I set in the past: to bring our dreams to fruition.' His words were sharp, laced with an anger that Lucrezia had not heard before.

'And what if you don't achieve those goals? What if you don't succeed, and Cardinal Sanchez wins the next Conclave? You will fade and fall silent, and you will suffer.' She saw the look of amazement on his face. 'You will suffer even more than you do now. Yes, your health fails, doesn't it? You were in pain when you came here tonight.'

'I was a little breathless maybe, but only from running from my pursuer. My exhaustion is the result of old age, not ill health.'

'But there is more, isn't there? Your exhaustion should make you sleep more, but you lie awake at night unable to rest. There is pain deep within you: I see it, I feel it. It is always there: an incessant ache, day and night, that you speak of to no one.'

The Cardinal's skin blanched, adopting a sallow hue in the firelight. He looked grey and tired, as if his life was being slowly leached from him and he was fighting to hold on to it. Despite his strong spirit and harsh words, he was worn out: Lucrezia half expected him to fade away before her eyes. There was no solution to his problems; no happy resolution to reach. Only the hard, abrupt end that they both feared.

'How long have you known?' He asked.

Her eyes focused once again on his face, and she took his hand in hers. 'I have worried about you for so long that I don't know when it began. Perhaps I have always known, deep inside. Perhaps I have known I would lose you, for as long as I have loved you.'

'Whatever do you mean?'

Lucrezia sighed, 'Look at me Carlo: really look at me. I am a frail old woman with no one to look after me. My family wish for me to return North and spend the last of my days with them, though I would rather stay here to assist you. I want to stay here for as long as possible. I have spent most of my life here: raising my family, telling fortunes, tending the sick, and easing the passage of people from this world to the next. I have seen friends marry, move away, grow old, and die, but I have been happy. I have been here, with you. Yes, I am old, yes I am frail, and yes there is no one to look after me, but I do not feel alone. I belong here, with you.'

'You should do what is best,' he said, patting her hand, 'best for you, not best for me. Your family can look after you better than I can.'

'And who will look after you, Giancarlo?'

The clock marked the silent seconds between them, accompanied by the soft sounds of their breathing. Lucrezia turned her face to the fire and glared at the clock.

'Time slips away from us, and we don't even see it. Midnight approaches Carlo; you should make your way back.'

He nodded and got up from the table. 'I wonder if I shall be followed again. Is my stalker still out there?' He pulled back the curtain and stared into the gloom beyond.

'I cannot help feeling sorry for the young man,' she answered, 'he is very much a small boy lost in this big city, and home is far away. In his short time here, he will have to grow up a lot. Fate has drawn him into a web of events, of which he has no understanding. His coming here has pushed him into the hands of the powers that govern this city, and he will play an important part in all of our lives.'

'Why he is so important to us?' The Cardinal grunted in reply, and pocketing his pen and notebook, wrapped himself up in his coat. Pulling up his hood to obscure his face, he planted a last kiss on her forehead, and for a moment there was a spark between them of a flame that had never been adequately tended; one which they both believed had burned out long ago.

'Remember my warning Carlo: you cannot win all your battles, nor fight them unscathed. Do not be afraid to put aside your ambitions and change your plans. Pay attention to the events happening around you, for they are to determine the consequences of your actions.'

'One thing: do you know what is it that you saw in the bowl tonight? Do you know what is coming?'

'The end.'

They parted, and she waved him off from the doorstep, watching as he picked his way across the flooded square. He turned once he had crossed under the strings of washing and waved back. With a smile, he ducked into the arched passage and was lost to the darkness. The sound of the gate groaning on its hinges came echoing back through the courtyard like the scream of a train derailing. When she was sure he had gone, Lucrezia closed the door, and returning to the fireside, wept until her tears were all spent.

19

'How did you know to find me there?' Lorenzo demanded, as Serafino escorted him out of the dark passage.

'You're pretty easy to spot.' Serafino said, kicking a discarded pizza box out of his way, 'You make your presence known.'

'Have you been following me?'

'You were following someone; is it such a surprise that you were followed yourself?'

'Why did you stop me from going into that building?'

'It was not your time, not yet. Leave the Cardinal to his business tonight; other matters concern you.'

'Such as?'

Serafino guided the young reporter through the labyrinthine streets that seemed surprisingly alive in the dead of night. They seemed to be drifting with a flow of people away from the river and into the heart of Renaissance Rome; were it not for the occasional brightly-lit designer window display, Lorenzo would have thought they were headed back in time.

'You are still searching for the thief, Amadeo Bertoli?' Serafino asked as sirens raced past them, returning Lorenzo to the present.

'Yes, but tonight-'

'Tonight, I fear you may be too late.'

'Why do you say that?'

The sirens increased in both number and volume as they crossed over the main thoroughfare, Serafino marching across one piazza after another, with Lorenzo struggling to keep up.

'Where are we going?'

'Where you *should* have been tonight.'

'And where is that?'

'Right here...'

Lorenzo smelled the smoke through the dark before he saw it. People were running now; some with cameras or smartphones held aloft. Serafino's pace quickened again as they rounded the corner to see the curved shape of the Pantheon rearing up towards the clouds, with smoke belching out of the roof.

'What in God's name?' He began.

'Not in God's name,' Serafino cut him off, 'this is the work of a man.'

'Not Amadeo Bertoli?'

'No, although I was told that he was here.'

A crowd of distressed faces had gathered, tears streaming from tired eyes as tourists and locals alike witnessed a symbol of Roma Eterna that had withstood the ages engulfed in smoke and flame. *Poliziotti* ensured that the public maintained a safe distance from the blaze as teams from the *Vigili del Fuoco* dealt with the inferno itself.

'He was inside?' The exasperation scratched at Lorenzo's voice as did the ash in the air.

Serafino nodded, 'Something tells me that he didn't make it out alive.'

'This is terrible.'

'The building will survive, but the artworks, the furniture, the interior; ruined.'

'You're sure he was there?'

'I had a call from a contact at the Vatican who told me as much. Apparently, someone from the Holy See came here tonight to see Bertoli.'

'So there's someone else in there?'

'I suspect that the other man escaped with his life.'

'Who was it?'

Serafino looked both at him, and through him, for a moment, 'I think you already know.'

One last fireball belched out of the Oculus into the night before the emergency services began to gain control over the flames. Lorenzo watched the firelight dissipate into the night air and shook his head with disbelief.

'It couldn't be.'

'Why not?'

'Because he is a man of God.'

'Was the man you followed tonight not also a man of God? Yet you suspected his motives. Then why should his colleague, any of his colleagues for that matter, be beyond suspicion.'

Lorenzo's mouth gaped open as he tried in vain to search for an answer.

'Many bad men have been known to hide in plain sight as men of God, Lorenzo. Taking Holy Orders doesn't necessarily change their nature; doesn't make them better men.'

'But why? Why would he?'

'Why indeed? Why would your Cardinal friend send you to follow his colleague on the same night when he himself was hunting the very man he had tasked you to find?'

Lorenzo's world began to disintegrate as the sounds of scaffolding collapsing inside the Pantheon drew cries of anguish from the crowd.

'The Cardinal sent you on a fool's errand, furthering his own ends as he himself obstructed your investigation.'

'But he was the one who started me on that path?'

'Perhaps you have outlived your usefulness? Perhaps he is already in possession of the Relic?'

'Then why send me out into the city tonight?'

'Perhaps because all along, he has been using you to fulfil his agenda.'

'Which is?'

'To discredit his rival and eventually ascend to the See of Peter as the next Pope.'

'The next Pope? Is the Holy Father dying?'

'Every man is born to die, Lorenzo,' Serafino growled, pulling out a cigarette and attempting to light it, before taking in the scene before them, and rethinking his action, 'including the Holy Father. He is not ill that I am aware of, but on occasion, the Papacy has been known to move on, before its incumbent is ready to vacate the seat. The men who have their sights on becoming the next Pope are soon to reach an age where they will no longer be able to achieve that ambition, so it would not surprise me if the current Holy Father's health were to deteriorate rapidly in the next few years.'

'Seriously?'.

'Timing is everything,' Serafino smiled grimly, 'and these men have waited a long time.'

News crews were beginning to arrive at the scene, and Lorenzo could see fellow journalists arguing with the officers present about gaining access to the site. It was strange watching his peers fighting to secure the best angle, the best interview that could be broken down into soundbites. Watching them from across the piazza, he suddenly felt as if he didn't belong among them.

Serafino followed his stare, 'Shouldn't you be joining them? I sense a story developing.'

'I'm sorry, Serafino, I'm chasing something bigger.'

'What could be bigger than an inferno at the altar of all the gods?' Serafino raised his arm in a theatrically-wide sweep that took in the smoking dome of the Pantheon, but when he dropped his hand Lorenzo had disappeared into the night.

Pulling his smartphone from his pocket as he ran, Lorenzo scrolled through the notes that he had made for the Cardinal. Anger and frustration spurred his feet on as he copied the details of Amadeo Bertoli's studio and pasted them into a search engine. Bringing up a map of the city, he followed the directions to the marker pinned to the studio's location within the narrowest of alleys in the city's Jewish Ghetto. It took him a while to find the doorway in the dark, and then what seemed like an hour exploring the building until he came to the apartment on the top floor with the plaque identifying it as Amadeo Bertoli's studio.

'Hello?' He called from the threshold, before cursing himself for being so predictable. If Bertoli was dead, as Serafino had suggested, then surely the place would be empty? Nudging open the door with a foot he could see the place had fallen into disrepair, so it had likely been empty for some time.

Using the torchlight on his phone, Lorenzo combed the apartment methodically, paying attention to each squeaky floorboard, and checking the walls behind every painting. In the largest room, he shone his light over the words scrawled on the wall; the ravings of a mad man. The relic had driven Bertoli mad, but the gnarled graffiti seemed to suggest that he had indeed possessed the Bowl of Pontius Pilate.

The night passed by, and Lorenzo had all but given up when the dawn began to dilute the darkness. He paused, watching the sunlight stealing in through the window shutters. Birds began to wake the world, but other than that, the city seemed silent, expectant almost. Silent, except for the sound of dripping water that Lorenzo suddenly realised had accompanied his entire search.

Water. The bowl in which Pontius Pilate had washed his hands, thus condemning Christ to the death demanded by the Sanhedrin. As the night shrank away from the encroaching day, the light came back to Lorenzo: if Amadeo Bertoli had been driven insane by the relic that had been used to wash away Pilate's responsibility, perhaps he too, had tried to wash away his guilt?

He followed the sound of the water to a sink in an anteroom that was piled high with paint palettes, brushes, and assorted crockery. The tap was indeed dripping over the sink, but all of its contents looked modern. Nothing jumped out at him as being especially ancient. Lorenzo thumped his fist down on the side of the sink in frustration, causing the cupboard door underneath to open with a squeak. He shone his phone downward, and opening the door, found a miniaturised bust of the statue of Madama Lucrezia.

His heart thumping in his chest, he reached in and closed his hand around the neck of the sculpture. His fingers brushed against something cold and wet in the process, and so Lorenzo crouched down, pointed the light from his phone directly into the cupboard, and gasped.

There, behind the face of Madama Lucrezia, was a collection of small clay fragments. They could have come from anywhere, they could have been any old scraps dug out of the earth, but he knew. As his finger touched the first piece, a shiver ran through him, as if the guilt collected within somehow passed up his arm. Lorenzo suddenly felt conscious that he was breaking and entering; that he shouldn't be snooping around the dead man's property; that what he was doing was wrong.

He dropped the terracotta shard on top of the others, where it landed with a slight clink. He instantly felt better. It was just earthenware, old pottery, like any of the pieces that were to be found littering Monte Testaccio: the hill in Rome that had was made of broken amphorae. He had been tasked with finding the relic, and he had indeed found it. Cardinal Sanchez would be pleased.

20

Cardinal Sanchez was not pleased. In front of him was the morning's copy of the Vatican newspaper, L'Osservatore Romano, open at the double-page spread dedicated to Cardinal Romano's missive against the gene therapy experiments. The article reiterated the Church's opposition to Professor Rossi's work, as well as demonising the Professor, and painting Cardinal Romano as some kind of Defender of the Faith. His rival had gone to press without discussing the diatribe with the senior cardinals, which would not work in Romano's favour, but the article painted him in such a good light that Sanchez couldn't help but feel outmanoeuvred. Cardinal Romano had played his next move in their game, and after the events of the previous night, Cardinal Sanchez was tired.

He turned the page to find a small, hastily-gathered eyewitness account of the Pantheon fire, incorporating the grisly discovery of the charred body within. No one knew who the unfortunate victim was, and some were already speculating that it was the arsonist himself, having perished in his own conflagration. The Cardinal knew differently, however.

According to the article, experts were still trying to assess the damage, but the restoration work would cost millions: there was considerable damage to the tomb of Raphael, the frescoes were ruined, much of the decoration was either burnt or covered in soot, and the plaster was falling from the walls. Surveyors were to be sent in to check on the stability of the roof, and a hotline had been set up for any witnesses, who were promised a reward.

The telephone on his desk rang, making him jump. He answered, shouted, and replaced the receiver. The door opened shortly after, admitting Lorenzo to the room.

'Buongiorno,' he said, eyeing his godson suspiciously, 'to what do I owe this unannounced pleasure?'

Lorenzo stopped in front of the Cardinal's desk, and brought a small wooden box out from behind his back; the sort of flimsy container that stallholders filled with chocolate and a postcard to hawk to tourists.

'What do we have here my boy?'

'I visited Studio Bertoli.'

'Oh?' The Cardinal's eyes fixated on the box as Lorenzo set it down on the desk, 'What did you find?'

'Devastation. The man went mad over his possession of the relic.'

'Poor Amadeo Bertoli, ever the suffering artist.'

'You know him then?'

'Well, I knew his reputation; I can't say that I knew the man.'

If Lorenzo picked up on the Cardinal's use of the past tense, he didn't show it. For his part, Cardinal Sanchez cursed himself internally and decided to backtrack.

'Bertoli once had some paintings exhibited in the Pinacoteca at the Vatican Museums, I believe, but they weren't of much renown.'

'I did some digging online about the artist and his work,' Lorenzo said, sitting down, 'and I discovered that there was only one painting, oil on canvas, that was ever judged to be of any merit. A magnum opus that he titled *Aracoeli*. A painting that apparently, you own.'

Cardinal Sanchez sat back in his chair and bared his palms momentarily.

'It is true; I do love that painting. But I had no idea that the artist was the same individual who stole the relic.'

Lorenzo pushed the wooden box across the desk; watched the Cardinal's eyes widen, and the pulse quicken at his neck.

'I don't know what these pieces are worth to you, Your Eminence, but are they truly worth a man's life?'

The Cardinal looked up, 'His life?'

'You haven't heard about the Pantheon fire?'

The Cardinal gestured towards the newspaper in front of him, 'I have read about it, yes. Such a tragedy.'

'The body they found inside may be the remains of Amadeo Bertoli.'

Lorenzo watched the grief rupture the Cardinal's face, only for him to recompose himself in seconds. What he couldn't tell was whether it was a genuine shock, or if the Cardinal was putting on a show.

'Such a waste of a life.'

'A life wasted by the pursuit of these small bits of pottery,' Lorenzo spat, as he opened up the wooden box. Cardinal Sanchez leaned in to take a closer look, and then pulled his desk lamp towards the box to illuminate its contents.

The clay glowed in the electric light as if it were possessed of an earthly fire deep within. The centuries had laid down dust and dirt in feint fissures across the surface, blackening the ancient terracotta pieces. To the untrained eye, they seemed the charred remains of any old pot but to Cardinal's eyes, that beheld them now in awe, the chips of pottery betrayed a history of neglect that had been visited upon the object.

The Cardinal daintily selected a piece and rubbed it between his fingers, the whorls on his fingertips caressing the surface. It was smooth on one side and coarse on the other, with a delicate web of dirt traced across the clay where moss had grown at some time in the past. He scratched away the dirt with a fingernail and returned the piece to the box, where it stood out clean and bare among its filthy brothers. The individual shards seemed like jagged flames sculpted from the earth, together forming a model of fire forever captured in terracotta for the delight of the owner.

No one glancing at it in a museum collection out of context would ever have guessed that the broken pieces, were the remnants of an important relic. None would have realised that, although created for a simple and humble purpose, it had become a bowl of ancient infamy. Plenty of similar specimens existed from the same era, some in much better repair, but none were as significant as this.

'This bowl of broken clay, ' the Cardinal whispered reverently, 'this vessel of earthly fire is all that remains of the basin used by Pontius Pilate to cleanse himself of the responsibility for the death of Christ.'

'So you said before,' Lorenzo added drolly.

'That simple act of ablution transformed this mundane piece of earthenware into a reminder of mankind's inability to accept accountability. A witness to the primal urge that convinces us to cast the blame from ourselves and lay it on the shoulders of others. It represents the instinct of survival, the need to dominate, and once held enough power to condemn the Living Word to death.

'I have searched for it for years, and at last, it is in my hands. If this bowl absolved the Roman Governor of the sin of Our Lord's death, then it can absolve any sin. Think of it, Lorenzo, the responsibility for the worst deeds of your life, just washed away.'

'I don't think that's the kind of power any man should have,' Lorenzo answered, 'I think it would do strange things to the mind. On the walls of Bertoli's studio, he had scrawled words saying that he wasn't innocent, over and over. And when I picked up the pieces of the relic, I felt...guilty.'

'How interesting,' the Cardinal mused, 'is there much that you have to feel guilty about?'

'Not as much as others.'

A moment of silence passed between them. The Cardinal moved his desk lamp back, plunging them into momentary darkness as their eyes adjusted.

'I also found the sculpture of Madama Lucrezia at Bertoli's studio. It was in front of the relic as if she was hiding it.'

'Who?'

'Madama Lucrezia. I'll see to it that the bust is returned to Signore D'Eustachio at the antiquaria. He said he'd kept it for luck.'

'Yes, of course. The sculpture is of no importance,' the Cardinal waved a hand dismissively and drew the relic closer.

'Of course, you'll have to inform Professor Rossi that the relic has been found. It is still his property after all.'

'Yes,' Cardinal Sanchez said dreamily, 'his property. I'll have it authenticated first, and then it shall be presented to the Holy Father before I decide how best to deal with Rossi. The revelation of this relic's existence will relegate the gene therapy experiments and those who oppose them, to the back page.

'Thank you so much for bringing the relic to me, Lorenzo,' I will make sure that you are adequately compensated. Name your price. Anything.'

'One question answered honestly.'

'Go on.'

'Where were you last night?'

21

Matteo donned his crisp white lab coat and shrugged twice so that it settled onto his shoulders. It was newly washed and pressed and had been starched until it was almost rigid. It would take a few hours before it moulded to the shape of his body. For now, the material rasped against his bare arms, making him itch. He adjusted his collar and buttoned up the coat.

Putting on his lab coat would usually have been the last action in a routine that transformed him from an average man into a scientist. Wearing the coat, feeling it around him, and listening to the pens clicking together in the breast pocket, would bring him closer to his work. Closer to his calling.

Wearing this uniform identified him with his vocation, with his desire to use science to help and heal others. They made him a scientist, and as a scientist, he was afforded the ability to step back from his environment and observe not only his work but the rest of his life as well, with the detached, critical eye of the observer.

Today was different: the coat was freshly laundered and didn't feel right. There were no pens in the pocket that knocked together like his own, private metronome to regulate the pace of his walking, his thinking. His head was full of the comments and criticisms he had heard during the Board Meeting, and as he walked along the corridor he mouthed the words silently, trying to find some hidden compliment or comfort in the harsh words of his superiors. He found none, no matter how hard he tried to manipulate the vague insults and veiled threats that had been made. With each thunderous heartbeat, his blood pumped through his head; his ears glowed, and his cheeks boiled.

He had to swipe his access card through the scanner twice because the sweat from his hand had greased the magnetic strip. The door clicked open and he pressed against it, leaving a palm print on the glass. As it swung shut behind him, he leaned against the door and sighed with relief. He was back in his domain, his private little world of test tubes and Petri dishes; back in the laboratory where he could forget the world outside. Once inside, he could conduct his research in peace, away from the demands of the Board of Directors, slowly piecing together his dream of a new, revolutionary treatment.

Karin watched Matteo emerge from the booth, and studied his body language: the stoop in his shoulders, the pale tired face, and the twitching hands. She figured out that the Board Meeting hadn't gone too well. She had known him for eight years, working alongside him for almost six of them, and with a twinge of sadness, she realised that the man entering the laboratory was a mere shade of the person he had once been.

Since taking on the project, she had watched him become consumed by the intricate workings of genetic manipulation, and the politics that surrounded such a bold leap into controversy. He had dropped everything else in his life to concentrate on his work; accepting the setbacks as well as relishing in the progress. He lived, breathed, and if what he had told her was true, dreamed the project. It was an obsession of his: a mission that had gnawed at the bright, positive and idealistic man he had been not so long ago.

Karin hated to think of what would happen to him if the whole thing fell apart at this stage. She feared that he would become trapped in the limbo of the unfinished experiments; that he would continue to pursue the cause of genetic manipulation and give his life to it. Of course, she hoped that if the facility were closed down, he would be able to pick himself up and move on, but the lines of his face and the grey hairs now streaking his head made her think otherwise.

'What happened?' She asked, guessing how well it had gone.

'I got my ass kicked.'

'How bad was it?'

'Awful. All they could talk about was Cardinal Romano's newspaper article, which they see as a renewed opposition from the

Church. Whenever I brought up the actual *work* that we're doing, the consensus was that we've done well, but could do better.

'They're more obsessed with what they call the "optics" of the Vatican's opposition, and how it makes things look bad for investors. They want better results, concrete evidence that the money is well-spent, and they want it faster.'

Karin snorted and pulled on a pair of latex gloves. There was a snap of latex against skin, and then hushed squeaking noises as she wormed her fingers into the gloves.

'It's always the same;' she said, 'they want more evidence; they want conclusive evidence; they don't understand the evidence; they want it presented in cartoons and flow diagrams. Why is it that Nature dictates that those who occupy senior management positions should be morons? Is it a genetic defect, do you think?'

'Who knows: maybe we'll be able to cure them of it soon enough?'

'Maybe,' she bit her lip, afraid of asking the inevitable, 'Do you think they'll shut us down?

Matteo shook his head as if rousing himself from the nightmarish thought.

'I've dealt with worse before now. I've worked in harsher conditions and under more restrictive covenants. I can deal with the pressure from the Board; the problem I have is dealing with myself.'

Karin nodded sympathetically and motioned for him to continue his catharsis. It seemed as if he was cleaning a blockage in his mind; reading what was written somewhere on the inside.

'Of all the things in life I fear, I fear failure above all else. The very notion of not being able to achieve my ambitions, to have to make a living from a job I don't enjoy, tears me up. To think that I could not achieve my best, that either myself or some other would stand in the way of my dreams, almost paralyses me. I cannot fail: I won't allow myself to back down. Not now, not after all the work I've put into these experiments. I won't permit it. Not here of all places, not here—'

'Not in the country where your father was so successful.' Karin interrupted. 'Not in the place where he thought you could have no future. After all those years growing up in America, working to become the man that you are now, you have to prove him wrong; you have to show him that you are better than he ever could have imagined, and you have to do it here. Admit it Matt: you wanted to base the experiments here to prove him wrong, to show that you could make something of yourself.'

'In my home country.' Matteo closed his eyes and looked inwardly. 'Although I grew up a long way from here, this is still my home. It doesn't matter what my father thought: I will make something of myself here. I have to succeed Karin. I can't fail.'

'The home crowd is the toughest to play,' she said, 'even Jesus found that. None of us are here to fail Matt, and it's unlikely that we will.'

She put her arm around his shoulder and led him gently towards the workbench where she had spent the best part of the morning. A large microscope sat on the work surface; a metal armature holding a small plate before the lens. Karin bent down and retrieved a petri dish from a freezer under the desk. Cold clouds rolled out from the freezing interior and sank to floor level before dissipating in the fluorescent light. Wiping away a film of condensation that was daubed over the dish by the warm air, she placed it on the plate under the microscope.

'Take a look at these and then tell me you fear failing.' She said with a half-smile.

Matteo bent down and peered into the microscope, studying the contents of the dish in silence. He refocused the lens once or twice, then stood up and rubbed his eyes. He checked the microscope over, looked again., and gasped.'

'How old are these?'

'Nine days.'

He looked up, the shock plain on his face. 'Seriously?'

She nodded and placed another dish under the microscope. 'This one's the best so far: no degradation at all. If we can make them all like this, then we'll be able to initiate cell division within days.'

'My God Karin we've done it! We've really done it! There's nothing wrong with this embryo! It's perfect! It's fixed!'

When he looked up from the microscope the lines on his face seemed to have softened, and the shadows under his eyes had fled in fear from the light now glittering in his pupils. He was close to tears, although his face spoke only of happiness. Gone were the slouched shoulders and pained expression; he had come to life again in front of Karin's eyes. He was fixed.

'This is wonderful! Really wonderful!' He said, turning from Karin to the microscope and then back again. 'We'll be able to produce the results the Board wants to see. And once they've been placated, we'll be able to progress to the next stage of the experiments. We're getting closer Karin: I can feel it!'

His jubilation was interrupted by the chirrup of his phone. 'There's another delivery in reception: let's go and have a look.'

The two of them walked to the reception, talking excitedly about the new development. Matteo asked for a message to be sent to the Board informing them of the news and then fussed enthusiastically over the delivery of yet another diagnostic machine. Karin stood back and enjoyed the benefits of his elation: when Matteo was happy, everyone else was. When things were going well, the whole place pulsated with energy. Looking at him now, she found it hard to recall the glum person who had walked into the laboratory mere minutes before.

Her attention was drawn to a window that looked out over the back courtyard of the Ospedale. Beyond the gates, a crowd of protesters had gathered to wave placards and chant in the street. Angry faces looked out from the throng, shouting and swearing things that she couldn't bring herself to understand. Some of the younger protesters were marching up and down a short section of pavement and chanting the slogans painted on their banners.

Matteo joined her and opened the window a little. Fresh air blew into the room, cleaner and cooler than the recycled air coming down through the vents. He bent his ear to the window and listened to the shouts.

'They say that we're heretics, that and agents of Satan.' He turned and gave her a grin. 'Where did they get that idea, I wonder? How much did Cardinal Romano pay them to stand out in the rain all day and shout themselves hoarse?'

'You don't think they're doing it simply because they believe in what they're shouting?' She reached forward and closed the window, hugging herself against the cold.

22

Il Capitano dipped a crusty *baicoli* into his coffee and used it to stir the drink, pulling the biscuit out at just the right time so that it was firm enough to tap against the cup to remove any excess liquid. He put half of the biscuit into his mouth and sucked the coffee from it gently, allowing the crumbs to dissolve onto his tongue. It was a process he had perfected over decades that called for patience and impeccable timing. As he ate the second half of the biscuit, he scrolled down his computer screen, narrowing his eyes at the online article he was reading.

A knock at the door heralded Rodrigo Fuentes, who walked into the room with the words, 'I have some news.'

'Do you indeed? Take a seat, Deacon Fuentes, and do tell.'

Rodrigo sat in the seat that Il Capitano indicated; like many in the room, it was stiff and uncomfortable, designed to discourage guests from overstaying their welcome.

'The Pantheon fire.'

'What of it?'

'It was me.'

Il Capitano lowered his coffee cup and set it on the saucer deliberately, 'Should we take this to the confessional?'

'Perhaps, but there are things that you need to know about the incident.'

'I'm listening.'

'I drove Cardinal Sanchez into the city that night.'

'Sanchez? Why? I thought it was Cardinal Romano who was roaming the Centro Storico in the small hours.'

'They both had business in the city that night. Cardinal Sanchez had arranged to meet a contact from the art world, Amadeo Bertoli, who he believed to possess a relic of great importance.'

'I am aware of his obsession with the relic, although Amadeo Bertoli is a name with which I am unfamiliar.'

'He was a small-time artist, not of any repute, although Cardinal Sanchez did procure a painting from him some time ago.'

'Painting?'

'Its name is *Aracoeli*.'

'A painting of the church?'

'No: it is a painting of Caesar's visit to the Tiburtine Sybil.'

'A pagan painting for a prince of the Church?'

'I've always thought that, but according to Cardinal Sanchez, it was the meeting at which the prophetess foretold the coming of Christ to the Roman Emperor.'

'*Haec est ara primo-geniti Dei.* But what does the legend have to do with the Pantheon fire?'

'After meeting with Bertoli in the Pantheon that night, Cardinal Sanchez returned to the car and asked for my help. When I accompanied him back into the building, Amadeo Bertoli was lying in the centre of the main chamber, dead.'

'Dead?'

'Removing the body would have meant carrying it through the main doors out into Piazza della Rotonda, in full view of late-night tourists and the CCTV from the nearby restaurants. So I chose to clear up the Cardinal's mess by setting light to the corpse.'

'Was Sanchez responsible?'

'I'm not certain: I was unable to get a clear answer from him. His state of shock made me want to believe that it was an accident.'

'How very interesting. Of course, you may both be on camera, having entered and left the building that night.'

'This is indeed a problem.'

'For Cardinal Sanchez, yes, but not for you. I'll make some enquiries, and if there is footage of you, Rodrigo, I'll see to it that it's scrubbed.'

'Thank you, Il Capitano.'

'I cannot promise the same for Cardinal Sanchez.'

'Of course not, nor would I expect it.'

'I only hope that this relic proves to be worth the trouble that Sanchez has gone to in his attempts to secure it.'

'I understand that it has finally been delivered to him, by his godson, a journalist by the name of Lorenzo L'Oscuro.'

Il Capitano looked to the computer screen on his left-hand side, where, scrolling up, he found Lorenzo's name at the top of the article that he had been reading.

'What an interesting coincidence, Rodrigo. The same journalist has today published an article about the struggles of the Roma population in the city, and the attempts by the local authorities to rid Rome of their scourge.'

'Has he really? I thought that he was reporting on the gene therapy experiments? The Cardinal had set him up with interviews with the scientists; one of whom is connected to this relic.'

'Perhaps it's no coincidence at all, then. This article mentions a woman: Madama Lucrezia. A leader of the Roma community, it seems. I have heard the name many times in my career, yet she has always eluded me. For years I considered her an urban myth, but it seems she is indeed flesh and blood. I cannot have anyone else controlling the streets, Rodrigo. If there is another power working against me, I must snuff it out.'

'What will you do?'

'If I can find her, I will pay this Madama Lucrezia a visit, and find out just how powerful she is.'

23

'Darkness, gentlemen, can represent many things. Ignorance. Confusion. Evil. The absence of light renders us blind: blind to the truth, blind to what is right. Darkness can be deceptive, can be inviting, and draws many men into its seductive embrace. Under the cover of darkness many evils awake, many wicked deeds are conducted, and good men are turned away from what is right. Darkness is our enemy. From the Darkness, it is hard to see the Light. It is hard to know Truth. It is hard to find God.

'I say these things because it is quite often the case that we forget what it is like to live without the light; what it is like to live outside of the One True Faith. Our minds must always be turned to those who live in darkness, with the view to leading them towards the Light. And tonight, I ask that we turn our minds to one of our own number who I believe has got lost in the dark, fallen prey to evil, and perhaps even turned from Christ. It sounds shocking, I know, but the one who is not among us tonight has fallen.'

Cardinal Sanchez paused and allowed his companions to soak up those last thoughts in silence. He examined his reflection in the window of a display cabinet and corrected his posture before resuming his route around the table, his shadow following him in the light cast by the single lamp.

'My friends, we all know that this is a strange time for the Church: the world is more secular in its processes and operations. Our flock has been reduced greatly by people looking to modern methods of gaining happiness and living lawfully. Governments around the world enforce their own temporal, humanist law over that given to us by God. People have turned to machines to ease their burdens, and to each other for solace and companionship. The role of the vicar or priest is often thought diminished as people abandon the sacraments and choose to lead their lives in the darkness.

'Yet even as people turn away from us, there are many who return to the fold upon recognising the harsh realities of the world we live in. The threats of terrorism and war, the deaths of loved ones, and feelings of betrayal and loss drive people back into our arms looking for comfort, for penitence, and for salvation. Our human sides caution us against rejoicing in their return, yet the divine in each of us tells us that they too are entitled, despite their past mistakes, to worship the Light again. God does not abandon them, nor does He go away when they stop believing, and He is there to help them when they lose their way.

'These are confusing times indeed, my brothers. We must fight against the darkness, and yet heal those who have actively embraced it. We must show love to those who would only offer us hate. We must work for the souls of those who work against us. We must sacrifice for them to gain. In these times, gentlemen, perhaps we are finally beginning to understand the ministry of Christ and to fully appreciate what it means to be one of his disciples. Yet just as we come to realise what our purpose is, there will be others among us who are denied that revelation: others who will look elsewhere for the Light, and such scandal could easily turn people away from us. If one of our members were to embrace that Darkness, he might tarnish us all.'

Sanchez took a moment to glance at each of the faces gathered at the table: old faces, tired faces, troubled and confused faces. Cardinal San Marco was slowly fanning himself with a piece of paper; the temperature of the room had risen since the men had taken their seats. Sanchez would have opened a window, but the fresh air would have served only to make his colleagues more alert, more focused. If the meeting was to go as he wished, then they needed to remain drowsy and uncomfortable.

'Are you saying that Cardinal Romano has suffered a lapse of faith, Luis?' Cardinal San Marco asked.

'I am saying it may be possible. What I know for definite is that he has made a grave error of judgement, one that may have far-reaching repercussions in the coming months.'

'I know of no such errors: his work in opposition to the gene therapy experiments has been exemplary, and I have yet to hear of any lapse in his duties as a Cardinal.'

'Of course,' Sanchez said placidly, 'in some areas, Romano's work has been faultless: his behaviour in that field is, as you say, exemplary. Unfortunately, there is another issue where his conduct has been less than satisfactory; maybe even to the extreme of discrediting the Church.'

'How, exactly?'

Cardinal Sanchez completed his circuit of the table and sat down in his chair. Before him was the damask-covered dossier he had compiled about Cardinal Romano's activities. With one eye on Cardinal San Marco, he opened the volume and distributed a typed sheet detailing Lorenzo's findings from the assignment he had been given.

'Gentlemen, I am sure many of us have become aware that our friend Giancarlo sometimes makes excursions into the city late at night.' Some of the Cardinals nodded their heads, others exchanged perplexed glances, and it was for their benefit that Cardinal Sanchez proceeded to explain the matter in depth.

'Once every month or so, Cardinal Romano leaves his residence, or his office if he has worked into the night, and then walks through the Borgo in the direction of the river. In the summer months, he can be glimpsed walking downriver; in the winter, and indeed for the last three or four months at least, he has chosen to take a car to his destination.

'I have cautioned him many times about using drivers unknown to our Administration, and have often recommended that he take one of our official vehicles, accompanied by an escort. It would not do for him to get into some kind of trouble in the city and have no means of protection. However, he continuously refused to disclose his business, or accept any of my proposals: I became concerned about his behaviour, and so, after much deliberation, I decided to have him followed.'

'You had him followed?' Cardinal Beauclerc shouted across the table, 'Outrageous!'

An argument broke out between the two Cardinals with Cardinal Beauclerc demanding to know whether Sanchez made a habit of stalking his colleagues and accusing him of breaking the bonds of trust that held their exclusive group together. It was Cardinal San Marco who eventually brought peace to the room, rapping his glass against the table until the argument subsided.

'Having another Cardinal followed is a questionable action in itself, Luis, although you must have had considerable suspicions if you had to resort to such a drastic measure. Tell us what you discovered.'

'Thank you,' Sanchez said graciously, 'please understand, my brothers, that it was out of concern that I had Giancarlo followed. For his protection, I had a friend follow him, at a distance that would not encroach on his activities: it was merely an observational exercise. Giancarlo was not harmed or disturbed in any way. I have, however, been quite disturbed by what he did get up to.

'He was driven along the riverbank before crossing the river and parking in Via Giulia; he was followed through the streets to a small courtyard inaccessible to the traffic. He was seen entering through the door of a house that had a red light shining in the window.'

'And what of it?' Cardinal Beauclerc demanded. 'Perhaps he has friends in the city.'

'Perhaps, but I was concerned by the description of the house: you can read it for yourselves in the handout. It's a private, secluded place; the kind of place you might find belonging to an organised crime family. It was the red light that worried me: I was worried about what it might represent. I can only surmise that the house in question was a house of ill repute.'

'Cardinal Romano was seen entering a brothel?' Cardinal Beauclerc asked over the collective gasp that arose among his peers.

'It is certainly possible.'

'That is a very serious accusation, Luis,' Cardinal San Marco chided, looking up from the piece of paper he had been handed. 'I see very little here to support it; the evidence is weak.'

'It doesn't make sense,' Beauclerc added, 'Giancarlo would never visit such a place: it would be out of character for him. He would never indulge in such, such–'

'Sin?' Sanchez suggested.

'Perhaps he was trying to make them see the error of their ways.' Cardinal Beauclerc said. 'Maybe he was converting them.'

'Believe that if you will, but he could do that at any time of the day, even with an escort: his behaviour suggests some darker purpose. I made enquiries about the property and discovered something more heinous. The woman who lives there is a woman who tells fortunes, known to the criminal underworld. Worse still, she apparently has a reputation for practising the Black Arts.'

As one man the assembled Cardinals crossed themselves, save for Sanchez and San Marco.

'The Black Arts?' Cardinal San Marco asked. 'As in witchcraft? Are you sure?'

'From what I have heard, she is a woman allied to the Devil, who surrounds herself with varied miscreants who are thought to indulge in demonic worship. It sounds dire, I know, but I believe Cardinal Romano discovered a Satanic cult in our city, and in his attempts to scour it, became involved in their devilry.'

'And you are sure this is the house he visited?'

'Yes, I am certain. I think that we must consider seriously the notion that Giancarlo has turned from the Faith. He has been seduced by this gypsy woman and the whores that dwell with her. We must find some way of dealing with this problem: this nest of vipers must be exposed, yet we must look after Giancarlo. He is, after all, our brother, whatever his vices may be.'

'This is terrible news.' Cardinal Beauclerc said woefully. 'Perhaps it is not as bad as it seems. There may be another explanation?'

'I have tried looking for one, but the deeper I look, the worse secrets I uncover. It grieves me to inform you of this, but I understand that this very house is under investigation due to a possible connection with the Pantheon fire.'

'How so?' Asked Cardinal San Marco, rubbing his chin thoughtfully and narrowing his eyes.

'I'm not sure of the particulars, but if his involvement with the mistress of this house is discovered, the police will want to question him. We may end up facing a scandal we have no way of containing.'

'We must take precautions to try and protect him,' Cardinal Beauclerc said, 'perhaps we could suppress the official investigation in some way, at least until we have made our enquiries.'

'The Holy Father will have to be informed.' Cardinal San Marco added gravely. 'Have you spoken to Giancarlo about this?'

'Not yet, no.'

'Then until we know otherwise, we must give him the benefit of the doubt. There is still a chance that his activities may not be what they seem.'

'Then by all means speak to him,' Cardinal Sanchez said, 'but I cannot begin to think of a way of reasoning with a man who has embraced the Darkness.'

'We are not certain that he has, Luis. I will speak to Giancarlo myself, but before then, I suggest that this matter be referred to the office of the Cardinal Major Penitentiary, and commence an internal investigation. |The results can then be passed onto the police or buried if needs be. Are we all agreed that this is the best course of action?'

They held a quick vote; the collective nod of heads confirming that Cardinal Romano should be subjected to investigation by the Penitentiary Office, and sanctioned in any necessary way. For Cardinal Sanchez, it was a victory, and an outcome that he had been hoping for: the senior Cardinals had reacted just as he had expected and played into his hands by deciding to keep the investigation private.

'What about the gene therapy experiments?' Cardinal Beauclerc asked. 'Shouldn't Cardinal Romano be relieved of some of his more public engagements? We have been fortunate of late to have such staunch support for our cause; if there is any hint of Romano's recent actions, the tide of opinion may turn and we might find ourselves on the receiving end of the opposition. We cannot afford to risk that outcome when so much ground has been gained in this campaign; nor do we want to upset or anger the faithful. I motion that we transfer the responsibility for this issue to someone else, and give Cardinal Romano something more menial to occupy himself with.'

'But who would take over from him?' Cardinal Beauclerc asked.

'I would be more than happy–' Cardinal Sanchez began.

'As I have said before,' Cardinal San Marco interrupted, 'the issue falls under my jurisdiction as Prefect of the Congregation for the Doctrine of the Faith; although I cannot afford to dedicate the same time to Giancarlo's campaign that he has managed to, I will take on the running of it, and delegate it to some of the workers of the CDF. That way none of us has to worry about spending the time and effort on it.'

'Surely something this important should be handled by one of our number, and not delegated to others.' Sanchez said, 'I would be more than happy to take on the burden, and would endeavour to find the necessary time to manage it.'

'No Luis, I think it's better if we concentrate on our respective duties, and spread those of Cardinal Romano across several different workloads.'

The other Cardinals nodded in agreement, Cardinal Sanchez folding his arms and abstaining from the following vote. He closed the portfolio in front of him and moved it aside to reveal another slim folder, containing a few glossy pictures.

'Might I suggest that we adjourn this meeting for the time being,' Cardinal San Marco was saying, 'and re-assemble in a fortnight to assess how the new arrangements are holding up? I will speak to Giancarlo to inform him of the changes, and also refer the matter to the Cardinal Major Penitentiary. If there aren't any other items for discussion…'

'If I'm to be completely honest with you, there is something else I would like to share with you; something positive, after the shock that I have given you this morning. What I am about to share with you may prove to be of use to us in maintaining our level of public support, should Giancarlo's antics become public knowledge.'

He shared out the pictures: photographs that he had taken of the relic and its casing. One of the other Cardinals blew his nose into a handkerchief, sending a cloud of dust motes swirling around in the light penetrating the gloom through the small window at the back of the room. The dust swelled in a tide of age and disuse that washed over them; time caught up with them as they looked upon the images of the bowl that had survived for centuries.

'My brothers, these pictures show the relic which I gained possession of recently. The contents of the casket, are the remains of the bowl in which the Roman Governor Pontius Pilate washed his hands before the Crucifixion.'

Cardinal San Marco raised his eyebrows.

'My inspection makes me think it is genuine, although that is merely an opinion: I don't have the authority or the expertise to declare it as authentic.'

'Why do you think it is genuine?' Cardinal Beauclerc asked, excitedly wringing his hands.

'The intricate reliefs of the casing, and the sturdy construction of the casket, along with the materials used suggest that it was held in great esteem. Whoever commissioned the creation of the casket clearly revered the relic. Finally, as I inspected the clay fragments themselves, I discovered some faint carvings on the outer edge that I believe might be Aramaic.

'The translation of the inscription would be the key to authenticating the relic's identity. I suppose the clay could be carbon-dated to further determine its age. At first, it struck me as strange that the inscription was not in Latin if the dish were part of Pilate's household. I can only surmise that it would have been of little importance to Pilate or any of the other Romans in Jerusalem at the time: for them, it was just another dish. It could be possible that the dish was procured by early Christians and then inscribed in a language that they themselves spoke.'

'It's an interesting hypothesis Luis,' Cardinal San Marco said, shuffling the photographs round in his hands, 'and an exciting find. I would dearly love to believe that this relic is what you say it is, but only rigorous testing will be able to determine its authenticity. We must not let our initial excitement affect our judgement of the relic. There are many relics in the world, belonging to faiths other than our own. That any of them have survived to this day is remarkable: that many of them are what they claim to be is nothing short of miraculous.'

'I believe that it is the Bowl of Pilate: every part of me tells me that I am right and that this is a great find for the Church.'

'Belief sadly is not enough.' Cardinal San Marco said. 'Belief alone cannot make it authentic, and we need something more permanent than belief before we release any kind of statement about the relic.'

'Still, it should be brought to the Holy Father's attention.' Sanchez said defensively.

'Perhaps, but not at the moment: it would be presumptive of us to inform His Holiness of the relic if it turned out to be a fake.' San Marco countered.

The other Cardinals agreed with him, which made things a little difficult for Cardinal Sanchez. Cardinal San Marco had been quite vociferous during the meeting; it was something Sanchez had half-expected. Benedetto San Marco had become increasingly active in past weeks, notably since the commencement of the gene therapy experiments; if left unchecked, it was more than possible that he would become another rival. Although San Marco had tried to be the voice of reason during the meeting, Sanchez couldn't help but think that he was deliberately opposing him; a fear that he related to Rodrigo that afternoon.

'At times I found myself wondering what his motives were,' he said, 'and whether they would be likely to come into conflict with my own. I have no problem dealing with opposition among my colleagues: Cardinal Romano and I have been engaged in healthy opposition for years. But Giancarlo is weak: Benedetto is an altogether different animal; stronger and potentially more dangerous to my plans.'

Rodrigo nodded intermittently as he listened. It was his way of dealing with Cardinal Sanchez: acknowledge what was being said, placate him, and commend him when he finally reached the point of his conversation. All the while, it was important to absorb what the Cardinal was saying, and mentally file it away for later analysis.

'What would you do, to see that he doesn't become a nuisance?' He asked him.

'I don't see what I can do without declaring openly to him that I fear his opposition. He would perceive that fear as a weakness to be exploited, and I might find myself in a worse situation than the present one.'

'How so?'

'If I reveal my suspicions of Benedetto and his actions, to him or any other, it would compromise my position. I am held in great esteem by my colleagues: if I am seen to be choosing and declaring a new rival so soon after Cardinal Romano is deposed, then their opinion of me would suffer, and Benedetto could easily use it to his advantage. I do not want to be seen to be picking fights with my peers, or alienating them: conclusions might then be drawn about my aims for the Papacy.'

'Cardinal Romano is to be deposed?' Rodrigo asked, almost disinterested.

'Of course he is, after what he's been up to lately. There is no way he will be able to carry on as normal with this investigation hanging over his head. If he does not resign from his post, it will only be a matter of time before he is forced out of it. Unfortunately, I can't be seen to have anything to do with it: I must now consolidate my position with greater stealth than ever.'

'Why?'

'So that I don't alert the other Cardinals to my plans.'

'What are you going to do?'

'To start, I will leak a document about the Bowl of Pontius Pilate, although for now, I will keep the relic's identity a secret. With rumours of a newfound relic in the public domain, the Holy Father will have to be informed of it. This, I am hoping, will quicken the pace of the examination of the relic, thus enabling us to disclose both its identity, and mine as its finder.'

'Why go to all this trouble?'

'Rodrigo, you know as well as I do that all purported relics have to be thoroughly tested and verified before we can even declare our interest in them. And although that is how it should be done, it takes a long time, and during that period I could be distanced from it, and others may take the recognition. If it is revealed to the public whilst I am still thought to have discovered it, and still have control over it, then the attention and reverence it receives will also extend to me.'

'Then let us hope that everything goes to plan.'

'It can go no other way. I have worked too long and too hard to obtain this relic for it to fail me now. I will be pushed to the pinnacle of our hierarchy, and you shall be elevated with me. This relic is what I need to improve my position, and steer attention away from Cardinal Romano and his campaign against the experiments.'

'Do you think he will sit back and let someone else take over his work?'

'He will have no choice. He will be removed from office: relegated to menial duties, demoted, shamed, scorned and spurned. He has been an irritation for too long, and now comes the time when I can dispose of him. His spirit will be crushed, his faith tarnished, and his mind broken. He will come to learn that when a person dares to oppose and offend me, there can be no hope of them winning.'

'And how will you achieve all of this?'

'I will frighten him...'

24

The rain continued to fall all day, flushing the streets and saturating the parks of the city. Clouds passed across the sky from South to North and were replaced by thicker successors dark with rain. The downpour continued into the early evening; daylight drained into the West as if leached by the continuous rain.

Cardinal Sanchez climbed the stairs, rehearsing the conversation in his mind, anticipating what his rival's reaction would be. He planned to taunt Romano, mock him even, then scare him, and if needs be, threaten him. Upon turning a corner to walk down the corridor to Romano's office, he heard a door open further along. Cardinal Romano stepped out into the gloom.

'Giancarlo!' Sanchez cried, increasing his pace until he caught up with him. 'I must speak with you urgently. I have terrible news: news that it upsets me to have to share with you.'

'What is it, Luis?' Romano asked with genuine concern. 'It sounds important.'

'Indeed it is of the utmost importance. I came to find you as soon as I heard it for myself. I have barely had time to think it over myself: see how my hands shake. Can we step into your office and speak in private? I would not have these walls listen in on words not meant for their hearing.'

Cardinal Romano's eyes gleamed in the last light of the day. 'Is it His Holiness? Has something happened?'

'No, no, His Holiness is in good health I assure you. This does not concern him, but you. I have learned of something that may endanger your position in the hierarchy.'

'What do you mean?' Romano replied, narrowing his eyes.

'Our colleagues have plotted to remove you from your post and divide your workload between them. Cardinal San Marco wishes to take control of the opposition to those experiments.'

'What? Absolute nonsense! Where did you hear this?'

'They are saying that you are not fit for your duties: you were seen entering a house in the city last week that they claim is a den of vice.'

Cardinal Romano stepped back and looked up and down the window. A peevish smirk appeared on his face, and he waved a finger in front of Sanchez's face.

'I have been waiting for you to use that piece of information against me, Luis, ever since the night that you had me followed. Yes, that is right: I know you were behind it. I have known for some time of your desire to remove me from my office. For your information, you will not find vice of any sort in that house. What story have you concocted to turn the others against me?'

Sanchez frowned. 'I don't know what you mean, Giancarlo. I only–'

'You know exactly what I mean! And I tell you now, that neither you nor Cardinal San Marco can depose me. Save your energies Luis, and let me do my work in peace.'

'Maybe the house isn't what I told them it was,' Sanchez said, dropping the façade, 'but there is something about the woman who lives there. She may be free of vices, but I know a dangerous person when I see one.'

Cardinal Romano raised a hand to his mouth and gasped. Cardinal Sanchez grinned and began to laugh.

'Really Giancarlo, did you think I wouldn't find out? Well, I have: I have found the secret woman that you have visited all these years. And I tell you that not only is she dangerous, but she is also powerful: she claims to influence the less desirable inhabitants of the city. She is a gypsy queen: a charlatan and a criminal, and her existence is a threat to all you hold dear.'

'She is not what you think she is.' Romano muttered defensively. He looked toward his office door, only a few steps away, and wished he was settled comfortably in his chair. A nagging pain began to creep along his arm to the whitened knuckles he held in front of his mouth. He leaned against the wall for support, his gnarled hands grasping the windowsill behind him. Pain broke free in his chest and rampaged wild through his body. Scrabbling at the wall, he sank to the floor. He felt as if a hole had opened in his chest, and all his energy was seeping out of it.

Sanchez circled him, walking closer and closer, dropping his voice to a whisper as he did so. 'I will teach her the lesson that she never learned, the one you couldn't bring yourself to impart on her. I will show her the price to pay for worshipping the Devil, for corrupting a man of the Church. A man of the cloth, a Cardinal no less, spending these long years tainted with her sin, and never doing anything to repent those evil ways. How dare you,' He struck him with the back of his hand, 'insult your God so!'

Romano fell backwards clutching his chest and cracked his head on the marble floor. Sanchez leaned over him, checked his pulse and walked up the corridor slowly. When he came to the landing at the end of the stairs he began shouting for help. By the time his calls were answered, Romano had stopped breathing and slipped out of consciousness. Doors opened along the corridor; various priests and lay members came to see what all the fuss was about. Cardinal Sanchez stepped to one side and admired his handiwork: it had all been so easy.

Twenty minutes later the ambulance was pulling away from the Palazzo del Governatorato as the rain drove hard into the side of the building. The water fell in sheets against the third storey window where Cardinal Sanchez stood watching and congratulating himself inwardly. The blue lights of the ambulance shrunk into the dark distance, the occasional light in the gardens catching the fountains of water sent up by its wheels. A bell chimed the hour and fell silent. Content with the result of his actions, Cardinal Sanchez withdrew from the window, and the rain outside that washed away the sins of the world.

25

The car came to a halt in the narrow street outside Vicolo della Notte. A streetlight flickered into life at its sentry post against the back wall of a medieval pilgrim hostel that had been converted into apartments. A dull thumping sound echoed from a thick rug being beaten over the edge of a balcony somewhere above; behind that sound lurked the omnipresent growl of the city traffic. Music played in the piazza that the car had passed through at the far end of the street, where people sat eating and enjoying themselves, many drinking, some dancing. All of them were blissfully unaware of the car door opening, and the man who stepped out into the dusk.

Il Capitano caught sight of his reflection in a shop window staring back at him amid an arrangement of drab oil paintings. At the sight of the painted canvas, his mind recalled the Bertoli painting that Rodrigo had described, and he made a mental note to seek it out at some point. Emperor Augustus and the prophetess; the soldier and the seer. As he raised his umbrella it obscured the oil paintings from view, refocusing him on the task at hand.

He looked up and down the street and up to the balconies above, and, satisfied that no one was watching, turned his attention to the gate and the deep shade of darkness beyond. A rat darted out from the passage as he opened the gate, splashing over a puddle and taking refuge underneath his car. Il Capitano stepped into the small passage that led to the disused kitchens and defunct servant's quarters of a Rome that no longer existed.

He manoeuvred through unseen debris in the diminishing glow from the flickering streetlight behind him: webs caught hold of him and small, unseen fingers clawed at his ankles. His senses felt threatened, assaulted; by what, he knew not. The orange glow of the city became apparent as he exited the passage, and his eyes slowly grew accustomed to the new light. The courtyard revealed itself as if appearing out of a melting fog; his eyes marvelled at the dark walls wrapped in dead ivy, the blind windows shuttered with splintered wood, and the cobble-studded pool of water that covered the floor.

With wonder, he saw the patterns made by the rain of water falling on the square, and following the droplets upward, found the lines of damp washing, ascending over one another to a burnt orange sky studded with the dark shapes of clouds. Small patches of the orange light managed to slice down through the clotheslines, but for the most part, the walls, water, and statue in the centre of the courtyard were only afforded light by a red lamp in the farthest window.

Of the four buildings that formed the square, one at least was inhabited. The glass of the window was unsullied by dust or grime, and behind the lamp were thick red curtains, more like those seen on a stage than in a window. The lamp itself, though dwarfed by the size of the window, and all the buildings of the square burned with a brilliant light that blazed through a chaotically-painted glass shade. Drawn toward the lamp, Il Capitano crossed the square, the wet cobbles sucking at the soles of his shoes.

Figures of men and beasts had been crudely rendered over the glass surface of the lamp, surrounded by a swarm of illegible symbols and lines. The design both fascinated and frightened him; the occult motifs repulsed him, yet the spiral that they were all drawn into reminded him of his own net of influence that he had cast over the city.

Enthralled as he was by the lantern, he pulled himself away from the window, and with a deep breath tried the handle of the door beside it. With pleasant surprise, he found it unlocked, and let himself into the house. He chuckled to himself as he thought of the simple-minded ordinary folk who thought it safe to leave a door open to all the criminals lurking in the passage beyond; little did they know that worse people were stalking the streets than a few dirty vagabonds.

The house was dark inside, save for a line of red light that glowed beneath a door on the left. He reached forward and pushed it open, revealing a small room lit by the embers of a dying fire, and an old woman sitting beside a table, staring at him blankly. He looked at the old woman and tried to read her posture, her mannerisms, and her expression, but gleaned nothing. Like the lantern on the windowsill, he found her presence intriguing, yet unsettling.

'I'm not sure I understand what you mean,' he said, 'perhaps you have mistaken me for someone else? Let me introduce myself: I am Cardinal–'

'At last; a face for the name,' she interrupted, 'I have known of you for a long time, Il Capitano.'

'My dear,' he protested, 'I think you have me confused with someone else: we have not been introduced before, otherwise I would remember it.'

'A man of your influence needs little introduction. I know of you, and perhaps you know of me, although we have not, as you say, been introduced. My name is Madama Lucrezia.'

Il Capitano smiled. 'Lucrezia. I *have* heard the name before.' He walked into the room and pulled a chair from beside the table, unoffered. 'It is quite common, is it not? Found also in the forms Lucretia and Lucrece. It is a name that sometimes reaches my ears, often connected with small events in the city, and I have often wondered as to its importance.'

She laughed loudly; the force of the sound pushing her backwards in her chair. 'And now you have found me: old Lucrezia, sitting alone with barely a fire to keep her warm, or a candle to light her darkness.'

'You are alone?'

She nodded.

'No family to look after you?'

'I have sent them away tonight, to keep them safe.'

'Safe?'

'I knew you were coming.'

Il Capitano raised his eyebrows. 'How is that possible? Who warned you I was coming?'

'Rome.'

'I'm not sure I understand,' he said, scratching his chin thoughtfully.

'Of course not, and that is why you and I have never met. We occupy the same area, but we live in different worlds. We have each known the other's work for decades, and yet our paths have never crossed.'

'You have been hiding?'

'As have you. Clothed in a Cardinal's attire, hidden behind the walls of the Vatican, shrouded in ceremony and secrecy: a life spent pretending to serve God when you only serve yourself. I have known you a long time, Il Capitano.'

'And still, you hide behind the identity of Madama Lucrezia; a statue within a myth. Who are you really?'

'I am Rome: where the fountains sing in the square, I am there; where the birds roost in the ruins, there am I also. When the sun is gone and the cold damp creeps up the banks of the river, I offer warmth to those in need. When the rich tourists step over and ignore the crippled and the dying without a second thought about their poverty, I am the one who picks them up and comforts them. When knives draw blood among the cobbled streets of this ancient city, my eyes are watching.

'My influence is far-reaching in the city. I bring people into this world, I help them through it and ease their passage from it. I know all the souls who walk these streets; the dreams in their heads, the fears they keep inside. Every coin that falls into a beggar's bowl, every hooded shape that passes among the palazzi. Every pizza served, and every cappuccino poured: I am told of it all. Priests and politicians; teachers, thieves and tortured souls; whores and housewives, they all come to the ears of Lucrezia. I am always watching, always listening, always feeling the streets of the city. There is nothing that I do not come to know of in time.'

A lump of coal cracked to her left as the fire burned down; the tips of the flames barely reaching above the grate. The only substantial light came in between the curtains, casting the room in hues of blood and shadow. Opposite her, Il Capitano's pupils were almost completely dilated, making him look like the demon that she suspected he was.

'From what you say, I think we want the same things, you and I. I can set you up in a grand palazzo. I can give you money to help the poor; I can give you political influence. I can give you power.'

'Perhaps, but it is not power that I seek.'

'Then what is it?'

'My eyes see even into the corridors of the Vatican. I know of the rivalries among a select group of Cardinals; I have heard of meetings in which certain Cardinals make decisions in the name of the Holy Father without his consultation; I know of the struggle for power within the administration of the Holy See.'

'Ah. Cardinal Romano,' Il Capitano noticed her face soften as he mentioned the name, 'yes I have been told of his frequent visits here. Cardinal Sanchez seemed to think that this place was a house of ill repute.'

She laughed at the suggestion. 'What Cardinal Sanchez thinks, and what *is,* are often very different things. The world does not conform to his perception of it.'

'And Cardinal Romano?'

'He comes here to talk about my work, about his work, and whenever he needs guidance that cannot be found within the Scriptures.'

'And how does he receive this guidance?'

Lucrezia swiped her arm over the table between them, spreading a deck of tarot cards in an arc before her.

'*Tarocchi,*' he mused, picking one up.

'You know them?'

'I am aware of their usage. A parlour trick to convince simple-minded folk to part with their money in search of answers to their problems. Cardinal Romano is not as clever as he likes to portray.'

'There is no trick involved, and no money changes hands. The tarot is an oracle; a way of communing with the spirit within. Those with strong spirits may learn to direct them to focus on the future, but for most people, they convey the facets of the self and how we will react to the obstacles that life places before us.'

'What does this one mean?' He asked, and threw the card at her, so that it came to rest face up, showing a picture of a man seated between two pillars.

'That is the Hierophant. The Pope.'

'How interesting,' he mused and picked up the card once more before throwing it from the table. Lucrezia watched it curve in towards the fire and settle just behind the grate, where it curled, blackened and burst into flames. She smiled to herself and turned back to the Cardinal, suddenly filled with renewed vigour.

'What's so funny?'

'The first card you select is the one you choose to represent yourself.' She replied, and a grin broke up her worried face.

Il Capitano frowned and looked at the card on the fire. The crossed keys beneath the Throne of Peter had burned away, and the flames were now consuming the seated Pontiff. Within seconds even the great pillars on either side of the card had fallen to ash.

'You see your dream burning away, don't you?' She asked. 'You have come here tonight, not knowing what you would find, and you have discovered your adversary, at long last. Staying here to banter with me will do you no good; neither will running away for that matter; you won't be able to run from me, not after tonight.

'I know you now, and from now on I will keep you in my mind's eye, always. I will watch and listen for you, I will monitor your actions, and I will move to obstruct your plans. During your worst nightmares, and even your deepest sleep, you will think of me: I will find you in the darkness and I will make sure you stay there.'

'Why do you assume that I will even let you live?' He asked, taking a fistful of tarot cards and throwing them at the fire. 'If you truly know my reputation, you will also know my methods. The things that I have done to my adversaries. The things that I still do.'

'I know, and see, and hear much, Your Eminence,' she hissed, 'including the words that you whisper to the darkness. As you sit in your study, listening to that old gramophone, listening to the speeches of the dictators of your youth. How many nights have you thumped your fist against the desk in time to the Fascist march?'

Her voice deepened to a sepulchral groan, and she began to chant the word that had once been a mantra adopted by Il Capitano and so many others: 'Duce! Duce! Duce!'

The words became louder and stronger until each was like a bullet that tore through his composure. She had somehow invaded his private moments and was aware of his past as one of Mussolini's Blackshirts. In one swift movement, he stood up, and bringing his hand in an arc through the air, struck the old woman so hard that he knocked her out of her chair.

He hollered, and picking up the hurricane lamp from the windowsill, turned and hurled it at the table. Shards of glass darted out in all directions, skittering across the floor like shrapnel, and puncturing the flames in the hearth.

'You know nothing of Il Capitano!' He shouted at her. 'Nothing of the work that I have invested; of the long years spent building up my empire! You know nothing! You are nothing! Nothing but a stupid gypsy woman and a child of the Devil; one who plays with her cards and believes she can charm and control people!'

'A child of the Devil?' She propped herself up on one arm, groping around at the glass with the other. 'You still cling to the medieval mindset that God lives above you, the Devil below, and that they are constantly at war. You still think that the Catholic Church is the House of God and that the Devil sits on God's doorstep trying to lure the faithful out into the darkness. Know this: God and the Devil are both part of the one divine force; the Morning Star and the Light are one, and that One resides in the heart of each man, woman and child. The House of God is the human being, be it Christian or otherwise. It is not the Devil, nor God, that influences whether we do wrong or right, but our own selves, and the choices we make. We are accountable for the lives we create, for ourselves.'

He crossed the room in two strides and raised his hand to hit her again. Lucrezia looked him squarely in the eye, watched him advance, saw his hand moving rapidly towards her face, and moved her hand up to catch his arm, below the wrist, in a hard grip. He cried out, in both amazement and pain: in her hand, she held a fragment of glass from the broken lantern, that she now pushed into the thin skin of his palm.

'I know who you are; I know what you are.' She said coldly. 'You may be clothed in the robes of a Cardinal, but I see the monster that you are, and I also see the man you once were. A man who bleeds.'

Il Capitano stood over her with his mouth gaping, nursing the fresh wound. He wanted to punish Lucrezia for her insolence; wanted her to know the true meaning of suffering, suffering as he knew it, but he felt a sudden vulnerability that was swiftly followed by an overwhelming urge to escape.

He walked to the window and pulled the curtain aside; the courtyard was quiet, empty but for the fall of water from above. He squinted to make out the passage, to try and see if people were waiting for him in the dark. His eyes looked up at the windows looking over the square, hoping to see some other way out.

'Your car is waiting, Your Eminence and the crowds are starting to leave Campo dei Fiori: you must leave now if you wish to avoid being seen.'

'What time is it?' He asked, gesturing to the clock on the mantelpiece.

Lucrezia turned her head and looked at the clock. 'It is now.'

'I will not leave here without silencing you,' he hissed through the pain.

'You have no choice: there is nothing more for you here. Of all the things that you learn tonight, keep this in mind: on both banks of the river, in the parks and alleys of this city, a forsaken people live their lives without the rich trappings of your existence. Some steal, beg, and sometimes even kill to stay alive; others sell handicrafts and tell fortunes; but one thing unites them all. Madama Lucrezia is their queen.

'They are my people; my family; a race with empty stomachs and dirty faces who are loyal to me, not out of fear, but out of love. Love for the care and aid I bestow upon them; fear creates loyalty out of weakness, whereas love inspires strong loyalty. When I call them, they answer. When I ask something of them, they deliver; and when I command something, they obey. The streets are already whispering about your arrival, and no doubt there will be eyes watching your departure. Know this, Il Capitano: should you ever step into my world again, they will be waiting for you.'

The Cardinal took two steps towards her, lurching as if bereft of his strength. Under his hand, his pulse beat sluggishly across his wounded wrist. The pain was still intense; he was sure she had dug the glass into a nerve. When he reached the edge of the table Lucrezia spoke again; calm, and with great strength.

'Leave now and hide where none can find you.'

'I will not disappear: I will fight you for the power, and for the Papacy. I will be dead before I see your puppet Romano take the throne of Peter!'

The last coals on the fire guttered in the silence between them. Madama Lucrezia pulled herself up onto her feet, and looked into her assailant's eyes, almost through them.

'This is my house, and I banish you from it.'

Somewhere outside a bell began to toll, hushed by the old buildings, as if in deference to the place. The two of them stood looking at each other from either side of the table; Il Capitano knew it was time to leave.

'I am not finished with you, witch!' He spat at the table, and still clutching his wrist, backed out of the room.

'Our fight is never finished.' Lucrezia countered, following him into the hallway, and watching him slip through the wet courtyard and disappear into the passage. Soon after, she heard the gate as it was slammed back against the wall, followed by Il Capitano's footsteps diminishing in a hurry. As the distant bell ceased its toll, the anxious quiet of the night returned; a car engine started, and the sound of tyres rolled away across the cobbles.

She closed the door, and leaning heavily into the wall, shuffled back inside. Returning to her room, she collected the scattered glass fragments, fighting back tears as she pieced together the pattern that had once covered the lantern. Maddalena had painted the images with her fingers, many years ago. Lucrezia knelt on the floor and pieced together the stylised image of a young girl caught up in the tempest depicted on the glass. The fragments reflected the firelight, drawing her attention to the fireplace, where a few tarot cards still smouldered. She told herself not to cry over such material things, and getting up, brought a pitcher of water from the kitchen and poured it onto the fire. The last of the light went out, abandoning her to smoke and darkness.

26

A pigeon poked around in the window, cooing noisily enough to block out the sound of the traffic below. Lorenzo watched it moving around, closed one eye, took aim, and launched a crumpled ball of paper at it. The bird flapped away indignantly, leaving the paper ball to fall the three floors to the street, where a kaleidoscope of social groups passed by. Nuns drifting along in their habits, students with designer backpacks sniggering at bedraggled globetrotters who scrutinised dog-eared street maps. A mother scolding her child on one corner and a man attempting to sell counterfeit watches on another. A handicapped man lay on the pavement rattling a cup the men in couture suits, who casually stepped over him as if he wasn't there. The ball of paper was buffeted by the wake of a passing tram, dancing across the pavement and coming to rest at Maddalena's feet.

Lorenzo had spent the morning flicking through a rival newspaper, staring deeply into the pictures hoping somehow he would find evidence of Maddalena; a woman he wasn't even sure existed anymore. After a week spent scouring the usual tourist sites looking for her, going back every night to Piazza Navona to question the peddlers, the woman in the red dress remained elusive. No one seemed to remember her, and he had been trying to prove to himself, more than anyone else, that she did indeed exist.

He blinked and rubbed his eyes, afraid to trust his sight anymore. Looking down from the hotel room's Juliet balcony, he finally saw her again, stooping down to pick up the discarded ball of paper. He watched her unwrap the ball, eyebrows raised with surprise, and then look up to his window, notice him and smile. His heart fluttered in his chest and a new breath entered his lungs, making him feel giddy. He was half afraid to move, in case she was gone by the time he reached the street, but she beckoned to him and that was all the sign that he needed. Lorenzo flew from his room, fleet-footed, skimming down the marble staircase to the hotel lobby and out into the street.

The city was warm, although the afternoon was already showing signs of giving receding into the lilac skies of the evening. A hunchbacked woman rolled up the security shutters on her shop to display the latest lines of lingerie for the students to gawp at, whilst a cashpoint happily fuelled another afternoon of good food, fine wine, and high fashion. A small electric bus crawled past him humming softly as it went, as it moved out of his field of vision, he could see that Maddalena was gone from where she had stood. He felt like crying out but his panicked breathing wouldn't allow it.

Lorenzo turned to walk back to the hotel, and there she was leaning against the wall with a smile on her face. He tried not to smile, he wanted to tell her how frustrated and confused he had been, but with each step that drew him closer to her, his face began to beam.

'I've been looking all over for you,' he told her.

'In all the wrong places, clearly,' she said, one side of her lips curling up into a smile of her own that ignited the desire in him once again.

'I wasn't sure I'd ever see you again. I even began to doubt if you were real.'

'Maybe I'm not. At least, maybe not the woman in these drawings,' she held up the crumpled paper and he blushed as he saw the positions he had sketched her in from memory.

'Since that night I haven't been able to get you out of my head.' He said, taking a step towards her and leaning one arm against the wall beside her, 'After you ran off, I searched for you across the city; seeing your face reflected in windows, smelling your perfume on the breeze, but never finding you. It's like you're everywhere.'

'Maybe I am.'

'Why did you run? Did I do something wrong?'

'Lorenzo...'

'When I close my eyes I picture you, and it's hard to think of anything else. I can't focus, can't concentrate on anything but you.'

'I got scared.'

'By what? By me?'

'It's all knotted up, like strands of vermicelli. It's taken time to untangle and make sense of.'

'What is?'

'You. The Cardinal. The relic. It's all connected.'

'I don't understand.'

'That's because I'm not explaining it right. I can never put the pieces in the right order. I don't have the skill to untangle all of the threads.' She bit her lip, looking up and down the street cautiously, 'but I know someone who does.'

'Who?'

She took his hand, bringing the smiles back to both their faces. 'Come with me. You might finally find answers to your questions.'

27

Although it had been intended to raise spirits, the yellow paint on the walls of the hospital room seemed tasteless: it was too bright and too cheerful to look at all day, especially if a person was suffering. It served only to remind the patient how colourful and vibrant the world outside was, and how claustrophobic it felt to be kept inside. For some patients, a yellow room can be uplifting; reminding them of the things in life worth living for; for others, it is a last sick joke made before death: the sun streaming through the window catching the colour, reminding them that the world will carry on much the same as it always has once they are gone. For the patient who receives no visitors, it does little to lift the misery.

Cardinal Sanchez was confident that Cardinal Romano would share the latter opinion when he awoke and beheld the brazenly glorious yellow of his immediate surroundings. He had specifically chosen this room for his colleague; with its blinding colour scheme and its view across the rooftops away from St. Peter's; hoping that it would further his depression and increase his feelings of isolation. There was nothing familiar or comforting in the room save for the crucifix on the wall, and Sanchez was already thinking of a way to get rid of that. He wanted to drive Romano to distraction in this smallest of cells, and thus improve his chances of victory.

As far as he was aware, he was Romano's only visitor: the other Cardinals having distanced themselves as the Penitentiary Investigation started. He spent as little time with Romano as possible, but kept coming back to stamp his authority over the hospital staff, and remain in control of the situation. He sat beside the bed, watching the frail man's chest rise and fall slowly; watching his arteries pulsating underneath his translucent skin; watching his eyeballs moving under his eyelids as he dreamed. The hours passed with lethargy, and Sanchez often had to force himself to stay awake: he didn't want to miss the moment his adversary woke up.

Some days the sun would shine through the window onto Cardinal Romano's face, exaggerating the jaundiced tone of his skin. The occasional shadow of a cloud passing across the sky would turn his skin ash grey as if it were a glimpse of the man's future. Sanchez liked to think that the changing colours represented the struggle of the powers of Light and Dark over the man inside; pulling him this way and that as they fought over his immortal soul.

Life was all about struggle, he reflected, about the fight that never came to an end. Day fought night, the sea fought with the shore, and men fought each other. The Catholic Church fought for souls: for the salvation of those souls through the observation of those sacraments, and unwavering faith in God. Cardinal Sanchez had fought all of his life, and although it wasn't quite the Good Fight that he would have people believe, he believed it to be just, and worthwhile. He had been a soldier once and scared; of war, of death, and of his own cowardice. He had run away from his past and joined the priesthood looking for salvation: what he found was a battle of minds and souls, where blood was rarely shed. It was the kind of battle he could excel at.

And so, he had grown up fighting that battle: between Good and Evil; between Cardinal Sanchez and Il Capitano; between Heaven and Hell. Both sides cancelling out each other, the perpetual struggle bringing him peace, he found his salvation in the freedom to commit the worst of crimes and to perform the most perfect acts of charity. He was no longer afraid to fight, he was no longer afraid of himself: he had spent his life satisfying both sides of his personality. Cardinal Sanchez considered himself the perfect man.

When Cardinal Romano finally awoke from his coma, Cardinal Sanchez missed it: he was busy fabricating evidence for the investigation to use against his rival. One of the nurses left a message with his secretary, as instructed, and he tied up his business as soon as possible to make his way over to the hospital. When he arrived, he found Romano lying on the bed, his eyes blinking and a frown scarring his forehead. It appeared that he was still in pain: the small range of movement and occasional wincing confirmed as much.

'What are you doing here?' He croaked, his voice rising from a whisper to a growl.

'I've been worried about you,' Sanchez lied, 'I feel so terrible about what happened in the corridor.'

'No, you don't.' He winced again as if speaking had caused him pain.

'Maybe "terrible" isn't quite the right word, but I do feel I must stay with you and attend you in your hour of need.'

'Lies!' Romano hissed, spit bubbling down his chin.

'I'm telling the truth, Giancarlo: I will stay with you until such a time when you are ready to leave.'

'I am ready to leave now, Luis,' he spat, 'if you'll let me.' He attempted to get out of bed, but no sooner than he tried sitting up, a hot pain stabbed out from under his chest, hitting his heart before ricocheting within his ribcage, and slowly spreading out through his body like scalding needles. Through his drawn, wincing eyelids, Cardinal Sanchez could see eyes bright with fear, and fresh tears.

'What have you done to me?' Cardinal Romano exclaimed through tightly clenched teeth.

'What have I done?' Cardinal Sanchez asked mockingly. 'Why nothing Giancarlo: you have ended up in this state by your own doing. You are responsible for what is happening to you: the food you have gorged on, the wine that you drink each morning, have made you ill. Your sins and failures have poisoned your body, and now you are paying the price.'

'Leave me.'

'Oh no, my friend, I wouldn't miss this for the world. Not if the Messiah returned to Earth and all the angels of the heavens came and perched on the rooftops would I leave your side. This is an awful time for you, and I want to be with you to help you through it.'

Cardinal Romano frowned again, and tried to speak, but couldn't form coherent words: even the tiniest of movements were punished by a throbbing pain in his chest. His lips trembled feebly until he resigned himself to merely looking on in anger. Cardinal Sanchez took this as his cue to begin, and with great ceremony began reading the doctor's diagnosis from the clipboard he held in his hands.

'I assume that Dottore Riotta hasn't had time to visit you yet. Not to worry, I have your notes right here. Would you like me to read them to you? I thought you'd be like that. Let's go over them anyway. Well, it's no surprise to either of us that you've suffered a heart attack. Your heart isn't as young as it used to be, and it's operating under extreme pressure; you've been working too hard Giancarlo, and it's having trouble functioning properly. Have you had any trouble with your heart before? I thought as much. So the doctor was right in thinking that this isn't an isolated occurrence. Lord knows how you've been able to manage this all on your own.'

He sat down on the edge of the bed and patted Cardinal Romano's hand sarcastically. 'But do you understand why you are having these heart attacks? Your heart is having trouble functioning, Giancarlo, due to something called a cardiac angiosarcoma, which has attached itself to your right atrium.'

'What is it?'

'A cardiac angiosarcoma? It's a tumour, Giancarlo, growing on the side of your heart, and it's doing so rapidly. You have cancer: heart cancer. Now isn't that surprising? Apparently, it's rare: only diagnosed in less than half a per cent of patients. Just like you to be individual, isn't it?'

'Cancer?'

'That's right: you're lucky they've found it: it's not usually diagnosed until after an operation or after the death of the patient. The tumour is growing around your heart, feeding off it, encasing it, squeezing it. Symptoms are chest pains, hypertension, and an irregular heartbeat. Do they sound familiar?'

He looked sternly at Cardinal Romano. 'You've been ill for some time, haven't you? Fancy keeping it all to yourself and not letting us know! You sneak, Giancarlo.'

'I have been unwell for some months.' Romano groaned, almost in apology.

'All this time you have been hiding a secret, another secret I might say, from us. And it couldn't have been easy to cope with, especially with the added stress of your campaign against the gene therapy experiments. Why,' he paused for effect, 'you might have been making things worse for yourself all along. Why didn't you tell us,

Giancarlo? Why didn't you let us share your burden? We are your friends, your colleagues, your brethren.'

'You would have stopped me,' Romano whispered, 'and confined me to my office to concentrate on menial paperwork whilst you stepped in and stole the glory for yourself. I wasn't going to let that happen.'

'But look where that got you: here you are in hospital, too weak to get out of bed. Someone has to step in and do your work for you, take control of your operations, and yes, take the glory. And when you do manage to leave this room, you won't be able to go back to your work: you have that investigation to deal with, remember?'

'I will fight you even from my deathbed Luis: I won't let you win.'

Cardinal Sanchez smiled and put the clipboard down. Moments like these made him feel he was being rewarded for good service and strengthened his conviction that his actions were always righteous.

'I have already won, Giancarlo, and the competition is over. I think your little escapade must have affected your memory. Surely you can't still believe that you have the power and authority to challenge me? Don't you remember anything of the talk we had before you collapsed?'

'I remember it all: there is no need for you to recount it. I am innocent of any charge levelled against me. I have done no wrong.'

'Oh but you have: conducting secret meetings with that gypsy woman, a figure known among the criminals of the city. She is every evil that you should have resisted. I was both shocked and dismayed to find that she had lured you into her dark world and turned your eyes away from the Lord. It hurts me to think that a man so apparently devout in his adherence to the Faith was privy to the black secrets held by a woman so obviously in league with the Devil.'

'Madama Lucrezia is a good and noble woman, Luis. These things that you speak of exist only in your head.'

With great difficulty, he pushed himself upwards into a sitting position. Great fronds of pain unfurled across his chest, and he could feel the blood rushing through his heart. The rhythmic beating paused for a second, and his lungs faltered in their quest for air. His face creased with agony for a fraction of a second, and then the pain had passed.

'She is not allied to Satan,' he wheezed, 'she simply worships other gods.'

'There are no other gods! There is only one God! One true, just, and perfect deity who can offer us salvation, and he walked among us as Jesus Christ! How can you claim that there are other gods when you have devoted your life to His service? How can you possibly talk about Faith when you clearly have none?'

'I have more faith in me than you could ever hold yourself, Luis. I have dedicated my life to the service of the Lord, and the teachings of the Divine Word as recorded in the Gospels. I trust his plan and have faith in all His works. Everything I do is for Him, and everything I say is to continue His good work.

'However, I am also aware that there are other forces in the world: lesser powers that held sway over the world before He walked among us. There are saints, spirits, deities and angels that guide and help us throughout our turbulent lives: other forces that operate independently of the Lord, powers that are different from His, but at the same time, all a part of the One Whole, and True God.

'These are the things that Madama Lucrezia believes in: the unseen beings that touch our lives in strange and secret ways. Entities that are in the service to the same Lord; the like of which you will never be able to comprehend. You should open your eyes, Luis: there is a whole other world outside the Catholic Church, full of wonders and miracles that make ordinary life so special.'

Cardinal Sanchez picked up the clipboard and flicked through the pages. Romano watched him like a child trying to work out how a magician does his trick.

'You will have to stop visiting her Giancarlo, not only because the Church demands this, but also because your body does. You cannot risk walking about the city anymore, or even the Vatican gardens for that matter.'

'What then? Am I to be bedridden? That would be an over-reaction: I might not look too good now, but in a few weeks I will have recovered well enough to enjoy my walks again.'

'You might not: it says here that the majority of cases involving cardiac sarcomas prove to be fatal. Most tumours are inoperable, and like yours, grow rapidly. The secondary tumours that travel around the body can spread anywhere and are likely to be even more aggressive than the first. I'm afraid it may be inevitable, Giancarlo. At the very least, you will have to refrain from exerting yourself. Perhaps it would be best for you to retire and enjoy whatever time is left to you.'

'You're lying. I know you are. I can tell.'

'See for yourself.' Sanchez said, handing him the clipboard.

Romano took it with quivering hands, his eyes becoming distant and teary as he stared at the diagnosis that he had ignored for so long. He suddenly felt guilty for trying to brush it off: the headaches, the racing pulse, the pain. Something akin to shame came to mind as he confronted his foolish, but natural ignorance. Both the diagnosis and the likely outcome were as bleak as Cardinal Sanchez had said. He stifled a sob and tried to push back the thoughts of blame and doubt that blossomed in his mind.

'It could be a matter of months, maybe even a year,' Sanchez said as if reading his mind, 'or it could be any day now. Whatever God sees fit. I'm so sorry Giancarlo.'

'Are you?'

'Yes: sorry that you abandoned your faith and held counsel with that fortune-teller. Sorry that you were too weak to stay close to the bosom of the Mother Church. And I suppose I am sorry that God has seen fit to punish you for these shortcomings so severely.'

Cardinal Romano ignored the insults: his rivalry with Cardinal Sanchez was over, and he had lost. Whatever precious time he had left would be occupied with ensuring that everything would be all right once he was gone.

'What will happen to her when I am gone?' He mused quietly.

Cardinal Sanchez moved up the bed to sit closer to his ailing adversary. He took hold of his hand, squeezing it severely, and leaned into his ear.

'Don't worry, my friend,' he whispered, 'I will see that she is taken care of: that much I promise you.'

28

The wind tugged at the dry leaves on the withered vines in the courtyard, shaking them loose and sending them fluttering to the floor like dying moths. Lorenzo followed Maddalena out of the passage and beneath the web of washing lines now bare of clothing. He looked up to the sky, looking up through the cords strung between the buildings as if he were looking up through a rib cage, and above it: nothing, only the empty void of the sky.

The place felt different; it felt as if it lacked something. Something was missing; something *good* was gone. There was no red lamp in the window this time: no warm, inviting light to welcome him. Instead, the shutters had been drawn across the windows and bolted from the outside, giving the impression that the building had been abandoned for some time.

Maddalena knocked on the door twice, and they waited as three bolts were scraped across the far side. The door opened slightly ajar and then swung wide open, revealing a tall man who beckoned them in silently. Lorenzo found himself reaching for Maddalena's hand as they crossed the threshold. A womb of darkness enveloped them, and he was aware of a low ceiling and narrow walls enclosing him. The man closed the door behind them, keeping an eye on the passage across the courtyard, and dragged three bolts across the door again.

'You weren't followed?' He addressed Maddalena.

'I made sure of it.'

'Is this him?'

'It is him,' another voice answered for her; an older voice. Lorenzo looked to the door at his left which appeared to be opening of its own accord. As his eyes adjusted to the light coming from the room, he saw an old woman sitting at a table, shuffling a deck of cards.

'Benvenuto, Lorenzo,' she said, 'I am Madama Lucrezia.'

Lorenzo hesitated, and felt Maddalena let go of his hand, and give him a gentle push into the room. 'It's okay, Lorenzo,' she said, 'you are safe here with my Nonna.'

'This is your grandmother?' He murmured from the corner of his mouth, 'she doesn't look that dependent.'

The old woman chuckled, 'I assure you, Signore, I can handle myself when I need to. Take a seat; we have much to discuss.'

'We do?' More awe-struck than afraid, Lorenzo warily took the other seat at the table.

'You have nothing to fear from me,' she said, placing the deck of cards in between them, 'I am an old woman, a widow, and one who can do you no harm. You were looking for me, were you not? Before you were looking for my granddaughter.'

Lorenzo failed to bury his smirk, and the old woman met his growing smile with one of her own.

'Maddalena knows how to make herself scarce, so if you have found her again, it is because she wants you to see her once more.'

Lorenzo looked over his shoulder and saw Maddalena reaching into the room to close the door. 'I'll be right outside if you need me.'

'Thank you, bambina, that will be all.'

'I wasn't talking to you,' she replied and winked at Lorenzo.

'My granddaughter seems to have taken a liking to you,' Lucrezia said, drawing Lorenzo's attention back from the door, 'and I can see that you have taken a liking to her. Love blossoms where and when it needs to, even in the worst of times.'

'Is this the worst of times?'

'No, not by far, but it is certainly not an easy time. Not for any of us.'

'Who are you?'

'I am Madama Lucrezia: queen without country, mother of the unwanted, she who has loved...and lost.'

'What does any of that mean?'

'I am a shepherdess, Lorenzo; I have helped bring people into this world, I have aided their passage from it, and I have eased their pain as they leave it. I have taken care of those who cannot take care of themselves, and those who are not cared for by others. I have also been a spear in the side of those who do wrong to my people. One man, in particular, Il Capitano, has worked against me for years. He has ascended within the hierarchy of the Vatican, using the Church for his own, dark purposes.'

'Which are?'

'To sow discord, disharmony, and to gain control of the faithful who flock to the Church in times of crisis. Many years ago we struggled to maintain order on the streets of Rome: the brigands, the organised crime; all infiltrated, influenced and inflamed by Il Capitano.'

'And for your part?'

'I nurtured those in need and inspired love in a legion of outcasts who have helped me fight against him. We never met, never came close, until you.'

'Me?'

'After the news article you wrote about the Roma, the one that mentioned me, he came looking for me. He paid me a visit.' Lucrezia turned to one side, displaying a bruise running down her face.

'He did that? I'm so sorry. I wrote that article after I met Maddalena, and she told me about your people. I had no idea Cardinal Sanchez was such a bad man.'

'Sanchez? No, Lorenzo, Luis Sanchez is a deluded old fool who believes that possessing someone else's broken pieces will make him whole. He has struggled with a friend of mine, Cardinal Romano, for control of the Papacy, when all the time Il Capitano did his damage in the shadows. Both Luis and Giancarlo were so caught up in their ambitions to reach the top that they failed to realise it is not the roof of the House of God that is the most important, but the pillars that support it.

'And so Il Capitano spent years strengthening his foundation, reinforcing his pillars, and is now poised to topple the both of them to crown his temple: a church built within the organisation of the Church. With that kind of power, who knows what he might do?'

'What does any of this have to do with me?'

'What indeed, Lorenzo? Il Capitano found me at last because of your words; the words you wrote after meeting Maddalena. She found you when you were looking for me; we were aware that you had been asking about me, and so I sent her to seek you out.'

'So it was all planned?' Lorenzo stared at her in horror.

'No, love is never planned. That, I did not see coming. The flame that has been ignited inside you is real, and it is all yours. As is its companion that burns within her. You were looking for me because of my statue, no?'

'It was linked to the theft of a relic.'

'And how came you to know of the theft?'

'From Cardinal Sanchez.'

'How did he come to tell you? Why you of all people?'

'Because I came to Rome and asked if he could help me with my article about the experiments.'

She looked at him, and Lorenzo felt like an insect beneath a magnifying glass.

'Why?' She said, her voice suddenly deeper.

'Because I took the assignment knowing that my godfather might be prepared to use his influence to help me get access, and I could write something that would gain attention.'

'And indeed you did.'

'I just wanted to get my name out there. Make myself known for something right from the very start of my career.'

'Your ambition has led you to this very moment, Lorenzo,' she said, turning her head once more to display the bruise, 'to this.'

'I-I didn't know.'

'We never do,' was her reply, 'we never see all the outcomes; the repercussions of our actions. None of us knows how far our ripples spread beyond the stones we throw; but they spread, far across the surface of the world, and even beneath.'

'How do I undo what I have done?'

'You cannot. None of us can. We can only make new ripples, and hope that they interrupt the ones made before.'

'And how do I do that?'

'You begin by making a choice. You take charge of your fate, and you choose a role for yourself to play from now on. No more drifting, no more relying on others to get you what you want in life: you take charge of yourself, and for yourself.'

'How?' He whined, aware that she seemed to be reducing him to a complaining child.

'You make a choice,' Lucrezia spread the deck of cards out in an arc between them, 'pick a card, Lorenzo.'

'Aren't I supposed to pick more than one?'

'Just one. One card; one path to take. The card that you pick will be the one which best represents you.'

'How will I know which one to pick?'

'You won't,' she said, before adding secretively, 'and you will.'

Lorenzo looked down at the pattern printed on the back of the cards, trying to find meaning; to make sense of it, and to make the right choice. In the end, he closed his eyes and just picked one at random, hoping that it would make some sense to him.

He opened his eyes and flipped the card over with his thumb. It bore the image of a young man about to step off a cliff, with a small white dog gambolling about beside him. In one hand he held a white rose, and in the other, he held a staff with a small bag tied to it.

When he looked up, Madama Lucrezia was smiling at him.

'This man is The Fool,' she said, 'although not in the same sense as we may use the word today. He is the archetypal young man setting out on the rocky path of life, with all his worldly possessions tied up in his bag. He is travelling the world in the hopes of gaining the experience and wisdom he needs to satiate the desires of his unfulfilled soul. He is looking for answers, looking for truth, and looking to make sense of the world he finds himself in. It is one of the highest cards of the Tarot: the earth and all of the forces associated with it have little power to restrain him as he takes a leap of faith from the perilous cliff.

'The Fool represents the urge to start anew and to leave behind the problems of the past. To identify with this figure is to gamble all that is comfortable and familiar with oneself in the hopes of winning something better. It is a card that counsels us to let go of that which constrains us, and step forward into a new world with Grace and Virtue as our travelling companions.'

'And this is me?'

'This is all of us.'

'What must I do?'

'Trust yourself, and your instincts. Trust to Fate. You are on the right path, no matter how perilous it may appear. No matter how lost you may feel if you keep moving you will always find your way again. No matter how dangerous the journey, it is your journey. Remember this, Lorenzo: the hardest climb brings you to the best view.'

'He handed her back the card, 'So everything will be?'

'As it should be,' she said, accepting the Fool with a smile.

'Should I pay you for this? I don't know how it works.'

Lucrezia laughed, 'No, you do not cross my palm with silver. To those of us with true gifts, the payment is in the sharing of it. We don't ask for money.'

She shuffled the cards again, a frown creasing her brow, 'I would, however, listen to what I have to tell you.'

'And what is that?'

She set the cards down and fixed Lorenzo with another glare that bore directly into him; as if the wisdom she was about to impart would be planted somewhere deep inside, for him to call upon in the near future.

'In the Beginning, Lorenzo, God created the Heavens and the Earth, and all things upon it. Through Him, all things were made...'

29

Lorenzo walked along the corridor as if he owned it, maintaining a confident air so people would assume that he belonged there. As he climbed his way to the third floor, nodding with assurance at those questioning faces that seemed likely to impede his progress, a few of the staff trailed their glances after him, curious of the new face among the clinical shades of their world. It had been quite easy to gain access to the Ospedale Centrale; for a crisp twenty Euro note, a porter in the downstairs lobby told him that room 126 was on the third floor, to the left of the main staircase.

Three nuns drifted past him, staring downward. There had been priests doing the rounds on the ground floor, he recalled. On each floor, he had passed an elaborate crucifix carved of some dark wood at the door in the stairwell. Whispered prayers could be heard from open doors; echoes of Latin chanted along the corridors. This hospital, he suddenly understood, was a place for those affected by spiritual sicknesses, as well as those of the body. How on earth Professor Rossi had managed to set up his laboratory here, he didn't understand.

As he counted the room numbers, Lorenzo began to think of a plan to slip into Cardinal Romano's room undisturbed. A quick detour brought him to a staff room, and as luck would have it, the door was ajar just enough to allow him unhindered access to the cluster of white coats hanging on the coat rack within.

He clipped his L'Osservatore Calabria identity badge to the front of the coat, doing his best to hide the newspaper's logo beneath the wing of the lapel, and grabbed an empty clipboard from the corner of a nurses' station. Clutching it to his chest, he found Cardinal Romano's room, and pointing to his badge with a nod to the man outside the door, he entered. It had all been so easy.

Cardinal Romano stirred as Lorenzo walked in; the eyes that stared out of the old man's skull had little life left in them.

'Are you a doctor?' He asked. 'Do I know you?'

'Your Eminence, I come to you with words of comfort from Madama Lucrezia.'

Something flickered in the Cardinal's eyes at the sound of her name. 'Lucrezia,' he said with a weak smile, 'how is she?'

'She is well, although she asks that you think not of her, but yourself. Conserve your strength for yourself, Your Eminence, and not for others. You are what is important now.'

'I have never been important,' the old man croaked, 'not really.'

'You have one last chance to do something of great import, according to Madama Lucrezia.'

'And what is that?'

Lorenzo inhaled deeply, unsure of how the moment would proceed. He felt like the Fool, about to step off the edge of the cliff.

'I am a journalist, from L'Osservatore Calabria. She has asked that you share your story with me.'

The Cardinal watched with a glassy gaze as Lorenzo placed his phone on the bedside table, and pressed a red button to start recording.

'Tell us your story, Cardinal Romano. Tell the world whatever it is you have left to say.'

'Where do I begin?'

'Perhaps tell us how you came to be here?'

'How indeed?' The Cardinal wondered aloud. 'I suppose it is my ambition that led me here.'

Lorenzo tried his best to keep the shock from his face as Romano's words resonated with him; he wondered if the words had been put there some time ago by Lucrezia, or whether they came from somewhere deep inside the Cardinal.

'My ambition, since I first came to Rome, has been to serve my God at the highest level. I have always desired to see myself take the Throne of Peter, to lead the faithful as the Holy Father. My ambition has been foremost in everything that I have done, and it has consumed my entire working life. Looking back, I think that the stresses of the job, the weight of the responsibility, and the pressure that I placed myself under; those things weren't good for me. I have spent my life burning myself out, thinking that the fire would feed itself, but it hasn't. The ardour that drove me has exhausted my strength, and is likely responsible for my condition.'

'Your condition?'

The Cardinal indicated his medical notes at the foot of the bed, and Lorenzo reached for them, compassion welling in his eyes as he read the words there.

'I have, it seems, a cancer of the heart. Quite fitting, given that I filled my heart with ambition, jealousy at the success of my rivals, and a rage at my own shortcomings. I took a vessel built for love, and I filled it with the wrong desire. My ambition has poisoned my life, and now I have come to my end, I realise my error in judgement.'

'And what might that be, Your Eminence?'

'Seeking out the highest position, whilst assuming all other outlooks to be inferior. To focus so much on my intended destination that I failed to appreciate the journey that I made to get there. And in not caring about the steps made along the way, I failed to reach my goal.

'There is a part of me, a large part, that wishes to stay a little while longer in the world; to have time to put my affairs in order, say goodbye to old friends, and do things I always promised myself I would do before the Good Lord calls me to his side. All that is human in me yearns to survive, to prolong my life against the wishes of the Divine; the closer I come to death, the more reluctant I am to be accepted into His Host.'

'Why is that?' Lorenzo asked, with a glance to check that the phone was still recording.

'Because I am afraid that when I am asked what I did with my life, I will look back and not be able to remember any of it. All there is, is my ambition. The driving force. No love, no compassion. It has not been a life well-lived. I wanted something I didn't have so badly, that I paid no attention to what I actually had.'

'And what was that?'

'*Life*, Signore. The chance to do something, anything, with the time that God gave me. The free will to go out into the world and *live* in any way. And I chose this.'

'I'm sure you have done plenty of good in your life, Your Eminence.'

'But did I do enough? Could I have done *more*? Lying here now, looking back, asking if enslaving myself to my ambition was enough, I don't think it was. I could have done more, I could have done better.'

'You judge yourself too harshly.'

'Each one of us has the potential to do absolutely anything,' Romano continued, seemingly unaware of Lorenzo even being in the room, 'that is why I campaigned against the gene therapy experiments: not just because I saw the campaign as a way to boost my profile and further my ambitions, but because of Professor Rossi's work using embryos; I knew that if left unchecked, he would bring that work here somewhere down the line. The papers he has written in the past, and the lectures he has given; they all involve the human embryo. That is the future that he seeks to build here.

'The use of embryos in laboratory testing, whether animal or human, is deplorable. I firmly uphold our belief that all life is sacred, and that all beings from conception to natural death deserve the opportunity to live life to their full potential. The thought that these scientists are not only interfering with embryos but also destroying them once they have fulfilled their purpose disgusts me. It shows clear contempt for life, and the rights of all living creatures to live unharmed, and unassailed.'

'How can you say that an experiment intending to produce a treatment that will aid and prolong life is in fact contempt of life?' Lorenzo queried, with another glance at the screen of his phone for reassurance.

'Because the embryos that will be used are alive, and life means more than just the physical processes that mark it. They have enough genetic material to form a human being, and if given the chance, would develop into a human child. From the moment of conception, the moment that the ingredients for life come into contact with one another, those embryos are for all intents and purposes, potential human beings. From conception onward, they have souls: therefore destroying them would be murder. I can only shudder to think where those poor, wasted souls are sent.'

'You're telling me that a human embryo has a soul?'

'Of course, it does. Why shouldn't it?'

'Something so small that I can't even see it, something that can't see, or breathe, or touch, or feel…that has a soul?'

'Those things you have just listed are of the body; the soul is not the body, and the body is not the soul. A soul, that is capable of feeling and suffering, is present in each being from conception. The Immortal Soul: that piece of the Divine that is grafted onto every human being, that spark of light that comes from the One, and seeks to return to Him when our physical lives end. That soul is possessed of feeling and emotion long before the body it inhabits is capable of exhibiting such things.'

'So even before a person is formed, they have a soul?'

Lorenzo watched the Cardinal's eyes lose focus and slowly close, were it not for the old man's chest moving up and down, he would have called for help. After a while the Cardinal gasped, startling himself, and began to cough again, resuming his lesson after the coughing subsided.

'Just as the DNA strand contains the source of the physical structure, so the soul is the source of a person's spiritual life. The body is, as we are taught, the House of the Soul. At the moment of conception, when soul is grafted to cell in an act of divine unity, a human being is at its most pure. It suffers not, it feels not; it just exists. It is humanity in its simplest and most pure form. It is that which connects us to God; for we are formed through him, and in his image, just as he made Adam in the Beginning.'

'But that's a particular belief that you hold, and one that not everyone shares. How can you justify these claims to those outside of the Catholic Church; those in the modern world who might disagree with you? How can you prove it?'

'Science, Signore.'

'What about it?'

'Scientific observation has recorded that at the moment of death, a tiny electrical charge leaves the human body and is channelled into the earth. Science also teaches us that energy cannot be created or destroyed: it moves from place to place or is transformed from one form to another. The energy that leaves a person doesn't disappear, it simply returns to its source: it returns to the Creator. There have also been cases when bodies weighed before and after death, have lost a small amount of weight. What is that weight if not the weight of the soul, and where does that soul return if not to God?'

'It goes to Heaven?'

'Perhaps, but I have come to view God and Eternal life as something other than the Paradise we see depicted in our frescoes and paintings. I think of God not as a man, or person, but as a force: my Creator; the Supreme Agent behind my very being. And our souls; the intangible, eternal aspect of our beings which can be thought of as that first and last spark of energy; they return to Him and are absorbed into His being to exist with Him. That is the Salvation that I believe the followers of Christ are granted.'

'Really?'

'Just as the atoms making up the physical body are recycled into other forms, so the soul becomes a part of the One again. We are not the same with Him as we are here on earth: we have a different form and purpose. And whilst I would like to tarry here and live longer, unfortunately, my time is reaching an end. My body is frail, my mind wanders inside the myriad chambers of my brain, but my soul; oh my soul! It burns! How it burns: brighter, stronger, and harsher than ever before! I can feel it guiding me out of this shell, guiding me to He who is the source of my being: He who is Alpha and Omega, my beginning, and my end. Strange that as I approach my death, and I mourn for the things I will no longer be able to do, my soul awakens, and I feel more alive than ever before.'

'Would you agree then, if I said you were opposed to those measures that might allow a person to live longer?'

'In part, yes: I subscribe to the belief that it is for God and God alone to decide when our lives should come to an end. If he calls for us to join him, and we are held on earth by medicine or technology, are we not denying ourselves the joy of Eternal Life?'

'And for those people who don't believe in God or Eternal Life?'

'They deny themselves whatever rest awaits them at the end of their lives.'

'What about those who die before their time? People injured in accidents, or suffering from a debilitating disease for instance? Don't they deserve the chance to prolong their lives, to at least try and survive?'

'That all depends on the condition they are in, and the quality of life they would have if they survived. There are some for whom serious injury or disease allow them to suffer, and only suffer; in which case prolonging life would be to condemn them. However, since my health has started its decline, and my spirit begins to feel the pull of the next life, I have given more thought to my own mortality.'

The old man's breaths rattled softly in his throat, wheezing through his voice box.

'When you take yourself from this room,' he said eventually, 'take a good look at the people and the world around you. Cast your eyes over those who tend the sick and the needy; listen to the Last Rites as they echo through the halls. You will notice that in this hospital, suffering gives way to peace, and those who die, do so with dignity. There is no dignity for the voiceless embryo that is destroyed needlessly.

'When you leave the hospital, open your eyes to the world around you, and allow yourself to really see it. Observe the protective mother holding her child's hand at the roadside. Stand on one of the bridges and feel the breath catch in your throat as the breeze pushes you to the edge, and you stare down at the reflection of the setting sun. As you walk the streets of the city, pay attention to the life that courses through them. Taste the rich flavours of the foods offered to you here. Smile as you watch the waiters flirt with the passing young ladies. See their eyes meet and sparkle as they share the tiniest moment of private ecstasy and the promise of future pleasures.

'Whenever you move through the world, take the time to experience it, to enjoy it. Revel in the delights that are before you, and take pleasure from the company of others. And in all of these things, see the work of the Lord, and the existence of the human soul; that small spark of innocent life which connects us to the Almighty regardless of race, culture, or personal beliefs. See for yourself the emotions, the compulsions, and the intuitions that are the signature of the soul; the proof that the Hand of God is at work throughout our fleeting lives.

'Recall the words that I have spoken to you here, and never doubt your Maker.'

Lorenzo looked at the pale, aged face of the Cardinal, fallen against the pillows, his eyes closed, his breathing shallow. That last words appeared to have drained his energy considerably.

Lorenzo reached for his phone, pressed the stop button and jumped as the Cardinal coughed, and opened his eyes once more. Lorenzo sat back in the chair and regained his composure.

Cardinal Romano began to breathe deeply, and Lorenzo noticed a sudden change in his stare. There was a determination that hadn't been there before; a purpose, as if some decision had been made.

'Never doubt your Maker,' he repeated.

It happened almost in slow motion, and Lorenzo was powerless to stop it. The old man's arm reached out of the bed, and arcing through the air, came down to touch the screen of Lorenzo's phone at the exact point where the option to delete the recording was.

As the phone beeped, signalling the disappearance of the Cardinal's revelation, Lorenzo grabbed the phone and shouted, which alerted the guard at the door, who came into the room and ushered him out despite his protestations. His last sight of Cardinal Romano as the door closed was of the old man holding up his right hand; two fingers pointed at the ceiling, two fingers folded down to the floor.

30

The guard escorted him out of the Ospedale, and all but pushed him through the main entrance and out onto the street. His senses were assaulted by the sight and sound of the traffic in front of him: the roar of the vehicles tore at his ears, and the exhaust fumes invaded his nose and throat. He waited for a gap in the traffic and then crossed the street, finding himself walking in the direction of the river, as always. As he set foot on the nearest bridge, Lorenzo stopped in disbelief.

A young woman walked towards him, seemingly oblivious to the child skipping behind her, jabbering away. The woman appeared to be absorbed in the screen of her phone, unaware of the child, as they passed Lorenzo at the end of the bridge. He turned and watched as the two of them approached the side of the road. Still absorbed in her phone, the woman paused, and instinctively put her hand out for the child, who similarly came to a stop, and accepted it. As their hands met, the woman became disinterested in her phone, and looked down and smiled at her daughter.

A feeling like a cocktail of nausea and deja-vu caused Lorenzo's stomach to flip, and he turned to face the bridge, the feeling rising to his head, which spun. As the feeling subsided, his vision settled on the man walking across the bridge towards him.

'Buongiorno, Signore L'Oscuro,' Serafino drawled, 'how was your appointment at the Ospedale?'

'How did you know..?'

'I saw you being ejected out of the building.' Serafino said, with some smugness.

'I wasn't being ejected, and that still doesn't explain-'

'I often find myself in the place where I a need to be, at the moment I need to be there.'

They crossed over the river together, retracing the journeys that Lorenzo had made cross-hatching the city streets during the previous weeks.

'Like on the night of Pantheon fire?' He asked.

'Indeed. You ran off that night. Did you find what you were looking for?'

'I found the relic.'

'Well done.'

'And I delivered it to Cardinal Sanchez.'

Serafino grimaced, 'Was that the right thing to do?'

'I'm not so sure now. I wonder if it might be safer in the hands of Madama Lucrezia. She seems to think there is some master criminal at the Vatican.'

'Ah. Il Capitano.'

'Then she was right? It's true?'

'It is true, but whether or not she is right is another question.'

'I don't follow.'

'On the one riverbank you have Il Capitano,' Serafino said, stretching one arm back the way they had come, and then stretching the other out before them, 'and on this one, you have Madama Lucrezia.'

'The Dark and the Light?'

'The Good and the Bad.'

'And where do you fit in?'

'Right here, on the bridge in between, moving from one to another and back again.'

'So you know them both?'

'I do indeed.'

'So what is your role in all of this?'

Serafino smiled, and what he said brought Lorenzo to a halt. 'You mean to ask which card I chose?'

The traffic lights changed, and they found themselves buffeted by a crowd of tourists following a red flag.

'Which card did you choose?'

'The first time I met Madama Lucrezia, I did something she said no one had ever done before, and I believe hasn't been done since. She laid out the deck before me in one swift movement and bade me choose the card that best represented me. To her astonishment, I swept up every single card with one similar movement.'

'So which one did you choose? Which path was yours?'

'All of them.'

'I bet she didn't see that coming.'

'They never do.'

'They?'

'Both sides of the argument. Both opposing forces. The day needs the night as the night needs the day. One cannot be understood, or appreciated, without the context of the other. Madama Lucrezia and Il Capitano need one another; each needs an adversary to work against, but never to completely vanquish, for the fight is never over. That is why they have never met, never discovered one another.'

'Until now.'

'Until you, Lorenzo.'

'Why me?'

'Why indeed? Why did you choose to follow the story of the scientists? Why come to Rome?'

A young couple passed lazily between them on a small droning moped, serpentining through the surrounding traffic as Lorenzo followed it with his eyes, taking in his surroundings once again. Two teenage girls admired themselves in the boutique window, trying to superimpose their reflections onto the designer clothes on display. Yet another group of nuns flitted in the direction of the nearest church like moths drawn to bright light. A bus growled past slowly enough for him to see the faces pressed against the windows, staring out.

'My ambition brought me here. Madama Lucrezia said-'

'As I told you, whether what Lucrezia says is indeed right is up for debate.'

'So it wasn't my ambition that brought me here?'

'What do you feel? What is your answer to that question? Not an answer delivered to you through the words of someone else. Not an answer you have had to go out and seek. Look inside. What is it that brought *you* here?'

Lorenzo turned his face to the sun, feeling what little warmth that the Autumn day allowed, and then turned away from it, and felt the wind cool his skin. All around him the city moved; the river, the traffic, the people, the birds, the church bells, the music from the restaurants.

'You did,' he answered.

'Well done,' Serafino led him on through the streets, 'just as there are those on the side of the darkness, and those on the side of the light, there are others who are neither, and others who are both. Agents of chaos and balance, moving through the world; creating and destroying order. The hands of the scientists that create life in a petri dish; or the hands of a Roman soldier that destroy a terracotta bowl that condemned a god to death. People who live and die, seemingly without consequence, but whose actions help preserve the struggle between light and dark. Those of us who ensure that neither one side nor the other keeps a foothold for long. So that there is always conflict; so that there is always momentum.'

'People like you?' Lorenzo ventured.

'People like you.'

'Me?'

'We are as alike as we are unalike, Lorenzo. And as I age out of my usefulness, so you come to the fore.'

'I still don't follow.'

'Then lead. Don't be like the others; be yourself. Don't choose a side. Walk both in light and dark, and stay always in the shadows between. Live in both worlds, fitting into both, but never belonging in either.'

'What must I do?'

'Whatever you see fit; that is your choice. You have free will.'

'What should I do, then?'

'That is for you to figure out, and no one else. Take accountability for your actions. Never shrug off your responsibility for anything that you do. Your sins are yours to own, as are your blessings.'

'This is to do with Pilate's Bowl, isn't it?'

'You tell me.'

It was growing colder and darker a lot faster and earlier in the day than when he had first arrived in the city. You could see it in the way people began to quicken their pace, and pull their clothes tighter around them against the wind. Another summer was gone, and another winter was fast approaching.

'Madama Lucrezia told me that both Cardinal Romano and Sanchez were using the gene therapy experiments and the relic to respectively further their respective agendas within the Vatican. That they both want to become Pope, and they know that they have limited time left.'

'That much is is true: there is a limit of eighty years of age on both suffrage and the eligibility for a conclave. Cardinal Romano only has another two years left before he becomes ineligible; Cardinal Sanchez has four.'

'After speaking with him today I'd be surprised if Cardinal Romano lasted until the end of the week.'

'Then, should the Holy Father die within the next four years, Cardinal Sanchez will be most likely to succeed him.'

'Would that be such a bad thing?'

'Luis Sanchez was a man born during a time of many struggles in the world. So many conflicts in the Twentieth Century; so many worthless wars that still have repercussions today. He has spent much of his religious career hunting relics that might absolve him of the sins he committed whilst in his secular uniform. He seeks forgiveness, and seeks to offload the weight on his conscious, without having to accept the consequences of his actions.'

'Without having to take responsibility.'

'Exactly. A man such as he should not ascend to the throne of Peter.'

'Then how do we change that? I thought that the Pope was elected during a secret ballot?'

'Indeed he is: the conclave must meet within two weeks of a Pope's death, and each man casts his vote in secret, but the work to influence the conclave in someone's favour is done much earlier. There have always been ways by which a Cardinal who fancies himself a likely candidate could make that outcome certain.'

'How?'

'By forming alliances, and having the majority of his peers vote in his favour. A career of secret agreements, handshakes behind closed doors, strong political connections and life-long pacts can all help to secure the Holy See for one specific candidate. Not that it always works: if God himself chooses a more appropriate candidate, then no amount of dealing will sway the ballot.'

'God involves himself in the election?'

'Sometimes,' Serafino said with a wry smile, 'there have been signs that a candidate has been…favoured, shall we say?'

'Such as?'

'There is a story that both awes and amuses me; it concerns Saint Padre Pio da Pietrelcina, the stigmatic and visionary of San Giovanni Rotondo. In the September of 1918, he became the first recorded Catholic priest to receive the wounds of Christ's Passion: his hands and feet bled, and a wound opened in his side. Revered as a miracle worker, people would write to him and ask to pray for the healing of sick relatives.

'One letter, received from Poland, asked him to pray for a mortally ill woman. Upon receiving the letter, Padre Pio is said to have remarked "we cannot say no to this one." The woman was miraculously healed, and the words of the Saint were in the minds of many when the man who had written that letter, Bishop Wojtyla of Krakow, was elected as Pope John Paul II in October 1978.'

'That's an interesting anecdote.'

'It's even more amazing when one considers the circumstances: the Holy Father was elected after the short rule of John Paul I, who died after a month on the throne. He was, interestingly enough, referred to as "God's candidate" by Cardinal Basil Hume of England, although he refused to be crowned at all.'

'Perhaps that's why he died.'

'Perhaps,' Cardinal Romano said darkly, 'but after the turbulent Papacy of Paul VI, and the short rule of John Paul I, there were many who saw the words "we cannot say no to this one" as an indication of Bishop Wojtyla's eligibility for the post.'

'Do you think that he was chosen by God?'

'I think he was shown some favour by Padre Pio, and following Pio's death, the Pope had him canonized.'

'You said that he was the first recorded Catholic Priest to receive the wounds of Christ. Have there been others?'

'Only one other.'

With great solemnity, Serafino slowly pulled his gloves off, finger by finger, exposing a wound at each wrist that glistened with fresh blood in the last light of the day. With great discomfort wrought plain across his face, Serafino lifted the fedora from his head, and

Lorenzo saw that the colour that he had previously assumed was some form of rust was in fact blood, seeping from scratch marks gouged into the man's forehead.

Lorenzo's mouth hung open, and as he tried to fathom what he saw before him, a fresh cut seemed to open on Serafino's brow.

'I am Fra Serafino,' he said, bowing his head to show a black zucchetto ecclesiastical skull cap.

'You're a priest?'

'Of sorts.'

'So...you're one of them?'

'As I said earlier: I live in both worlds, yet I belong in neither.'

'Is it...are they painful?'

'Yes, and no. What I feel transcends what we conceive as pain. And the pain that I do feel...is not my own.'

'Have you always..?' Lorenzo trailed off, pointing at Serafino's hands.

'When I was a boy, my family planned for me to stay in the same village, and work on the family farm; reaping the benefits of their labour. Although that was satisfactory for a short time, I became bored of the work: I wanted to live my own life, not theirs. I wanted something to engage my restless spirit, something to interest and excite me, to set my soul alight.

'I received the first of the stigmata shortly after my eighteenth birthday, on my right wrist. The people around me; my family, my teacher, the village *dottore*; they all thought that it was something I had done myself. When the left one turned up a year later, they had me committed to a sanatorium "for my own protection". It was there, at age twenty-one, that the crown of thorns began to carve its likeness into my forehead. As you can see yourself, the thorns manifest themselves of their own accord. The staff at the sanatorium witnessed this, and a priest was called.

'I was freed from my incarceration at the sanatorium, but sentenced to life in the service of the Church. In some ways, I count myself lucky that I found God, and didn't succumb to earthly temptations which attracted the boys I grew up with. Had I stayed to work on the farm with my family, I would have ended up working the earth, and not the people on it. With each harvest, I would have gathered in the crops, but never reaped the benefits to the soul that life in the Church has given me.'

'But you still weren't able to live your life.'

'I said that I was a priest of sorts. I have still lived my life, not necessarily as I intended, but still with a presence in both camps. In the spiritual and the secular. Moving from one to the other. Shepherding those of the light and the dark in their struggles with one another.'

'Madama Lucrezia called herself a shepherdess.'

'She is one of many. There are good shepherds, and there are shepherds of evil, each tending their own flocks.'

'Who looks after the shepherds?'

'We do. You and I, and others like us. Custodians preserving the balance. There must always be a struggle. There must always be momentum. Without that, there is no progression.'

Serafino replaced the hat on his head, and the stares he had begun to attract from passers-by evaporated as they suddenly remembered their own business.

'And the stigmata that you receive? What are the signs of Christ's suffering for?'

'The Lord sent his Son to live among men as they lived, and to suffer as they suffered; to receive the pain of death. Through the Son, the Father clearly felt and understood the worst of our experiences here on earth, and in understanding our suffering, He is better able to judge us at the End of Days.

'I'm not saying that God condones suffering, nor that we should accept it in our lives. Rather, I believe he has given each of us the free will to do as we wish, and govern our lives as we see fit, to make of this world whatever we will. The suffering that we see in the world is our doing, Lorenzo, not His. If some of us are hungry it is because others are eating too much. If some are in pain, it is because it has been inflicted upon them.

'These are things that the human world has conjured up to test both our humanity and our humility; benchmarks of faith. We have a choice in everything that we do: and that is why our choices are so important.'

'I don't know what I should choose.'

'That makes your choice even more important. Whether Pilate's Bowl stays with Cardinal Sanchez, or whether you take it from him, is up to you.'

'But why me? I'm just a journalist. I report the news.'

Serafino chuckled, 'And that, Lorenzo L'Oscuro, is why it must be you. The word *gospel* comes to us from the Old English word meaning "good news", from *evangelion*, a Greek word for "the bringing of good news". Your career path, your interest in reporting the news, has brought you to here, to now.'

'I thought I'd be able to get an extra article out of my talk with Cardinal Romano, but after giving me such great words to work with, he deleted them all.'

'There are some things that God doesn't like to see in the papers.'

'Are you telling me that the almighty reads newspapers?'

'The Good Lord doesn't need to read, Lorenzo, he is omniscient: he sees and knows all that is going on in the world.'

Lorenzo looked up.

'Do not look to find God in the heavens,' Serafino chided, 'Look inside. He is ever-present in our hearts and minds, whether we recognise that presence or not.'

Never doubt your maker.

Lorenzo felt, rather than heard Cardinal Romano's last words to him before he deleted their recording. When he looked back down from the sky, Serafino was gone. Instead of feeling the frustration that had followed their previous encounters, Lorenzo laughed to himself. The laughter subsided when he saw the building in front of him: at eye-level was an advertisement pointing down a flight of steps to a basement level shop. The fluorescent letters promoted a data recovery and backup service. Lorenzo looked down at the phone in his hand and made a choice.

31

Cardinal Sanchez looked down at the stricken figure of Cardinal Romano laying on the bed, and briefly gave thought to his own mortality. He had known the man for a great part of his life, and it was difficult to imagine the world without him. Even now, as close as he was to achieving his goal, he found it hard to think of the Vatican without his most fierce opponent. He realised also that his own life was in danger of finishing the same way: there was work to be done before he finally reached his goal. Death would come for him one day, sooner rather than later given his age; but so long as that day was not today, or tomorrow, or any day soon, he was content.

He was a little annoyed that Cardinal San Marco had seen fit to move Cardinal Romano to a room that faced St. Peter's; he would have preferred him to die out of sight of the Vatican. His rival whimpered in pain, twitching involuntarily on the bed. He took Romano's hand in his own and feeling the faint, intermittent pulse, suppressed a smile.

The rasping breaths became fewer and shorter as the life of Cardinal Romano began to slip away into the evening. To his weakening eye, the first stars beckoned through the window. He could almost make out the statue of Christ looking over St. Peter's Square, more because his mind knew it was there, rather than through his sight. The pain was now a hot searing shock that hit his body regularly like the blows upon a smith's anvil.

A small part of him still prayed, despite the pain, that he might be saved from his Fate. After a life of devout adherence to the Faith, and diligent service to the Holy See, it was the least that he felt he deserved. Cardinal Romano prayed to the Father, to the Son, and to Mary the Mother. He prayed to the miraculous Saints whose statues graced the colonnades of Piazza San Pietro, and in his desperation, he also prayed to the Spirit ebbing and flowing through every living being. To that supreme force that lit the stars and sculpted the moon, and first set the world turning, he offered the last of his prayers.

Cardinal Sanchez sat by his side and looked in fascination at the sweat beading on his adversary's brow. Romano, he decided, was no doubt feeling the heat of the first flames of purgatory: he was to be punished for allying himself to the gypsy woman. Sanchez nodded; it was just and right that a man such as Romano should be punished for the lapses of faith brought on by his own blindness. He reached forward and removed the napkin from Cardinal Romano's throat. Romano had had just enough strength to receive the Host, but now his strength was leaving him rapidly. Sanchez turned and gave the napkin to a nurse, and dismissed her with a wave of his hand, leaving the two Cardinals alone.

'Giancarlo,' he said solemnly, 'you have already taken confession. I ask you now: is there anything else you wish to confess before your soul departs this mortal coil?'

Whether it was another agonising twitch, he wasn't sure, but Romano seemed to nod. Sanchez waited patiently as, pain allowing, Cardinal Romano turned his head slowly. For a moment the two rivals regarded each other without the hate and jealousy that had marred their working relationship for decades. With tears in his eyes, Cardinal Romano uttered the last words that the agony would allow.

'I loved her.'

'I thought so.' Sanchez hissed, and sat back in the chair, contented. 'It was as I have thought all along.' Watching Romano turn stiffly to look out of the window, he decided against his judgement, to offer some words of comfort to the dying man.

'Then there is nothing you have to confess,' he said, 'for love is not a sin. Christ bid that we love, Giancarlo. It would be a sin to not take the time to love during the course of one's life. If we have not loved, and hated, someone at one time, then we have not lived. There is nothing to pardon: you are free of sin.'

Cardinal Romano was vaguely aware that the attendants had returned, and the Latin chanting had resumed. He paid little attention, instead directing his mind to the night sky. Slowly, the convulsions crept upon him once more: his chest lurched upward from the bed, and his mouth spasmed with a silent scream as the tumour gave one last, tight squeeze around his heart. His last heart attack was the worst: the pain spread everywhere: it burst in his head, shot to his hands and feet, and tore down his side from his chest to his abdomen.

Through it all, however, his mind was elsewhere. He stopped feeling the pain, stopped feeling the bed underneath him, and could no longer sense the presence of others in the room. Instead, he beheld the moon rising above the city; he saw the river sheathed in silver flowing through the city; he saw the trees ruffle in the wind. As the stars called him, he heard the voice of a friend and companion speak out as clearly as if she stood beside him.

'*Arrivederci, mio caro*. God speed.'

On hearing those words, all that was Giancarlo Romano left the world and became part of a darkness deeper than night, and a light brighter than the midday sun. No longer a Cardinal, no longer a man; he was freed from the pain of his last months and returned to the Source, where he rejoined the One and found his beginning and end.

32

The moon emerged from behind a cloud and illuminated the dark corners that the streetlights failed to reach. Silver light glazed the cobbles of St. Peter's Square, worn flat by the footsteps of faith. Glazed eyes drunk on poverty and misfortune gaped out of the corners up at the pale glowing disk that crawled through the sky. Trees genuflected to the pagan orb that gazed down upon them, and stray dogs barked up at the goddess whose name their lips could not utter.

Jean-Baptiste Phillippe, *hellebardier* of the Vatican Swiss Guard, stepped back from the exposing moonlight and retreated into the shadow cast by the arch stretching across the road behind him. He adjusted his uniform self-consciously: the city food had added pounds to his frame, yet he was too ashamed of his expanding waistline to ask to be measured up for a bigger size. Still, it did the job: people knew who he was, and what he represented. His uniform commanded respect from those who looked upon it, even if it was a little too small for him.

'City living will make you fat.' His brother had teased him before he'd left home. 'When you come back on leave we won't recognise you.'

He'd been wary of coming to the city: if it could make him fat, it might be able to change him in other ways. He had dreaded arriving in Rome and was nervous about how it would change him. During those first tense weeks, he had lain in bed listening to the sirens and exhausts, the shouts and the slammed doors, longing for the gurgling streams and goat bells of his native Alpine town. Estranged from all that was familiar to him, it had taken him a while to fit into his new life, and to feel comfortable in the uniform. Now, although he was used to the city, he felt more uncomfortable in the uniform that seemed to shrink every time he put it on.

No one who walked past him would have guessed that he wasn't meant to be there. None of the nightwalkers, drunks or prostitutes could know that he wasn't meant to be out: that he should have been tucked up in his warm bunk inside the Barracks. If any of his superiors approached him, he would explain calmly that he had swapped shifts with his friend Henri, which was at least partly true. Henri had sneaked a girl behind the Wall and was, by now, most likely releasing the pent-up aggression he had accrued from weeks of chastity.

Jean-Baptiste looked to Henri for inspiration: he was someone who took full advantage of the perks the city offered to an officer of the Swiss Guard, and yet still managed to reconcile it with his Faith, and respect for his position. Henri knew the best bars, he knew people at some of the most exclusive restaurants, and most of all, he knew that the city girls loved a man in uniform. Henri used his uniform like a weapon: a little flash of colour, or a quick peek at his plumed helmet, and he disarmed them. He charmed them, wooed them, and sneaked them behind the Wall. There were so many notches on his bedpost that it resembled Jacob's Ladder.

Half in and half out of sleep, Jean-Baptiste dreamed of Switzerland. His mind recalled the sloping fields and the sun shining through the clear mountain air. He dreamed of lonely milkmaids high up in the mountains, with only the goats and snow to keep them company. He thought of barns, tucked out of view and warm with the musty smells of straw and sex. He imagined going home in his uniform, and the local girls treating him like those of the city treated Henri. He thought of anything but the noisy, congested streets of Rome, and the tall smog-stained buildings that flanked them.

It wasn't that he disliked the city, or his job: he considered himself lucky; honoured even; to have been accepted into the Pope's private army. He just found himself longing for a view unspoiled by city buildings; a line of sight that lasted longer than a few blocks. He longed for the simpler life he had left behind in Switzerland: a life with a slower pace, a life with more free time. Sometimes he was completely bewildered by the pace of events and the clockwork regiment that now controlled his life.

His mother, though, was proud of him: she'd always wanted one of her sons to join the ranks of the Swiss Guard as her uncle had, and Jean-Baptiste had further endeared himself to her in fulfilling her dream. In the weeks before he had taken up his position, she had treated him like royalty; he could do no wrong in her eyes.

Since he had left, however, she'd fallen ill: the weekly letters he received from home painted a worsening picture of her health. What he heard from his brothers was a horror story of the pain that she was living with: she was so ill that she could barely speak over the phone to him. She had just enough strength to give him strange instructions: there was someone in the city who needed his help. At her request, he had sneaked through the Apostolic Palace to the concealed entrance to the *Passetto di Borgo* the ancient covered passage leading from the Vatican to the Castel de Sant'Angelo on the banks of the Tiber.

Now he stood, just inside the main entrance to the castle, having crept through the millennia-old fortress that was originally built as a mausoleum for the Emperor Hadrian. When Alaric the Goth had sacked Rome, preceding the eventual collapse of the Empire, the ashes of the Emperors stored in the castle had been scattered by the invaders. Jean-Baptiste wondered whether the rulers of Ancient Rome were still present; grains of dust in between the cobbles at his feet. He lifted a food delicately to examine the floor beneath.

His thoughts were interrupted by the approach of footsteps pattering up the street like dry rain. Jean-Baptiste stood to attention and peered into the darkness. The footsteps grew louder and clearer until he could identify a multitude of strides and shoe types. Like one of the phantom Roman Legions that he had been told walked the city streets, the noise rattled along the cobbles of the unlit street that opened up opposite his hiding place. A bead of cold sweat set out from under his arm and made its icy voyage down his side. He wasn't afraid of what was going to happen; rather, alarmed by the consequences if he were to be discovered.

He thought about his mother again, and the words that her frail voice had recited through the phone to him. He had promised her that he would not dishonour the family by forgetting the odd lines, but now his nerves threatened to undo those good intentions. The footsteps stopped at the junction before him, and the silence threatened to snatch the words from his memory. He thought he saw a hand stretch out to halt the group and prevent them from going any further. From both sides of the street, the two parties peered at each other through the lamp-lit darkness.

A moped growled along the road, ripping through the darkness and momentarily cutting off his line of sight. His heart pounded in his chest, and more sweat escaped his skin to move through the fibres of his uniform. When the moped disappeared from view and the street became silent again, the footsteps resumed. Jean-Baptiste thought of Henri in bed with his girl and thought of his mother in bed with her illness. The moment he had been waiting for had arrived.

There were five of them: two women, and a young man; all of them wearing black and moving as one from lamplight to moonlight, their shadows dragging the darkness behind them. Even their faces seemed dark; all set in a grim expression; save for the young man, who looked as nervous as he, himself, felt. The two women wore scarves of black over their hair, although the younger one needn't have bothered: her hair was as dark as a night in the mountains.

The older woman, in contrast, had silver-grey hair that glittered in the moonlight through the lace of her headscarf. Long coils of hair, white as the frost decorating the windowpanes of home, snaked about her neck where a string of jet beads glinted with a minuscule moon in every facet. Her hard expression was rendered even more fierce by the lines carved into her face by time, and the dark shadows that haunted her shining eyes. Although he was still hidden by the darkness, she appeared to be looking straight at him. As crossed over to the castle, Jean-Baptiste left his hiding place, and remembering his mother's orders, knelt before the old woman and took the hand she offered.

'Hail Madama Lucrezia,' he said, kissing her hand, 'Queen without Country, Oracle of God, Mother of the Unwanted. My service is yours this night: what is your command?'

Lucrezia looked down at the feather in his helmet and a smile parted her lips. 'I command that you be less nervous, soldier, and know that you will do nothing wrong tonight: we work with God, not against Him.'

Jean-Baptiste stifled a sigh and mumbled an apology. Guided by Lucrezia's hand, he stood up and looked into her eyes, waiting for her to speak.

'Your mother is well.' It was a statement, not a question.

'Thank you,' he said, relieved of pressure, 'I thought the illness might be her undoing.'

'Not this time, Jean-Baptiste, son of Eloise. You will hear from her in the morning.'

Fighting back tears, he nodded and allowed himself to relax a little, but not so much that she might think he was slacking in his duties. Lucrezia looked past him to the ancient building that loomed up majestically into the night sky. Although she had been careful not to show it, an intense pressure had been building inside her head for hours, as if the hands of all those who had handled or used the Pilate's Bowl pressed down on her now. Distorted shapes writhed on the edge of her vision and danced through the shadows of her mind; some urging her onward, others demanding that she turn away, and admit defeat.

'We go on,' she said to the group, as well as to those shapes not present. She gestured to Jean-Baptiste to lead them on, and then as one, they crossed under the gateway and were inside the walls of the Castel de Sant'Angelo. They followed the Swiss Guard up the internal ramp that spiralled around the bulk of the building to the fortress buildings above. Sculpted busts of long-dead Emperors looked down on them as they climbed the path laid out in *sampietrini* cobbles beneath their feet.

As they entered the castle proper, Maddalena thought she could hear whispers; each time she tried to listen to them they disappeared into the sounds of their footsteps echoing against the lamp-lit brick walls. She could almost feel the slightest of touches brushing past her shoulders, but once again, when she tried to focus on them, they vanished.

'You feel them too,' her grandmother said at her side, 'those from the past.'

'What do they want?'

'To be remembered,' was the answer, 'and to be left alone.'

They crossed a drawbridge spanning a chamber that seemed to reach deep down into the dark heart of the building. Lorenzo looked over the safety railing and wondered where the bottom was, and with a shudder, found himself wondering how long it would take to reach it.

'Do not listen to them, Lorenzo,' Lucrezia ordered, her voice drawing him back from the edge, 'your business is with the living tonight, not the dead.'

Lorenzo gulped and righted himself with a nod before he followed their guide out into a courtyard, and a chamber opposite. Looking up, he could see that a security camera above a door had been switched off.

'This is it,' Jean-Baptiste announced, pushing the door open, 'Il Passetto di Borgo.'

'And this is the way into the Vatican?'

'For you, yes,' the Swiss Guard replied.

Lorenzo turned to Lucrezia, seeking reassurance. 'We will wait here for you Lorenzo. Follow Jean-Baptiste's directions and do as he says; you will be safe, you have my word.'

Lorenzo nodded, and then looked at Maddalena. He was trying to think of something clever and fundamental to say, but she took the words from his lips by stepping forward and kissing him. His courage renewed; he followed Jean-Baptiste through the door.

Maddalena watched the two men go, hugging her elbows for comfort. She saw them walk away across the open roof of the Passetto until it disappeared into the covered walkway that stretched almost a kilometre to reach the Vatican. As the echoes of their footsteps were swallowed by the sound of the city, she began to bite her fingernails.

'He will be safe, Maddalena,' her grandmother assured her, 'but there is something for you to do, too.'

'Me?'

'Lorenzo will take care of Cardinal Sanchez tonight; you will deal with Il Capitano.'

'*Nonna*, I am not strong enough! I can't face him.'

'You are both younger, and stronger, than I. You must do this, Maddalena, for all of us to be safe.'

Maddalena looked along the Passetto and back to her grandmother. 'How will I find my way?'

'Here, *bambina*, this will guide you,' Lucrezia gave her a piece of paper, which she unfolded to reveal a blueprint of the Apostolic Palace, 'find the Tower of the Winds. It is there that you will find Il Capitano, and you will give him this.'

She handed Maddalena a velvet bag with the words, 'Go, and come back to us in one piece.'

Maddalena stepped through the doorway and out on the open-air section of the Passetto. The moon moved across the sky, following her path, as if peering around the side of the building to see what was happening, spilling light across the stonework, illuminating her path as she ran through the night air.

Behind her, Lucrezia left the chamber and stepped out into the courtyard. She looked up at the statue of the Archangel, silhouetted against the moon, and removed her headscarf. Her hair seemed to glow silver in the moonlight as if the light came from within her, and not from the sky. Like a droplet of ice, a shining tear formed and streaked down her face, melting into her skin.

'Arrivederci, mio caro' she whispered to the moon, as the wind suddenly dropped, 'God speed.'

33

Jean-Baptiste pushed open the door a little and peered out into the room beyond. The room beyond was quiet, as would be expected at this time of night, but he wanted to make sure. In the Vatican, there were sometimes eyes among the frescoes that were more than paint on plaster. The cold air from the Passetto bled slowly into the room, chilling the temperature within, and guttering the wick of the lamp that he had left burning earlier in the night. The lamp hadn't aroused suspicion; curious hands had not disturbed its position. He nodded to Lorenzo, and they proceeded into the Apostolic Palace in silence.

They could hear soft footfalls in the corridor outside; Jean-Baptiste held up a hand to stay Lorenzo until the sound receded into the distance. The Swiss Guard stuck his head through the doorway, looked left and right, and then gestured for Lorenzo to follow him. They walked quickly, keeping to the carpet whenever they could, trying to reduce their noise imprint in the empty corridor. By day Lorenzo could have been any tourist who had lost his way among the tapestries and alabaster, being escorted back through the building to the public galleries. At this moment he was a literal thief in the night, being escorted by a guard; someone he had only just met and had no idea whether he could trust.

Madama Lucrezia had placed her trust in the guard, and he had chosen to place his trust in her. He remembered now her words to him on the night they had met, the night in which he had chosen The Fool's card:

'In the Beginning, Lorenzo, God created the Heavens and the Earth, and all things upon it. Through Him, all things were made. He created Light and Darkness, he made the waters flow and bade the trees reach up unto the sun. God made fish and flower, bird and beast; he filled the mountains with precious metals and the fields with golden grain. He gave the sea its waves, He gave the desert its dunes, He gave the winter its snow, and the summer its fruit. Last of all, He made Man.

'Man took it upon himself to master the world around him and use it to better himself: he yoked the oxen and ploughed the fields: he ate the beasts and dug deep into the mountains. These were done so that he might taste, wear, mine, and farm the things in the world that were created before himself. In doing these things, man gained control of the things older than he and thought that he would be closer to God. He ruled the earth in God's stead, lived in his image, and populated the land with his children.

'So long as there have been men and women on the earth, they have coveted the things that God created: the feathers of the birds, the hides of the beasts, and the hearts of the mountains. It is this lust, this urge to own and control the basic elements of God's Creation, that has been man's undoing; this desire that gives Pilate's Bowl its power. If we strip away the legends that accompany it and push aside the actions of Pontius Pilate, disastrous as they were, we finally reach the source of the relic's strength.

'It is not the silver casket, so intricate and pleasing to the eye, that has the power. It is not the metal, so strong and resilient as to resist the ravages of time. No, it is the clay within, taken out of the earth to make a simple bowl: that is the source of its power. Clay that Christ used to make the blind man see. Earth that God used to make man himself. If it is one thing that man covets, it is the earth itself: its power to create, to generate, to recuperate: the very act of Genesis, of mastering our destiny. That is what we desire, above all.'

The Swiss Guard stopped outside of a door and knocked cautiously; when there was no answer within he opened it. Lorenzo waited patiently as his guide checked the room and then ushered him in, closing the door and then switching on a small light.

They found themselves in a large office. Thick, luxurious carpet pushed up against their feet, combining with the soft curtain drapes covering the windows to absorb all sound within the room.

'This is the office of Cardinal Sanchez,' Jean-Baptiste whispered, 'I do not know what it is you have come to do, and please do not tell me, but whatever you seek will be through that door, in a private antechamber that the Cardinal keeps to himself. It is known to be in his personal art collection, though I have never seen it for myself.'

Lorenzo nodded.

'I will wait here,' the Swiss Guard said, 'watching the door. Try to be quick. I don't know how long we have.'

Lorenzo exhaled his doubts and inflated his chest with what he hoped was certainty, and then crossed the room to try the door handle to the antechamber. It opened easily; Cardinal Sanchez was evidently so confident that people knew not to enter that he didn't see a need to lock it.

The room inside was a shrine to decadent opulence. The floor was covered in a warm, high-pile scarlet carpet, the walls and window frames rouged with a rich colour red, and adorned with exquisite heavy-looking drapes. A wrought iron chandelier with stained-glass panes hung from a ceiling painted the colour of an autumn sunrise, vying for space with various models of machines that seemed to have leapt out of the pages of a Da Vinci notebook. The room was adorned with sculptures and paintings that overloaded Lorenzo's eyes.

One wall was decorated with a collection of elaborate crucifixes carved of different woods polished so much that they shone like glass, and beneath it was a delicate glass-topped curio table. Looking down through the glass he saw it: the silver casket, the centrepiece of a tableau of icons and paraphernalia relating to Christ's Passion. Scraps of cloth and splinters of wood had been seemingly pushed aside to make room for the casket, which the Cardinal clearly showed supreme reverence.

Lifting the glass pane, Lorenzo once again thought of the request that Madama Lucrezia made of him after she had explained the relic's power:

'You must leave behind the silver casket; disregard the casing and take only the clay pieces. Cardinal Sanchez must not suspect any interference. Replace the pieces of Pilate's Bowl with these clay shards I give you, that have been dug fresh from the ground here in the city. Let Cardinal Sanchez have his piece of earth to dominate and control. But let him have the wrong shards: deny him the Bowl of Pontius Pilate, and deny him his desire. Give him pieces of clay not linked to Christ, and not marked with any inscription to authenticate them. Let him pin his career on them, on the earth itself, and let him fall.'

Lorenzo drew a small velvet bag from his right-hand pocket and emptied it into his hands, replacing the shards one by one to ensure that the new pieces were in the same positions as their original counterparts. He picked up the last fragment and sighed with relief as he dropped it, the resultant drop in his shoulders causing the fragment to fall to one side as he let go of its weight. He cursed under his breath as the piece of pottery bounced twice across the carpet, landing with a deep, ominous thump that belonged to a much heavier object.

He stooped down to pick it up, and on straightening his back, found himself in front of an exquisite painting. Lorenzo beheld a Roman clad in purple; an Emperor, he assumed. The man seemed engaged in discussion, perhaps arguing or bartering, with a woman clad in some kind of veiled material that exposed her breasts. Lorenzo stood there, taking in her shape, and the look of ecstasy on her face. It was a strange scene for a prince of the Church to have in his personal collection. The Emperor's sword thrust upwards at the woman, brutal and dominating, and Lorenzo began to wonder just how many sins Cardinal Sanchez was seeking absolution for.

He placed the last pottery shard carefully within the velvet bag this time and drew the drawstring tight. No longer trusting it to his pocket, he gripped it tightly in his hand as he left the zealous art collection behind. The Swiss Guard checked the corridor outside and then led him back through the Apostolic Palace, which seemed to darken around them as they walked.

With great relief, Lorenzo left the Vatican behind and followed Jean-Baptiste back along the Passetto. He was right to trust his guide; he had delivered him both to and from the place he had needed to be, when he needed to be there. They moved from the covered safety of the Passetto into the open-air section leading up to the Castel de

Sant'Angelo, and he saw the angelic statue illuminated above it with its sword pointing downward to the building. Lorenzo recalled Serafino's words at their last meeting, and the choice that he had decided to make for himself:

'There must always be a struggle. There must always be momentum. Without that, there is no progression.'

Although he believed that he could trust Madama Lucrezia. more than he now believed he could trust Cardinal Sanchez or any of his colleagues, there was still something that didn't feel completely right about the night's events. A growing suspicion that something was wrong. Something made Lorenzo pause, and look back down the Passetto.

'There are good shepherds,' Serafino had said, 'and there are shepherds of evil, each tending their own flocks.'

As Jean-Baptiste reached the door leading into the castle, Lorenzo drew a small plastic bag from his left-hand pocket. In the moonlight, he saw the collection of dull pottery shapes that he had picked up that afternoon from Monte Testaccio. With one eye watching Jean-Baptiste as he opened the door, Lorenzo tipped the contents of the velvet bag into his pocket, and then replaced them with his own pieces of clay.

He felt guilty for betraying Madama Lucrezia's trust, and for working against her, but as he stepped into the castle and saw her standing there alone with the Swiss Guard, he knew he had made the right choice.

'Where's Maddalena?' He asked her.

34

Maddalena looked down at the map and then up again at the door. On the map, the room behind it bore the words *Torre dei Venti*, but the sign in front of her read *Torre Gregoriana*. She had already checked the other doors further along the gallery, but they led to the rooms of the wrong shape. She looked once again in each direction and tried the handle.

She found herself in a small square room filled with floor-to-ceiling frescoes portraying oceanic scenes. A dim light coming from one corner illuminated a spiral stone staircase ascending through the ceiling. Maddalena stepped onto the marble floor, treading lightly to try and reduce the noise she made. She climbed slowly, waiting for each footstep to stop reverberating up the staircase before she made the next one.

A voice stopped her as she reached the floor above: a loud Italian voice that startled her at first until it was accompanied by the wild roaring of an enthusiastic crowd, and she realised it was a recording. The speaker was animated to the point of being comedic, and the crowd rewarded his performance with enthusiastic applause that filled every pause in the speech. When the crowd was whipped up into a proper frenzy, loud brash music would begin, giving the whole recording and the room above a carnival atmosphere. Maddalena crept delicately up the staircase and into the room above.

What she saw made her head reel and her stomach heave; she had to clench her teeth together to stop herself from gasping. She found herself in a small room little more than a store cupboard, the walls of which were filled with shelves adorned with artefacts that upset the very foundation of her soul. There were handguns, rifles, knives, a gleaming bayonet, and a dagger fashioned out of a dark stone flecked with small white snowflakes.

Two skulls sat on the corner of one shelf, with empty boots beside them. On the shelf above them were pictures of Christ and the Virgin Mary, alternated with those of Adolf Hitler, Benito Mussolini, and other figures she didn't recognise.

Bones were piled along the edge of one shelf; she hoped they were animal in origin, but the chill running the length of her spine told her otherwise. There was some kind of feather headdress on another and the Vatican Flag hung from the topmost shelf, flanked by that of the Third Reich, and the Italian Fascist Party. There were candles everywhere, in various states of use, some of them nothing but piles of wax frozen as they dripped down the shelves. She saw a cross-bow and rusted bolts and below them gold bars marked with swastikas. Looking over the shelves, she finally grasped the madness and the hypocrisy of Il Capitano: a man who had mixed Catholicism with Fascism, order with chaos.

In the centre of the room, next to a table with a battered grass gramophone that played the Fascist speech, Il Capitano relaxed in an armchair with his eyes closed and half a glass of red wine dangling from the fingers of one hand.

The orgiastic excitement of the crowd coalesced into a single-word chant that barked out of the gramophone over and over:

Duce! Duce! Duce!

Il Capitano remembered vividly the crush of bodies, the feeling of excitement, the smell of perspiration, the sore feet, and the chorus of voices made hoarse by cheering. He had been full of hope that day: hope that the Fascists would indeed be able to impose order and alignment on the country, and from there build a new Roman Empire that would crush the Allied Forces. Rome would be great once more, and he was to be a part of it.

He smiled to himself as he recalled the naivety of his youth. In the years since, he had learned that empires of land and dominion of people, were always destined to fail. Empires of the soul, however, were a different story: domination of people's minds could last, and did. And nothing controlled a person's mind quite like organised religion: the promise of salvation in return for following a particular code of conduct. Keep the Faith, and the Faith would keep you. Il

Capitano had simply jumped ship, swapped Mussolini for Jesus, and had achieved more than he could ever have done following a false idol like Il Duce.

He began to tap a finger from his free hand to the rhythm of the chanting crowd, wincing slightly as it irritated his wound from a few nights before. Decades of planning and plotting were coming to fruition. He, of all of the Cardinals, would fulfil his ambitions. He was certain of that. As certain as the cold, sharp steel that now pressed against his throat.

Il Capitano opened his eyes to see a young woman standing over him, holding a blade against his skin. Neither of them said a word as the record came to an end with a crackle and a hiss. His eyes moved to the gramophone, and hers followed. He wondered how long she had been there, how much she had heard, and he began to calculate in his head. Her pupils were wide, her arm was rigid as it pointed toward him. He could sense fear, determination, and behind that: anger. He watched her shoulders rising and falling as she tried to control her breathing, and raised an eyebrow to goad her.

'Earlier this week you attacked a woman in the city.'

'Ah,' he said, 'the witch.'

'My Nonna is no witch.'

'You are kin to Madama Lucrezia? That makes you her weakness.'

'She is strong. As am I.'

She pushed the blade harder against his skin, the second woman in her family to draw blood from him. Il Capitano snarled against the pain, baring his teeth.

'Try the artery instead,' he said, 'you'll kill me faster.'

Maddalena looked down at the knife, and in the instant that she shifted her focus he brought up his arm and smashed the wine glass into the side of her face, sending her falling into the gramophone, losing the weapon in the process.

As she scrabbled around for purchase on the floor, Il Capitano pushed himself out of his chair and retrieved the knife. She rolled onto her side, pulling pieces of glass out of her cheek, and gasping through the pain that lanced at her face. The recording had long since finished, but she still heard the chant. With horror, she realised that it was coming from Il Capitano, standing over her, the blade raised above his head:

'Duce! Duce! Duce!'

'Fascista!' She spat, and kicked at the old man's leg, causing him to stumble sidewards. As he fell, she pushed herself up and ran for the door. A roar from behind preceded the knife, which flew past her head and clattered down the stairs. Maddalena stopped to collect it as she passed, and ran on.

She descended the Tower of the Winds with all the noise that she had concealed on the way up. She didn't care if she was discovered; didn't care if someone else caught her. Just as long as it was anyone but him. She understood her grandmother's fear now; she had seen him with her own eyes. She had seen into him, and she was afraid.

Her fear drove her on. She had to get out, back to safety, back to the real world, back to Lorenzo. The thought of him stopped her just as she reached the corridor below, and she realised that her map had gone. Maddalena ran the length of the corridor, hearing Il Capitano shouting behind her. Lights flickered on in rooms as she passed, trying to remember her way back through the galleries. Her pulse pounded in her ears as the pressure built in her face from the swelling where the glass had broken her skin. There were footsteps somewhere far behind her, but whether they belonged to him, she couldn't tell. Too scared to even look over her shoulder, she ran on.

There were more shouts, other voices somewhere up ahead, and Maddalena realised that she was trapped. The Vatican was a fortress with its own private army, and she was stuck behind its walls. She had become lost in the Apostolic Palace, trying to find the hidden entrance to a passage that was supposed to be a secret. Only one option remained: hide until morning. She stopped and took in the unfamiliar surroundings. The corridor to the right seemed familiar, but something about the plain wooden door directly in front of her caught her attention. It looked new and was unvarnished, unlike the others she had passed. She followed her instincts and opened the door.

Inside was a small, plain chapel, stripped bare of finery; a complete juxtaposition to the pomp and luxury that she had just run through. A simple wooden cross was suspended above a white altar graced by two lit candles. In front of her, lying prostrate before the altar clad all in white, was the Holy Father.

The Pope looked up at her, his expression changing from surprise to concern as he saw her standing over him, bleeding, and holding a knife.

Maddalena followed his eyes to her knife and hid it behind her back self-consciously. With her other hand, she crossed herself.

'Buonanotte,' he said.

'Mi scusi, Beatissimo Padre.' She tried to control her breathing and keep her voice down, but with the adrenaline coursing through her, she almost shouted at him.

He pushed himself up onto his knees, and then brought himself up to stand in front of her, and reached out to touch her wounded cheek. 'Your face...'

The concern in his voice was obvious. Maddalena closed her eyes, and tears drew lines in the blood that was already drying. For a brief moment, she felt safe; she felt at home.

'Holy Father, there is a man here; a man with an injured hand.'

'What man?'

'One of your Cardinals. You cannot trust him. He-'

Her words were interrupted by a knock at the door, and a voice asking to gain admittance. Maddalena's brow crumpled with anguish, but once again, instinct guided her.

'I'm trying to find my way to the Passetto,' she said, opening her eyes, and seeing benevolence in his.

The Pope indicated another door, 'The entrance is in the room beyond that gallery, but it is always closed.'

'Not always; not to all.'

'Who are you, child?'

She slipped away from his touch, and ran for the door, crossing the gallery into a room that at last looked familiar, with the burning lamp inviting her to enter the Passetto. With one last look at the interior of the Apostolic Palace, Maddalena blew out the lamp and pulled the door closed behind her, sealing herself into the Passetto.

She ran with renewed vigour, discovering a strength and a warmth in her muscles that she hadn't felt before. Her footsteps rebounded off the flagstones, the walls and the ceiling until she burst out into the cold night air and the low rumble of the traffic. Behind her, the bells of Piazza San Pietro announced the midnight hour and the passage of one day into the next. Still, she ran, forcing herself on, trying to forget the words of Il Capitano, the shouts in the corridors far behind her. There were voices ahead of her now, raised in anger.

'You sent her to confront your enemy!' She heard Lorenzo shouting, 'The man you fear yourself!'

'It is she who must confront him!' Her grandmother protested, 'Maddalena is the one who exposes him.'

'How can you be sure? You may have sent her to her death!'

Maddalena screamed with effort as she lunged through the doorway and collapsed between the two of them. Lorenzo looked horrified, her grandmother triumphant. He helped her to her feet, then hugged her, kissed her and hugged her again. She pulled away from him.

'My face.'

'What about it?'

She felt her cheek with her hand, and slapped it lightly, feeling no pain. When she pulled her hand away there was no blood.

'Well?' Lucrezia asked, as Maddalena calmed her breathing.

'It is done.'

35

Rodrigo Fuentes knocked gently on the door, and opened it when Cardinal San Marco called him in. Large windows looked over the gardens and let in the sun; one of them was open, allowing some of the last birdsong of Autumn to filter into the room. The furniture shined with beeswax, and an oil burner perfumed the air with the scent of citrus fruits.

'Buongiorno Rodrigo! Please take a seat,' the Cardinal said, looking up from his newspaper, 'Please, sit down. You know why I've asked to speak with you? Have you had chance to see any of the papers this morning?' Cardinal San Marco asked.

'Not yet, is there anything in particular that I should direct my attentions to?'

'Since you ask: yes.' Cardinal San Marco replied, unfolding his newspaper. 'This is today's L'Osservatore Calabria: a little-known newspaper from the South that has become infamous among these corridors since it began covering the gene therapy experiments a while back. It seems their reporter, Lorenzo L'Oscuro, who has been covering the experiments somehow spoke to Cardinal Romano before he passed away.'

'I know that Lorenzo secured access to report on the experiments through Cardinal Sanchez, who is his godfather.'

'How interesting. Not as interesting as some of the content of this article. Among the ravings of his last thoughts, Giancarlo seemed to have grasped some fascinating insight into the nature of the soul.'

'I'll be sure to buy a copy.'

'Take mine,' the Cardinal said, passing it across the desk to him, 'I have learned what I need from it. This is the same reporter who wrote of Madama Lucrezia, and who, I have also been informed, was recorded by the security cameras roaming the Apostolic Palace late last night.'

'How is that possible?' Rodrigo asked, wide-eyed.

'I'm not sure yet, but both the *gendarmerie* and the Swiss Guard are on high alert this morning. Apparently he was not alone: a woman is also captured on camera. She somehow managed to find her way into the Holy Father's private chapel.'

'Did she speak with him?'

'It's uncertain. She certainly interrupted his prayers in the early hours, but he seems confused as to some of the details. I'm sure he will remember more about her in time.'

'Who was she?'

'I believe it's more than a co-incidence that both incursions into the Vatican took place on the same night, so they must be linked somehow. I understand that the polizia are going to search the city for the reporter, and I would assume that wherever they find him, they will find this woman also.'

'What if they go to ground?'

'Then I will set the Dominicans on their scent,' the Cardinal chuckled, 'speaking of which, Fra Serafino has deigned to show his face within the walls today.'

Rodrigo grimaced, 'I have little time for that man.'

'He is an acquired taste, I'll admit.'

'He comes and goes as he pleases, with little thought to the organisation and structure imposed upon him by the Faith.'

'Yet he remains committed to his suffering; the Faith may well impose on him in ways that do not touch the likes of us.'

'That's if his suffering is genuine,' Rodrigo grumbled, 'there have been many fraudulent stigmatics exposed by the CDF.'

'You're not a believer?'

'I believe the Lord only graces the most deserving of our brethren with his sufferings.'

'Indeed,' the Cardinal held up his bandaged right hand, 'suffering is wrought upon those who are most deserving. Like Amadeo Bertoli, for example.'

Rodrigo's head jolted on his neck as if Cardinal San Marco had struck him, 'What of him?'

'It seems the remains discovered after the Pantheon fire were indeed that of the artist Amadeo Bertoli. Just this morning, I was handed a copy of a report from the ongoing investigation which links Bertoli to Cardinal Sanchez. Thankfully there is no mention of yourself, but I feel perhaps may be an opportune moment for you to confess.'

'Confess, Your Eminence?'

'Confess that Cardinal Sanchez told you of his involvement in starting the Pantheon fire, fuelled by a long-standing animosity between he and Bertoli over a painting which I understand Luis still holds in his private collection.'

'Should we take this to a confessional after all?'

'No need; a written testimonial will suffice.' The Cardinal said, pushing a jotter and fountain pen across the desk, which Rodrigo duly accepted.

'Forgive me, father,' he said as he began to write, 'for I have sinned.'

'You needn't worry,' Cardinal San Marco assured him as he wrote, 'your place is secure. I give you my word. As long as you continue to cooperate with our internal investigations, and tell no-one outside the walls of this, you will be saved from sharing Luis' fate.'

'I understand.' Rodrigo said, signing his name at the bottom of the page with a flourish.

'Good. I am pleased to say that I have also been informed of your formal acceptance into the priesthood next month.'

'You have? That is news to me. When did you hear?'

The Cardinal looked at Rodrigo's signature and blew on the ink to help it dry. 'Oh, less than a minute ago, my friend.'

'Thank you, Your Eminence. Will there be anything else?'

'No, that will be all for now, Rodrigo. Go with God.'

'I will try.'

Rodrigo stood and left with a bow, almost bumping into Serafino at the door. The two mean scowled at one another, moving in opposite directions as if each were repelled by the other's presence. Cardinal San Marco looked up in time to see the display in his doorway.

'Ah, Fra Serafino. Benvenuto. Please, take a seat. I am told you have made yourself busy in the city of late.'

'St Jerome bade us to "do something, so that the Devil may always find you busy".'

'*Fac et aliquid operis, ut semper te Diabolus inveniat occupatum*...is that correct?'

'You know it is.'

The Cardinal opened a desk drawer and selected a slim cardboard folder.

'I had to keep myself busy whilst you made me wait, Your Eminence,' Serafino huffed.

'I am sorry that it took so long to get your results; please understand that the Pontifical Academy of Sciences has been busy dealing with an added workload caused by those experiments at the Ospedale Centrale.'

'I appreciate you taking the time to chase up the paperwork.'

'And I appreciate you taking the time to sit for the tests in the first place,' San Marco simpered, 'now, with the pleasantries out of the way, shall we get down to business?'

'Why not?'

The Cardinal opened the cardboard folder and glanced at the pages within. 'To briefly paraphrase, the blood tests proved your hypothesis that the blood from your stigmata is not your own.'

Serafino nodded, 'This makes sense to me.'

'Furthermore, the tests were able to identify two separate blood types: yours, being O-type negative, the most common, and the other, being AB-type negative, which according to this appears in less than one per cent of the world's population. Apparently the blood in your veins is known as a 'universal donor', meaning that you can give your blood to anyone.'

He handed the folder over to Serafino, who began to pour over the statistics on the front sheet.

'The blood in your wounds, however, is known as a 'universal receiver' in that it can accept a transfusion from anyone. The two types are apparently incompatible, which may give some indication as to why your body keeps rejecting the stigmatic blood through your wounds and lesions.'

The Cardinal stood up and walked to the window, closing it to expel the sounds of the outside world.

'If the blood is not yours, and your family records seem to indicate that there is little chance of a close genetic ancestor with the second blood type, we must ask ourselves, Serafino: might it be His?'

He turned away from the window.

'Serafino?'

'The room was empty. Cardinal San Marco walked back to his desk and opened the cardboard folder, to find it empty. He slammed his bandaged hand down onto it, and instantly regretted his anger.

36

The sun shone on Cardinal Sanchez as he walked under the trees, enjoying the tranquillity of the Vatican Gardens as Cardinal Romano had once done before him. Despite the decreasing temperatures of the season, much that was to be seen in the gardens was still green. The leaves clinging desperately to their branches, the ferns fighting against the yellowing of age, the shrubs standing proud through wind and rain and the grass determined to push up through a thin layering of leaves: all these things reminded him of life's determination to remain verdant and strong even unto the first frosts of winter. They reminded him that he would have to remain strong even as he moved through the last years of his lifetime.

Even the sun, although lower in the sky and somewhat lacking in its radiance, still made the effort to burn through the cold clouds. It was a pity, he thought, that Cardinal Romano had given in to death so willingly, and not fought the turning of his seasons like the stubborn grass and resilient trees. Sanchez was confident that it would be a long time before he surrendered to the ravages of age; and even then, he would never condemn himself to the rapid decline that his old rival had accepted.

He would fight to the very end of his days, and would be renowned for the things he had achieved during his lifetime. Giving a nod to a Priest walking across the gravel in the other direction, he entered the Palazzo del Governatorato. The windows of the building captured a sky full of reflected suns, perhaps a reflection of the Holy Light coursing through the corridors within. He felt better than ever: there was little he could think of that could harm either himself or his ambitions now.

The most notable difference he felt upon entering the building was its warmth: it made him appreciate how cold the world outside was becoming. A blast of hot air was pushed down his neck by a heater as he crossed the threshold, working its way around his body under the shifting folds of his robe as he walked. The warmth slowly radiated into his skin, and Cardinal Sanchez felt it infiltrate the chill in his bones that, until that moment, he hadn't even registered.

Barely conscious of the path he was taking, he made his way to the designated meeting room. His mind was busy ruminating over the tasks that needed to be done, both publicly and privately, and so he left it to his instincts to guide him to his destination. He turned the doorknob and entered; the atmosphere couldn't have been further from the Salome Room, which he himself favoured.

This was the *Sala del Getsemani*, a green study named for the garden at the Mount of Olives where Christ was betrayed by Judas and arrested by the Romans. It was a room favoured by Cardinal San Marco, decorated in lush green with gold fittings and large windows that looked out over the gardens. Small green desk lamps glowed before each of the chairs set around the huge table in the centre of the room, itself surfaced with green leather. Basking under the rays of each bulb were fresh new folios; the agenda of this meeting, the minutes of the last, and so on; printed on the crisp, pristine official Vatican paper that San Marco always used.

Cardinal San Marco himself was sat at the head of the table: something that greatly vexed Cardinal Sanchez, as he was the one supposed to be chairing the meeting. The relic had been his project: he had put in the hard work to secure it, and was determined to lap up all the glory for its discovery. He was to be in control of the meeting, and Cardinal San Marco had taken his seat.

Sanchez sat down at the seat furthest from the head of the table and began to flick through the portfolio. The validation of the relic was at the top of the agenda, followed by Cardinal Romano's passing, the preparation for the funeral, and the distribution of his duties. Lower down the list, Cardinal San Marco had added his own matters; regarding the Holy Father's health and the festivities for the approaching Nativity period.

The door opened and closed twice, admitting the last two Cardinals to the assembly. Sanchez looked around the table to make sure that the delegate from the *Archivo Vaticano* was in attendance, and noticed the absence of the relic. Cardinal San Marco coughed, and all the heads turned down the table to look at Cardinal Sanchez over the line of desk lamps. He gave them a moment or two, just to ensure that he had their full attention, then closed the folio, and with a sigh, stood up. Directly behind Cardinal San Marco's head, a painting of Christ praying the in the garden looked down on the table.

'Gentlemen,' he began, 'it is with sorrow that I open this meeting, and the admission that the Lord has seen fit to relieve us of one of our number. I won't delude you by saying that Cardinal Romano and I were great friends, but all the same, I do feel a sense of loss at his passing. In the days to come, I daresay we will find ourselves wishing that he was still among us to offer his advice and staunch support for our cause. I fear that without him, our circle has weakened, my friends.'

A murmur circumnavigated the table, low enough that Cardinal Sanchez couldn't determine whether it demonstrated support or reproof. One or two of his colleagues nodded, but most of them stared blankly at their respective desk lamps.

'Nevertheless, we shall have to be strong,' he continued, 'especially under the renewed attention from the world's press now that the relic of Pilate's Bowl has been delivered into our hands. It will probably be wise to postpone the official authentication of the relic until after Cardinal Romano's funeral, at such a time when we have all paid our respects and are ready to commit all of our resources to servicing our upcoming projects.'

There were more nods around the table at this suggestion, and the odd tearful eye. A vote was taken on it, and recorded in the minutes.

'Without further delay, gentlemen, I would like to introduce Don Giovanni Albano, Head of Reliquary Acquisition and Validation at the Archivo Vaticano, and ask him to deliver his report on Pilate's Bowl.'

Don Albano stood up, and bowed stiffly; once to Cardinal Sanchez, and once to the others,and began a long, protracted speech about the importance of proper validation of purported relics before they were revealed to the public. He made it clear through the tone of his voice that he disapproved of the way in which Sanchez had prematurely disclosed the discovery of the relic; knowledge of which had passed quickly along the corridors of the Holy See.

'The problem is, the public eye becomes trained on my department: the people anticipate the news that the relic is authentic.' He said. 'The very idea that something genuine has surfaced that would support the Gospel tradition of Christ's Passion in this modern day attracts the attention of the faithful, the sceptical, and fanatical alike. We have to be careful of how we go about handling the news; how it is transferred to the public domain. Since the news broke, my department has been inundated with calls, as has the Press Office: this increases the pressure on us to either confirm or denounce the relic's identity, and sooner rather than later. Increased pressure, of course, increases the likelihood of mistakes occurring.'

'Such as?' Cardinal San Marco asked. Cardinal Sanchez noted with interest that his colleague's left hand was bandaged.

'Such as misdating the piece, or perhaps the contamination of samples. We are all vulnerable to human error, and the more we are rushed to reach a judgement, the more likely it is that we might overlook something.'

'Not that that matters, because the relic is genuine.' Cardinal Sanchez stated without a hint of question in his voice. He was determined to keep the meeting on track, and drive the man to the crux of his speech.

'Well, we did manage to produce a set of preliminary dates for the three pieces in question,' Don Albano continued, pushing his spectacles back up his nose, 'and the results for the relic itself seemed to date it at around the year 30CE. When the relic was retuned to my department, it was subjected to more extensive testing to establish a more precise date.'

'And what did you find?' Sanchez asked encouragingly.

'First: the silver casket was undoubtedly produced in the First Century; the design conforms to early Christian symbols, but it seems to have been elaborated in the centuries since as metallurgic technologies developed. Upgraded over time, if you will. It is interesting to note that, despite its purported contents, the exterior of the casket shows no sign of Pontius Pilate in the act of washing his hands'

'Purported contents?' Cardinal San Marco asked with a single raised eyebrow.

'As for the relic itself, I am pleased to say that it was much easier to date. We have many samples of pottery from the same era, and the style of the bowl conforms to those produced in the Roman Empire during the First Century CE. It is, as expected, of Roman style and manufacture. Our preliminary investigation, as I said, dated it around the year 30CE, but since then we have been able to narrow down a date. Dust and dirt within the fragments seem to correlate with pottery that was made for the opening celebrations of the Colosseum in 80CE. It is more likely that the piece originates from this city rather than the Holy Land, and belongs to a much later date.'

'You're wrong!' Cardinal Sanchez shouted. 'It is Pilate's Bowl!'

'Please, your Eminence,' Don Albano said, 'I am only reporting what we have found.'

'Carry on.' Cardinal San Marco ordered. From the corner of his eye Sanchez watched his colleagues turn to look at him, and then to Don Albano. With trembling fingers he read down the page to the last comment: one that if true, would damage his reputation immensely. But it wasn't true: he'd seen it with his own eyes, even run his fingers over it.

'As for the identity of the relic,' Don Abano continued, 'I am sorry to have to say that here I must differ with Cardinal Sanchez. There isn't anything on the surface of the relic to confirm that it is indeed the Bowl of Pontius Pilate. My brief, that I received from Cardinal Sanchez, described some kind of carving in Aramaic, along what would have been the rim of the bowl. He translated it as "Pontius Pilate, Governor Judea....Jesus who is Christ."

'An interesting phrase to survive to this day, I'm sure you'll all agree, and if it really were written in Aramaic, it might prove that the early Christians gained possession of Pilate's Bowl. However, as I'm sure you have all read by now, there is no such carving. No words. No inscription. There is only a feint pattern around the edge of the bowl.'

'But it was there.' Sanchez protested to the room.

'A trick of the light perhaps,' Don Albano consoled him, 'shadows on the cracks, dirt on the pattern. But there is no writing, your Eminence: nothing that supports your conviction. There is nothing to say that the relic is what you claim it to be. In fact, from the condition of the clay, and the amount of moisture we've found, I would say that it hasn't long been dug out of the ground. I can only assume that someone found the casket and placed clay fragments in it to pass it off as a relic. Your hopes must have got the better of you this time.'

Cardinal San Marco harrumphed, and everyone looked at him, seeing anger in the look he aimed at Cardinal Sanchez. His frown deepened under the attention of his colleagues.

'It's fake Luis.'

'It can't be!' Sanchez protested.

'It is: you heard what the man said. You were duped: Lord knows how much money you've wasted in procuring it. Where did you get it?'

'My contacts wished to remain anonymous.' Cardinal Sanchez sniffed pompously.

'And I'm guessing if you went looking for them, you wouldn't be able to find them again. You've made a fool of yourself, and of us. The Holy Father will be most disappointed.'

'But it still is an important relic,' Don Albano interjected hopefully, 'and one that might interest the Holy Father. It is a relic from a time when Christians were martyred in the Colosseum: when men died for their Faith. And someone at some time considered it important enough to protect it in silver. If anything, it is evidence of the reverence with which we treat our history and our heritage. We all want to preserve the past, and decorate the painful, simple life of Christ into a beautiful, glorious time; a time when God walked the earth and touched the everyday people with his miracles. A time, the like of which, we have yet to see again.'

'So it might serve as a relic of the struggles of the early Church, but it has nothing to do with Pontius Pilate.' Cardinal San Marco intervened.

'It's highly unlikely, your Eminence: without any evidence of an inscription on the relic, we can't ascribe any identity to it, let alone the one Cardinal Sanchez would like us to. Yes it is the relic of a clay bowl from the proto-Christian era. Yes, it is of Roman origin, but it is no more likely to be the remnants of Pilate's Bowl than any of the other clay shards on display in museums from here to Jerusalem. To say that this is definitely the Bowl of Pontius Pilate would be to perpetrate a fraud that would undermine our Faith. It would be wrong.'

'Are we clear on that, Luis?' Cardinal San Marco said with a mocking tone.

The other Cardinals frowned at Sanchez, who chose to remain silent. It didn't bother him: he was past caring now. He realised that something had gone horribly wrong, and that somewhere along the line he had made a mistake. He knew that his dream was gone; his ambitions ruined. He'd probably end up sidelined with some mind-numbing assignment far from the seats of power.

Cardinal Sanchez stared across the table into oblivion, and watched as his plans collapsed, and his ambitions came tumbling down in front of him. Cardinal San Marco closed his copy of the portfolio on the relic, and said something which entirely upended the meeting.

'My brothers, before we move on to the tragic passing of Cardinal Romano, now that Luis' relic has been proven a fake, I feel like this may be an opportune time to discuss his involvement in the recent Pantheon fire.'

37

Matteo Rossi reluctantly signed the paperwork with a sigh, and looked at his laboratory being deconstructed around him. Units were being taken apart, shipping crates packed, labels peeled off the glass panels. Everything that he had helped to build over the months before they had announced their arrival in Rome was now coming apart all at once.

'I still don't agree with the Board's decision,' he said to Karin, 'we were doing so well.'

'It was that article about Cardinal Romano's death. I think the Vatican blames us for what happened to him, and to be perfectly honest, it's difficult to argue with them.'

'Why does this all feel so final?'

'It's not like we're quitting, Matt,' she reassured him, sealing the lid on a refrigeration unit, 'we're just moving on to pastures new. The experiments are evolving, just like our science. We need to evolve with them.'

'I wonder if it will mean the same, though, far from here?'

'Well, Geneva is still in Europe, and Switzerland seems to be a lot more open-minded towards our work than Italy.'

'It just feels wrong to me, that's all.'

'Well, setting up in Rome apparently felt wrong to the rest of the world, Matt. And our work is for their benefit, not ours, right? We won't get the widespread support that we want if we go against the masses.'

'You're right, Karin. I just thought that here-'

'Here you'd make the most impact. Well, we certainly did that.'

'Professor Rossi?' A voice behind them made them both turn to see a tall man in a dog collar, his shoulders slouching to bring him down to their eye level.

'Has the Vatican sent someone to make sure we're definitely leaving?' Karin quipped.

'I am Deacon Rodrigo Fuentes. Benedetto San Marco, Cardinal Prefect of the Congregation for the Doctrine of the Faith, requested that I deliver this to you personally.'

He held out a brown parcel the size of a small house brick, and as Matteo accepted it, he recognised the weight and knew instantly what was inside. He turned his back to the Deacon and set the parcel down on the worktop and tore at the wrapping, revealing the silver casket. He turned it over in his hands, the light bouncing off its recently-polished surface.

'What did you say the Cardinal's name was?'

'Cardinal San Marco.'

'The Cardinal who took this from me at the antique shop had a different name.'

'Yes, regrettably Cardinal Sanchez is currently indisposed, but the Holy See thanks you for your loan of the casket, and wishes you well with your future endeavours...providing they remain respectful of our doctrines, of course.'

'Of course.' Karin said with a long eye-roll.

'What of the contents inside?' Matteo asked.

'Our experts concluded that although the casket itself is an original First Century piece, the fragments of pottery contained within are of a much later date, and of less interest to the Church.'

'So it wasn't the Holy relic that Cardinal Sanchez thought it might be?'

'Alas, no.'

'What a shame.'

'Indeed. Should you have any further questions, or wish to donate the casket to the Vatican Museums, I believe someone left the contact details for Don Albano who conducted the evaluation of your heirloom within the wrappings.'

'Thank you.'

Deacon Fuentes bowed and left. Karin waited for him to disappear through the doors and mocked him with an overly-exaggerated bow of her own.

'So this is what all the fuss was about?' She said, looking down at the casket.

'This is it. You know, I've never opened it myself. I didn't even know it could be opened.'

'Shall we?'

Matteo tried to prise it open, as he had seen done in the antique shop, but the lid wouldn't budge.

'Shine that light over it, will you Karin?'

'Sure thing.' She pulled a desk lamp over and bent it above his hands, making the silver casket gleam.

'Scalpel,' he called.

She grabbed one from a passing tray of implements that was on its way out the door, 'scalpel.'

They looked at one another and laughed. Karin was relieved to see the old Matteo was back; the one who was able to find enjoyment in his work.

Poking the scalpel blade into the metal, he scored a line along the front of the casket. The line became a crack, which he then managed to widen enough to get his finger in and then lever the lid open. The two scientists looked down at the clay fragments. They looked like boring, broken pieces of pottery. Nothing of interest about them really. What was more interesting was the pristine white business card that lay beneath them.

Karin reached forward and picked it up, tipping the clay fragments off it. She blew a few grains of dirt off it and passed it to Matteo.

'What does Serafino mean?' She asked him.

38

The air smelled of oranges. Serafino sat at a cafe table in a small piazza in Trastevere, downriver from the Vatican. Children ran past on their way to school, and two deliverymen were unloading crates of fresh citrus fruit in front of the store opposite. No-one paid any heed to the man in the battered fedora sat reading the morning paper in the only patch of sunshine that had so far reached the piazza. A stray dog sauntered past, and stopped to give him a suspicious glance. Serafino narrowed his eyes at the dog, and it barked at him and ran off.

The patch of sunlight slowly grew to cover the whole table, and the adjoining seat. Serafino made a great show of finishing the newspaper, folding it, and placing it theatrically on the table in front of him. He drummed his fingers, counting down, until he felt a hand tap him on the shoulder.

'I bet you thought you'd never see me again,' Lorenzo said, sitting opposite him with smile.

A waiter appeared in an instant and deposited two espresso cups in front of them.

'Think again,' Serafino said smugly.

'So how does this work, then?' The young reporter asked.

'How does what work?'

Lorenzo picked up the espresso with a gesture that encompassed the entire piazza.

'Sun come up, sun go down,' Serafino said sagely, picking up the tiny cup of steaming brown coffee, 'that's all there is to it.'

'And the stigmata. Will I get those?'

'I hope not, for your sake.'

'I see you read my article.'

'I might have glanced at it; the sport pages are more interesting.'

'Careful you don't inflate my ego with all that praise.'

Serafino downed his espresso.

'Lorenzo L'Oscuro: reporter extraordinaire. You came seemingly out of nowhere cover the story of medical experiments in Rome, and in the process uncovered a fight for supremacy over the city's underworld, helped a dying Cardinal share his philosophy on the soul with the world, and also discovered his colleague's obsessed with an ancient relic from the time of Christ.'

'Alleged relic.'

'What did you do with it, by the way?'

'That would be telling.'

'Indulge me.'

Lorenzo took a deep, satisfying breath. 'Madama Lucrezia gave me some terracotta pieces from Monte Testaccio to swap in place of fragments of Pilate's Bowl. I had already made the decision to do a swap of my own, so I already had a bag of broken pottery. After I switched the relic for her substitute, I simply gave her my own decoy that I'd collected.'

'And the original?'

'Scattered across Monte Testaccio. What was made of the earth was returned to the earth. Nobody will be responsible for it now. The pieces will never be found.'

'That is good work indeed! Worthy of another one of your articles, perhaps?'

'My best work was highlighting the poor treatment of the Roma people in the city, and the government's attempts to evict them. That's worthy of a humanitarian prize all on its own!'

'Now your ego's inflated.'

'I also somehow found love along the way.'

'You go too far.'

'It's true. Maddalena is leaving the city with me.'

'Where will you go?'

Lorenzo shrugged, 'Home? Further South? Wherever I need to be, whenever I need to be there.'

'I hope you know what you're getting yourself into.'

'I don't, and that's what makes it so enjoyable.'

Lorenzo scoffed and picked up the newspaper, re-folding it to show a headline about a mystery woman who broke into the Papal Apartments.

'They will be looking for her; she will never be safe. Nor will you. You both took a risk, stealing into the Vatican that night.'

'We did it for Madama Lucrezia.'

'Let's hope it was worth it.'

'What will you do now, Serafino?'

The older man pondered the question, and then produced a sheaf of papers from inside his coat. 'I have some blood relatives I'd like to track down.'

'Will we ever see one another again?'

'I doubt it, but you never know how life will turn out. You never know what's around the corner.'

Serafino nodded at the opposite corner of the piazza, and Lorenzo turned, only to find it empty. When he looked back, his guide had disappeared, leaving only his empty coffee cup and the newspaper.

39

Cardinal Sanchez looked down at the pale skin stretched over his knuckles as he clenched and unclenched his fists nervously. His hands were wrinkled and worn, with calloused patches on his palms: soldiers' hands, with the fight knocked out of them. His reflection in the green desk lamp showed a sickly spectre of the man he had once been: a haunted soul now looked out of the dark hollows of his eyes.

The door to the next room opened, and Cardinal San Marco walked in with one of his verdant green portfolios.

'Ah, Luis. The Holy Father has decided it is best that he does not speak with you.'

'His Holiness has, or you have?'

'We were both in agreement. It's easier to work with someone than against someone, Luis: that's how you get things done.'

'If I cannot plead my case to the Holy Father, what am I expected to do?'

'A good question. The Swiss Guard will escort you to your car.'

'My car?'

'The Holy Father has decided to revoke your Papal Immunity, and to hand you over to the Polizia di Stato to assist in their investigation into the Pantheon fire.'

'Revoked?'

'As I said: we were both in agreement.'

Sanchez nodded; a slight movement that was barely noticeable. 'What will become of me?' He asked, more to himself that anyone else.

'The Swiss Guard will escort you from the Apostolic Palace: there is a car waiting to take you away. You needn't look so worried: you'll have a police escort, so you'll be quite safe.'

'What will happen to me in the long term?'

'That depends on you: if you cooperate fully with the investigation, and we can somehow find a way to bury the charges against you, then you might finish your days at a rural parish somewhere in South America. The Church doesn't want to see you imprisoned. The people, well, I do not know. But you should know this: you will never set foot inside the walls of the Holy See after this day.'

'What will I do?'

'Pray.' He said solemnly. 'One other thing Luis: it is requested that you wear these.'

A pair of shining silver handcuffs suddenly appeared at his side, dangling from the arm of a Swiss Guard.

'We are none of us loosed from the laws of this world Luis,' Cardinal San Marco said, 'we are bound to them like each and every other person.'

'God will be my Judge.' Cardinal Sanchez muttered.

Cardinal San Marco gave a nod to the Swiss Guard. 'See that he goes directly, and quickly, before the spectators grow.'

Jean-Baptiste Phillippe saluted Cardinal San Marco, and then gave Cardinal Sanchez a poke in the small of his back.

'One last thing,' Cardinal San Marco called out as they reached the doorway. Jean-Baptiste turned Cardinal Sanchez around. Sanchez pulled his arm free, giving the guard a look that he had hoped was withering, although Jean-Baptiste saw only desperation in his eyes.

Benedetto San Marco smiled. 'I wouldn't want you to worry, Luis. Be rest assured: once you are gone, the Holy See will be in good hands.'

Jean-Baptiste grunted and pushed Cardinal Sanchez along the corridor. Occasionally a side door would open, and someone coming out of a room would stop in their tracks and stare at the Cardinal. Whispers passed before him through the corridor like the wind, opening doors and windows, halting people in mid-stride. Heads turned to watch one of the most powerful men in the Vatican so humbled.

They reached a staircase and the Cardinal stopped at the top, staring directly in front of him. Jean-Baptiste followed his gaze to the elaborate crucifix mounted on the wall. Unlike most of the others he had seen, where Christ was portrayed looking upward, or at some obscure angle, this one had been carved so that the face of the Messiah looked directly at anyone who stopped at the top of the stairs.

'He died for my sins.' Cardinal Sanchez mused distantly, as if the thought was new to him.

'He wasn't the only one.' Jean-Baptiste remarked.

The two of them crossed the hall at the foot of the staircase and stepped into the bright morning light. The sunlight bounced off Jean-Baptiste's armour and blinded the Cardinal, making him stumble down the steps towards the waiting police car. The door opened for him, and he took his seat, cowering as the Swiss Guard slammed the door shut. His life, for all that he was concerned, had ended.

Jean-Baptiste Phillippe walked to the Porta Sant'Anna; a gateway between two countries. The place where the City of Rome met Vatican City. He relieved the guard on duty and attempted to move along the paparazzi who had come to photograph the fallen Cardinal. Minutes later, he heard the wheels of the police convoy licking against the cobbles behind him, as Cardinal Sanchez was escorted out of the Vatican, never to return.

The crowd parted before the motorbikes, and rejoined once they had gone. Cameras flashed and people cried out and stamped about, trying to get a better view. The convoy drove off past St. Peter's Square, and was gone. Jean-Baptiste looked along the Vatican Wall, and seeing a mother and child begging there, reflected that some things would never change. Here were a gang of paparazzi, milling around at the entrance to the Vatican, hoping to catch a whiff of scandal, when all along, they were ignoring the story of suffering that was being told just a few paces along the wall. Once the convoy drove beyond Piazza San Pietro and disappeared from view, the crowd dispersed quickly.

Jean-Baptiste stood at his post before the Porta Sant'Anna and saluted a Cardinal who shuffled in through the gate. The young Swiss Guard jumped at the sound of a car backfiring, momentarily thinking it was a gun-shot or an explosion, and gripped his halberd for reassurance. Henri came along shortly after to relieve him of duty and sped the day winking at young ladies. Jean-Baptiste saluted his friend, and marched into the Vatican, turning his back to Roma Eterna: city of a thousand fountains, cradle of culture and civilisation; a living, breathing monument to the past.

40

'*A*racoeli: The Altar of Heaven. The pagan temple dedicated to the goddess Juno, whom the Greeks called Hera, wife of Zeus. The temple wherein resided a most powerful seer, if tales are to be believed, who had the ear of the Emperor of Rome.'

Cardinal San Marco looked down at Don Albano, bemused at the sudden history lesson. They stood before the painting that Cardinal Sanchez had kept for so long in his private collection, now relocated to the Pinacoteca of the Vatican Museums.

'I still fail to understand why Cardinal Sanchez enjoyed this particular piece so much,' he said, 'yes, it is a fine work of art, but it is nothing compared to a Raphael or a Michelangelo.'

The painting reproduced in rich detail the imagined interior of the ancient Temple of Juno on Rome's Capitoline Hill, portraying the consultation of Augustus Caesar and the Tiburtine Sybil. It was a tableau of two worlds: the Emperor of Rome representing the secular, tangible world; the Prophetess representing the higher world of the spirit.'

'I believe his interest lay in what the painting signifies, Your Eminence.'

'Go on.'

'In a fit of giddiness inspired by the gods, the Sybil whispered the words *haec est ara primo-geniti Dei* into the ear of the Emperor.'

'This is the altar of God's first-born.'

'She foretold the birth of Christ to the Emperor Augustus Caesar. She knew that the Lord himself would take human form and walk among us!'

'No wonder she was giddy.'

'Few who have seen it appreciate the clash of the mundane and the enlightened; the meeting of the worlds of men and gods. Of course, those of us with prior knowledge of the subject understand the importance of the event that the artist preserved here.'

'Of course, but...humour me.'

'Consider this, Your Eminence. If Augustus had not visited the Sybil, she would not have shared her vision with him. She told him that her altar would be dedicated to the Son of God.'

'You have said, yes.'

'As the Bible tells us, it was Augustus who then called for the census in Judea. The census demanded that every man register in the town of his birth, thus ensuring that Joseph would travel to Bethlehem, and the Holy Virgin would give birth to Our Lord in the City of David, thus fulfilling what Scripture had foretold.

'Therefore, it could be argued that it was the prophecy of a pagan oracle that enabled our Lord to be born in Bethlehem, and carry out his ministry in Judea. Had he not been born according to Scripture, Jesus of Nazareth may not have been the Messiah.'

Cardinal San Marco regarded Don Albano from the side of his eye.

'What does this have to do with the painting?'

'The painting reminds us that it was the intervention of the Tiburtine Sybil, the prophecy that shared with the Emperor, that set the events of the Nativity into motion. Without the prophetess, there may have been no birth at Bethlehem, no Messiah, no Christianity, and no Church. This soothsayer, Il Capitano, is the woman who set the wheels of our religion in motion. Without her visions, Vatican City may never have existed. Oh that the world should still have such a woman in it...'

'Indeed,' Cardinal San Marco scratched at his chin with his bandaged hand as his eyes took in every curve of the Sybil's body, 'Do you see the sword that the Emperor is wielding at the pagan witch, Don Albano?'

'Yes, Il Capitano?'

'I have one very much like it, and if you dare to use my *nom de guerre* inside these hallowed walls one more time, you'll be able to ask Saint Peter himself what he thinks of this painting.'

'Yes, Your Eminence.'

'Good man.'

Epilogo

Like all of the others ,the car slowed with the traffic, coming to a halt next to an old brown nose fountain that spluttered water at its tyres. An old hand reached through the open window and opened the door from the outside. The driver stepped out to take the door and was pushed away angrily. A stick hit the wet ground with a splash, followed by two feet more frail than ever before. Independently and yet with great difficulty Madama Lucrezia got out and steadied herself.

'Leave me be,' she cautioned, 'I am well enough for this.'

She trailed one hand along the metal railings, her stick held tightly in the other. Maddalena and Lorenzo walked a respectful distance behind, trying not to be heard or felt. The sun warmed them both, dressed in black from head to toe.

Lucrezia stopped at the gate, closed her eyes, and looked up without seeing. Monte Testaccio, the hill made of clay jars, was waiting for her. A dense pack of trees barred access to most of the hill but two paths crawled the slopes to the summit.

Lorenzo leaned against the car, his arms folded across his chest. Maddalena linked her arm around his, and gave his bicep a squeeze.

'She'll never find them all,' he said, frowning.

'You don't know my Nonna.'

They watched as Lucrezia tapped the stick forward and found one of the paths. She walked forward, dragging the stick in a wide arc before each step, looking for all the world as if she were blind. No sooner had she stepped onto the path, she stopped rigid, and back straightened. With difficulty and a cracking of joints she lowered herself slowly to the floor. Her fingers splayed out, she patted her hand along the ground, lightly touching the shards of pottery. Her hands moved around the right side of her body, working, searching, until she found it. Her fingers closed around a single piece of ancient terracotta.

It was warm to the touch against the coolness of the others around it. Lucrezia pushed herself up and placed the shard into a bag. She moved the stick from left to right, and Lorenzo suddenly realised she looked less like a blind woman, and more like a treasure seeker with a metal detector.

'She can't possibly find them all. Even *I* don't know where I scattered them.'

Maddalena watched her grandmother lower herself to the floor a second time. In her mourning clothes and black veil she looked like some ancient ghoul scrabbling around a graveyard looking for ghosts in the amphorae. With the light becoming lost to the West it would soon be too dark to see the pottery shards among the grass. Not that she thought for one moment that her grandmother was using her eyes.

Lucrezia stood up and bagged a second piece.

'What happens if she finds them all?' Lorenzo asked.

'I'm not sure. She never spoke about owning the relic herself. I don't think she truly believed it existed. Not until she heard about Bertoli's theft.'

'Why do you think he stole it?'

'I don't think he meant to. I think that he intended on stealing back his sculpture, and happened to see the relic there. Maybe he felt something when he saw it, or when he touched it? Maybe he wanted to give it to her as a gift; he was devoted to her, after all. Amadeo Bertoli worshipped Madama Lucrezia, both the woman and the myth, almost like a goddess. Apparently he painted her once, in the style of a prophetess meeting one of the Emperors.'

Lorenzo's eyes widened as he looked to the dark shape scrabbling about on the hill, trying to reconcile that with his memory of the nubile woman in the painting.

'Who did he paint as the Emperor?'

'Giancarlo Romano, her lover.'

Maddalena laughed and reached her hand up to close his gaping jaw.

'They didn't. They couldn't! He was a-'

'They were young. It was a long time ago, long before either of them came to Rome. Decades before Bertoli painted them. Before she even assumed the mantle of Madama Lucrezia. When they were just in love.'

She drew his chin down to meet hers, and they kissed, briefly before he broke away and looked up the hill to where Lucrezia had found yet another piece.

'So who was she? Before Lucrezia?'

'I don't know. No-one does. She has only ever been herself.'

'But she doesn't have to be Lucrezia now, does she? With Cardinal Romano dead and buried, she doesn't need to stay. She's too old to continue her struggle with Il Capitano; I don't think either of them have enough energy or years left to fight on.'

The temperature rose suddenly, and Lorenzo felt the warmer air catching in the back of his throat, drying out his lungs as he inhaled it. A strange wind picked up, rushing past them and up the slope, where Madama Lucrezia rose slowly from the ground. As she straightened her back, her arm continued to rise, high above her head, pointing to the sky. Although he couldn't see from so far away, Lorenzo knew that two fingers pointed upward, and two folded downward, holding the last terracotta piece in place. A sheet of lightning flashed over their heads and spread out across the city, followed by a thunderclap so violent that it triggered car alarms and set the street dogs to howl.

Maddalena held Lorenzo tighter, and watched as her grandmother turned to face them down the slope, her hand still reaching to Heaven.

'Lorenzo, the fight is never finished...'

About The Author

Born and raised in South Wales, Daniel Lyddon is a creative entrepreneur whose business interests include film and television production, e-publishing, app development and hospitality and catering.

He is a co-founder of the independent production company Seraphim Pictures, and the founder of Gwion Press.

Printed in Great Britain
by Amazon

82317770R00140